THE SC

Also by Andrew Harman

THE
SORCERER'S
APPENDIX

Andrew Harman

ORBIT

An *Orbit* book

First published in Great Britain by Arrow Books Limited 1993
Reprinted by Orbit 1998

© Andrew Harman 1993

The moral right of the author has been asserted.

A CIP catalogue record for this book
is available from the British Library.

ISBN 1 85723 685 8

Typeset by Deltatype Ltd
Printed and bound in Great Britain by
Mackays of Chatham PLC, Chatham, Kent

Orbit
A Division of
Little, Brown and Company (UK)
Brettenham House
Lancaster Place
London WC2E 7EN

For Jenny, without whom . . .
love would remain a mystery.

Contents

Middin

In semi-darkness, the four figures sat.

In gloom; in half light, broken by a few candles flickering wildly in the draughts, they hatched plans.

In this room generations of kings had invented schemes of wickedness, stratagems of evil, and complex systems of crippling taxation to keep the royal larders brimming and the people under the regal thumb. This was the Conference Room of Castell Rhyngill and it was not designed for pleasure. Unless, of course, you are the type of person that can find thirty-two different ways to have fun with thumbscrews, experience hot flushes of joy whilst torching tiny villages and thrill with spine-tingling delight after adding the last clause to a grossly excessive extortion racket.

A huge oak table had squatted, for centuries, in the centre of the room. It was upon this that countless plans had been drawn up, agreements broken and fists slammed in frustration and/or anger. Behind the table loomed a tall, black monolithic throne whose austerity emanated dense waves of cold, harsh cruelty. It looked as if it had been hewn from a solid block of black slate. It had.

The walls of the Conference Room bristled, in angry sympathy, with that self-same cruelty. Instruments of torture were arranged in bleakly geometric patterns and weapons of pain and destruction hung nonchalantly in rows along the far wall. Swords mingled with tournee lances, fifteen-pound maces rubbed chains with the shafts of throwing spears and cross-bows stood ready to hurl bolts into suits of battle armour standing ready-at-arms in the corners. The effect was at once bleak, tastefully grim and very, very sharp. Well, let's put it this way: if a maniac mongol warlord, a psychotic murderer with a love of shower curtains and a Victorian killer of prostitutes had been scouring the small ads for a house to share, this room would have been perfect in every detail.

In choosing the decor for the Conference Room, King Stigg, the first, and so far cruellest, King of Rhyngill had remarked in response to an interior decorator's suggestion, 'Tapestries, TAPESTRIES! Pah! They're for Girlies!' The interior decorator had then been dismissed. Permanently. Right now, centuries later, four figures were sitting in deep debate. Around them the Conference Room almost hummed with centuries of accumulated wickedness.

'What if we taxed food, Sire?' asked Burnurd, a member of the Black Guards of Castell Rhyngill, in a moment of rare intelligence.

'We already do!'

'Wha'?' said Burnurd, returning to a more normal level of mental inactivity. The effect of the room already wearing off.

'We already tax food, imbecile!' repeated Snydewinder, the Lord Chancellor, with little patience for the lumbering castle bouncer.

'Oh!' intoned Burnurd, feeling a little put out that his idea, his brilliant idea, had been sat on so abruptly and so early in its development.

A thick silence fell in the room.

Suddenly, almost as if the room wasn't going to give up that easily, something began to happen in Burnurd's head. In the same way that certain concert halls can bring out virtuoso performances from visiting artistes, or that certain sporting venues can always be relied on to produce record-breaking times and distances – in that way the Conference Room worked its old peculiar magic on Burnurd. His eyes opened wider, allowing a glimmer of daylight to sneak under his heavy caterpillar eyebrows. His right index finger twitched, straightening. His hand quivered, his eyes slid slowly upwards, pulling his heavy head with them. The signals halting his train of thought had changed to green and his idea was now thundering recklessly down an uncontrollable incline powered by the racing engines of inspiration. A look of panic flashed across his crimson face. Beads of sweat appeared on his heavy forehead. His lips twitched.

Snydewinder looked up from the black leather-bound book.

The room was quiet . . . except for the slight hum of evil, at a pitch of approximately 50 Hurts.

Burnurd began to vibrate as inspiration took a firm hold of his right arm. It rocketed skyward.

'I know . . .'

It came like the release of steam from some immense volcanic geyser.

All five eyes were glued to Burnurd . . . waiting.

'W-w-we could . . .' he struggled, unused to the forces of inspiration.

Expectant silence gripped the other three men.

'We, we could ta – ta – ta – tax food more!' he blurted, collapsing with the strain of the mental effort.

'Oh dear,' murmured Maffew, the other half of the Black Guards.

'Tut, tut, too bad,' said the King.

'I've warned him before about thinking too hard,' sneered Snydewinder. 'It's bad for him! He was not born to think!'

Burnurd groaned.

'I fink it's a good idea,' said Maffew, timidly supporting his colleague.

'Shut up!'

'But . . .'

'Shut up!' repeated Snydewinder, waving his pointy, steel toecapped boots for effect.

'But . . . mmmfph!'

Maffew had been warned. He now sat and nursed a badly bruised shin, the unhappily throbbing recipient of a swift jab from Snydewinder's boot. Maffew muttered obscenities under his breath. The Lord Chancellor wore deadly boots.

'Snydewinder!' snapped the King, 'What is the level of food tax at present?'

'Could you be more specific, Sire?'

'What?'

'Well, Sire, do you mean Vegetable Tax – (1) Outdoor and its subclasses (a) growing tax, (b) fertilisation tax, or (c) harvest tax; or Vegetable Tax – (2) Indoor subclass (a) cleaning tax, (b) peeling tax, (c) preparation tax, or (d) eating tax; or Meat Tax – (1) Poultry Farming, subclass – (a) battery chicken tax, (b) free range . . .?'

'Stop!'

'Sire?'

3

'The overall level of taxation on food.'

'Global, Sire?'

'The bottom line.'

'Including P.A.Y.E.* Sire?'

'Yes.'

'With seasonal and climatic adjustments, Sire?'

'YES!'

'And Difficult Terrain Collection Increment, Sire?'

'Just tell me!' bellowed the King.

'Ahem . . . The overall level of taxation on food, as laid down by yourself, His Majesty the King of Rhyngill, on the 14th January OG** 1038, in accordance to the Kingly Laws passed by your Majes . . .'

'TELL ME NOW!'

'Seventy-four per cent, Sire.'

'Thank you.'

'You're welcome, Your Devastating Regality, Sire.'

'Stop wheedling.'

'As you command, Your Regal Altitude, Sire.'

'Hush.'

'Sire,' whispered Snydewinder.

Burnurd sat up but still looked a little pale and confused. The mental effort had been a great strain. Maffew still nursed his

---

* Pay As You Eat.

** OG – Original Gravity. This calendar system was invented by the philosopher Gren Idjmeen whose reasoning was as follows. If an inanimate object, such as a brick, is held out of the window of a very tall building and dropped, two things happen: (1) it falls, and (2) it gets faster. Both of these, he said, were due to gravity. He explained the acceleration as follows: '. . . and the brick, being without reason, cannot propel itself and so falls victim to the omnipotent force of gravitic attraction. Acceleration is a change of velocity with time. The brick cannot change its velocity by its own volition. Therefore, gravity affects time. Henceforth when calculating the time a gravitic attractor constant must be used and all measurements of time must be compared with that at sea level, on a sunny day. Henceforth this will be known as Original Gravity.'

Later it was found that the change in time due to gravity was so fiddlingly small as to be almost, but not entirely, irrelevant. The gravitic attractor was swiftly dropped from all temporal calculations and the time scale was renamed Gren Idjmeen Time in his honour.

throbbing shin and cast doubt on the parentage of the Lord Chancellor under his breath.

'Seventy-four per cent Food Tax,' mused the King.

Burnurd looked expectant.

'Well, I suppose seventy five per cent would make the calculation a bit easier.'

'Yes, Sire.'

Burnurd scratched his head.

'Make it so!' the King decided.

'Yes, Sire.' Snydewinder fetched his quill and put on his Tax advisor's hat, 'a wise decision, Sire,' he fetched the ink, 'an exercise in excellent judgement, if I may say so, Sire.'

'Just put it in the minutes, will you?'

'Yes, Sire.'

Maffew rubbed his leg and scowled at Snydewinder.

The Lord Chancellor opened the huge leather-bound Minutes book, adjusted his black leather eyepatch, cracked his bony knuckles noisily and began to write.

Burnurd smiled as he listened to the quill scratching over the rough parchment.

His idea was in The Book.

In the early afternoon of a late spring day, the young boy saw the chance he had been looking for. Without a moment's hesitation his arm shot out, snatching at Mote the Wood-Nymph, his hand huge against its tiny body. Effortlessly the defenceless creature was lifted brutally skywards. Mote did not struggle. Mote could not struggle.

Inevitably, the Wood-Nymph was lowered into Firkin's hand where Mote joined his brothers, Gnot and Phloem. Now Firkin had three. He needed one more. He released Murrion the Shepherd, tossing him away with a careless flick of the wrist.

Hogshead watched as the Shepherd tumbled slowly forward and landed on the tatty bedclothes below. He scowled angrily at Firkin, looked to his left and forfeited his turn.

Dawn, with a weak grin, reached out and picked up the Shepherd. She slid him in with the other three, tossed away Thrum the Weaver, and revealed the full set of Shepherds to her brother and his best friend.

'I won,' she said simply and then coughed violently, the colour draining from her cheeks as she doubled up on the bed.

Firkin looked pityingly at his sister, unable to help. He scowled at her cards, focusing his frustration elsewhere. 'I was so close! One more pesky Wood-Nymph and . . .'

'Yeh . . . but I won!' she answered, controlling her coughs momentarily.

'Another game,' whimpered Hogshead, desperate to win a hand. 'I'll deal.' He began collecting the cards eagerly from Dawn's bed.

'No, I'm sorry, but I've had enough today,' she said weakly. 'Maybe later, eh?'

Hogshead shrugged his shoulders as he collected a Black Guard and a pair of Jesters.

'Come on,' said Firkin, ushering Hogshead out 'Dawn needs a rest now.'

Almost as a reply, a fit of pathetically weak coughs drifted into earshot.

Dawn was the latest victim of a malady that was sweeping the tiny community of Middin perched high in the Talpa Mountains. Most of the other children and some of the older people had already succumbed to its effects.

It wasn't really anywhere near incurable, far from it. All that was required was a good feed. That was the whole problem in a nutshell. The new higher rates of taxes, set by the King of Rhyngill, were really crippling life in the village. It was hard enough growing enough food to feed yourselves, especially in these barren, heather-coated mountains. But having to send almost three quarters down the mountain as the King's Tithe was getting beyond a joke. The word tithe was used entirely for historical reasons, and because it sounds better than tax. It had started as a proper tithe, but had grown way beyond the official ten per cent years ago. The name hadn't changed partly to save confusion, but mainly because 'halfthe' or 'three-fifthsthe' is extremely difficult for guards to say through menacingly clenched teeth. Food, and nutrition in general in the village, was now sadly lacking. Most of the villagers hadn't had a decent meal in weeks. Even months. And it was beginning to show.

Watched jealously by Dawn, two boys ran through the tiny little

6

talpine village of Middin.

Actually, village is a bit of a grand word. Had a hugely successful Elizabethan playwright not stolen the word for the title of a tragic play, hamlet may well be more apt. It conjures up a place about the right size for the measly collection of scrotty wood huts perched high in the Talpa Mountains. But far, far too quaint. If you could view Middin from the air, the overriding impression would be that a very large, and particularly ineffective, raven had, several times, attempted to build a nest. Unsuccessfully.

The 'high street' in Middin was a patch of ground that had been left free of debris. It wasn't so much a deliberate attempt at civil highway engineering but more a bit that they hadn't got round to doing anything with yet. At the moment it offered a reasonable surface, but when it rained, well . . . mud is an understatement.

Either side of the 'high street' were the 'houses'. Nearly all of these looked more like something had fallen down than been built. This wasn't too far from the truth. One of the finest examples of the 'hastily-erected-bonfire-after-a-hurricane' school of architecture, beloved by the inhabitants of Middin, was Franck's Hut. The destination of the two boys.

Pushing open the rickety door to the hut, which appeared to be held up mainly by luck, the two boys entered the dim and dusty room. They blinked in the dark. Mysterious bottles lined rickety shelves and a mortar and pestle, filled with strange-smelling powder, balanced precariously on the edge of a wormy-looking cupboard. All the tools of the Wizard's trade seemed to be here. Glass jars, labelled with strange names in strange writing, housed even stranger-looking pickled and preserved creatures whose fate had been sealed long ago. Unlike some of the jars. Pools of sticky ooze congealed down the sides of some of the older-looking vessels. There were mysterious metal constructions scattered in corners whose purpose the boys could only guess at, theodolites, a sextant, two divining rods and one device that looked as though it had been made from the bottoms of two dark green beer bottles and several lengths of wire. A small piece of flint shone with a tiny auric spark. Shallow pots of coloured powder smouldered gently on most flat surfaces giving off a thick oily smoke, that always made the boys choke. In short the whole place had a very mysterious and moth-eaten air to it. Though what sort of a moth it

7

would be that would actually be hungry enough, or mad enough to even fleetingly contemplate eating anything even remotely associated with Franck's hut was a very difficult question to answer.

In the far corner of the Wizard's hut was a heap of dark grey rags, apparently flung on to the table and draped on the floor. The boys coughed in the dense dry atmosphere, breaking the dull thick silence.

'Eh, eh, what, what, what?'

'Hello, Franck,' offered Firkin, looking around for the source of the outburst.

'Eh, eh, what-what, what's that?'

'Hello, Franck?' suggested Hogshead vaguely.

'Eh, eh, wh- what, what's that noise?' repeated the heap of rags stirring up a small cloud of dust.

'Hello, Franck, its me, Firkin.'

'What . . . uh . . . oh. Come in then.'

'We already are.'

'What?'

'In.'

'Oh!'

Silence. Nothing moved.

The inside of the hut seemed to turn into a quick-drying oil painting as still life fell and the boys stood expectantly waiting for Franck.

Hogshead succumbed to the atmosphere and suddenly began coughing his head off.

'No, no, not another one . . . uh . . . oh. Oh!' cried the rags as they sat bolt upright in a shower of dust revealing Franck the Wizard, waving furiously to protect himself from the hundreds of falling somethings in his dream.

'Who's that coughing?' he demanded.

'Sorry, its Hogshead,' said Firkin.

'Hogshead . . . whatsewant?' said Franck dozily wiping his eyes.

'He came with me.'

'Whaddyouwant?' he yawned expansively.

'We came to see you.'

'Oh . . . Why?' said Franck, finally opening his eyes.

'We thought you'd tell us a story.'

'Give me a chance to wake up and . . .'

'Not another what?' interrupted Hogshead, controlling his coughing fit at last.

'Eh . . . ?'

'You said "not another one" and then sat up.'

'Oh. Did I . . . ?' Franck was obviously not with it. Several pieces of fluff hung messily in his tatty beard. 'Not another one?' He screwed his eyes up in an effort to recall the dream. Several hundred yellowish rodents, eyes gleaming in wild abandon, hurled themselves toward him in a flash rerun of the dream, causing cold beads of sweat to spring on to his forehead. 'Er . . . Nope. Haven't a clue,' he lied. 'Funny that.'

'Well, was it a magic dream?' pressed Hogshead eagerly.

'Eh? . . .' said Franck and Firkin together, looking at the small rotund boy bouncing up and down excitedly.

'A dream, a magic dream, a dream about magic, with magic in . . . I like magic, magic is exciting, Firkin doesn't believe in magic. I do, was it a magic dream? hey was it . . . Ow!' Firkin kicked Hogshead's shin and stemmed the babbling berk.

Actually, Hogshead was only a nickname. It was unfortunate that Billy Hopwood just happened to bear an uncanny resemblance to a small squat barrel.

'What's that, Firkin?'

'Er what, Franck?'

'About you and magic?'

'Er . . . well . . .'

'He doesn't believe in magic,' said Hogshead, rubbing his leg and pulling tongues at Firkin. 'He told me so, today.'

'Is this true?' Franck fumbled with his glasses.

'Yes,' said Firkin decisively. 'I've never seen any and I don't believe in it!'

Franck leaned across the table, looked at Firkin and listened.

'. . . And all the stories with magic in are silly and get the heroes out of a fix with the flick of a magic wand. It's all phooeey. Rot. Rubbish. Hocus-pocus. IT DOESN'T EXIST!'

'Have you quite finished?' said Franck, looking down at the red-faced youth.

9

'Yes.'

'Well, I'll tell you about magic.'

'Oh, no,' whined Firkin. 'I want to hear something real. Tell us something like . . . er . . . something like . . . Oh, anything but no magic!'

Hogshead shook his head in disbelief; Franck was good at making up stories but one without magic would be so boring. Nothing interesting ever happened without magic.

'. . . and,' continued Firkin, 'I don't want anything made up. I want the truth. Facts!'

Hogshead gasped.

'Oh dear, oh dear,' moaned Franck. 'Facts, eh? Does this mean that Firkin is growing up?' he asked, rhetorically. 'Do I take it,' he continued, 'that my tales of swords, sorcery, dragons and damsels are now no longer required . . .'

'No . . .' started Hogshead.

'. . . that the yarns I have spun are wearing thin . . .'

'No!' Hogshead's eyes were wide. He loved Franck's tall tales.

'. . . that I no longer have such an avid audience . . .?'

'No, Franck,' said Firkin. 'I like your tales. I just want something a bit more . . . er . . . bit more . . .'

'. . . real!' finished Franck.

'Yes,' nodded Firkin.

'Oh, very well,' he sighed in mock defeat.

The two boys settled down to listen.

'This is a secret. None but I know the truth of the marriage of Prince Chandon.' Had Franck been able to dim the lights, play low ominous music and produce swathes of foggy dry ice, this would have been the perfect time. ''Tis a strange tale: of adventure; fortune; shoe sizes.'

The boys' eyes widened. Franck had started slipping into his pseudo-old-fashioned speech. This normally meant it was going to be good.

Franck stared at the boys for a moment, just to add a little excitement, took a deep breath and began in the time-honoured way. 'Once upon a time, far, far away . . .

*

King Klayth's footsteps echoed down the empty-sounding corridor.

It probably sounded empty because it was.

Empty.

There were miles and miles of corridors like this in Castell Rhyngill.

Bare stone floors separated bare stone walls which ran for miles, broken only by the occasional door into an empty room, or crossed by another corridor which was . . . yes, empty.

The whole place was empty.

It had been this way ever since he could really remember.

It must have been so different once.

He could ever so dimly recall a time when the whole area rang with life. Over three and a half thousand lives. All sorts of shapes and sizes, from tiny chimney sweeps permanently grey with soot, through parlour maids, cooks, valets, right up to the bristling mass of the black-clad castle guards.

He stood now in the empty corridor and listened. Silence. Thick, deep, absolute silence. The silence of cotton wool. The silence before a thunder storm on a July day. It would never have been as quiet as that in the old, glorious days of his youth. Even in the dead of night there would have been a hum of life. Over three and a half thousand people can never be perfectly quiet. Why else call it '*sound* asleep'? There's always some noise: the gentle contented breathing of a young girl muffled by her scented pillow; the fitful breaths of a dreamer fighting dragons on a mountain top; and the steam-engine bellows of the snoring cook – a constant hum.

During the day it would have been deafening, with everyone busy with their daily tasks too numerous to mention, all essential for the smooth running of the castle.

The last days of preparation, before the War with the neighbouring kingdom of Cranachan, must have been impressive. People running, gathering, checking – readying. Of course, Klayth hadn't even known how to spell war then let alone know what it was. It didn't seem to matter though. People were going away and that was that. He was too young to know why. He could only dimly remember it, walking through the hubbub in quiet bewilderment,

11

close to it but not part of it, like a leaf on an autumn stream. There was an excitement, an electric tension in the air, as if some great god had rubbed the whole castle on a monstrous woolly jumper and tried to stick it to the ceiling. But this was different to anything else, it was a hollow excitement. A final excitement. An excitement marinaded for weeks in a subtle and potent blend of sadness, despair and plain old-fashioned fear.

But suddenly, it went quiet. In OG 1025 all the men left. The women stayed around for a few days, not knowing what to do after all the hectic preparation. Small groups of them would be found sobbing gently in corners. Gradually they drifted away, leaving just a few to keep the castle going, and the King safe. That was thirteen years ago and Klayth had been just over four years old. He'd been inside the castle ever since as it gradually emptied of staff, leaving now just the six of them in a castle built for at least four thousand. It wasn't, therefore, too surprising that for most of the time, most of the castle was, in fact, mostly empty.

Right now he stood in the middle of one of the hundreds of upper corridors and thought about the people he was left with. The two bodyguards, Burnurd and Maffew, probably had the physical strength but not the mental agility to save him from any willing and able assassin. They were faithful though. Devoted to Klayth and willing to die for him. But he was sure they hoped it wouldn't come to that. So did he.

There was the cook, Val Jambon, whom he saw on rare occasions and who always delivered the most splendid meals and snacks. He had a daughter, Courgette, young and shockingly red-haired. Klayth hardly ever saw her face to face but would occasionally spy her creeping out into the nearby woods.

And then there was the Lord Chancellor, Snydewinder.

He had, in no particular order, the roles of chief strategy adviser, chief accountant, book-keeper general, Lord Chancellor, tax adviser, teacher . . . the list seemed almost endless but, thought King Klayth, I expect that's what Lord Chancellors do.

Shrugging his shoulders he turned down the empty corridor and headed for the library.

'"Who-so-ever puts their foot in this tiny sandal is the true-born

12

Queen of my Kingdom," declared Prince Chandon at the top of his voice.

'All the guests who had attended the party moved forward and clamoured for attention. The Prince was the most eligible bachelor in the whole of the Kingdom. He was Tall, towering above most men even without his tournee boots; Dark: his mane of black hair was the envy of all men, knights and commoners alike, as well as a fair proportion of the women of court; Heroic: he was the champion of the tournee field and could defeat any man in a fair tournament contest, his feats on the battle field were legendary.

'Prince Chandon scowled and whispered in the chief guard's ear. There then followed a period of shouting guards and pushing and shoving as the men were separated out.'

' "All of you women shall try on this sandal and who-so-ever it fits, shall I marry," shouted the Prince, resplendent in his dress armour.

'Everyone was brimming with excitement and two women fainted. But soon . . .'

'Why?' asked Hogshead.

'Eh?' answered Franck.

'Why did they faint?'

'Oh – they wore their corsets too tight. Now don't interrupt or I'll stop. Now . . . where was I?' His eyes glazed over and he tugged at his beard. 'Oh, yes. But soon every single woman's foot had been pushed into the sandal. It fitted none of them. Not even the married ones.

'Prince Chandon was irate and . . .'

'What's that mean?' whispered Hogshead.

'Angry,' answered Firkin quietly.

Franck hadn't stopped: '. . . so he made a decree there and then to send for the Wizard Merlot. Two guards set out to bring him to the aid of the lovelorn Prince.'

'I thought you said there wasn't going to be any magic in this!' interrupted Firkin.

'W . . . w . . . well . . . yes, but . . .' flapped Franck.

'You always do that! You always bring in Merlot to magic the hero out of trouble or find hidden treasure or something. That's cheating. There's no such thing as magic. It's not real!'

'Firkin, it's only a story and I like it so let Franck finish,' said Hogshead, annoyed at Firkin's protests.

'Well, I bet I know how it finishes anyway,' said Firkin, crossing his arms and starting to sulk.

'Magick is more real than you think, young Firkin!' said Franck, his voice strangely serious and his eyes staring deep into those of the young boy. 'You'll find out soon enough. It's all around you! You'd see it if you only looked.' Then in a lighter tone he added, 'So, tell me, Firkin, how does it end?'

'Well,' began the cocky reply, 'Merlot comes in and using his powers of magic he finds the girl who the sandal fits and the Prince marries her and they all live happily ever after.'

'So who was the girl?' asked Hogshead.

'Easy!' shouted Firkin. 'It's the one who had to stay at home and clean the fireplace out.' The young boy grinned and sat back smugly.

Franck stroked his chin and said, 'Tell me, Firkin, how interesting do you think a prospective King, whose hunting and tournee skills were legendary, would find a girl whose life had been spent cleaning fireplaces, darning socks and mending tea-towels? Eh?'

'Well . . . er . . . probably, not very . . '

'Aha! So they wouldn't live happily ever after, would they?'

'Er . . . s'pose not.'

'So you've not got the right ending there, have you?'

'Hmmmm . . . s'pose not.' Firkin looked embarrassed.

'What's the proper end, Franck?' asked Hogshead, eager for more. 'Tell me, please!'

'Well, remember the decree that was sent to Merlot?'

'Yes,' said Hogshead.

'Yes,' said Firkin suspiciously, curious to hear what Franck was going to make up now.

'Do you know what it said?'

'No. You didn't tell us,' answered Firkin quickly.

'Well, it contained a message and a threat. Merlot came to the Prince's Court and obeyed because he liked to make people happy. The sandal had been ripped by a particularly fat and greedy woman who had tried three times to jam it onto her foot. Merlot remade the sandal to exactly the right size to fit on to the foot of the Princess Davina, who the Prince loved because she was beautiful, intelligent, rich and her dad owned the best tournament field for miles. They got married and threw a big party for everyone.'

'What happened to the other girl?' asked Firkin.

'Oh . . . er . . . er . . . she was a bridesmaid.'

Firkin looked at Franck and shook his head. 'You can't do it can you? You can't tell a story without magic. You didn't need magic in that. A tailor could have fixed the sandal. Like I said before, I don't believe in magic and it'll take a lot to convince me otherwise.'

Franck folded his arms, sat back in his chair and grinned smugly to himself. 'We'll see,' he said, 'we'll see.'

Strangely, Firkin began to feel rather uncomfortable.

Later that day, after Franck had told them a few more tales with varying degrees of accuracy, Firkin pushed open the door to the hut where he lived and walked in. The smell of turnip stew hit him full on the nose.

'Hello, Mum,' he called.

'Ooh, hello, love. Where've you been?'

'Franck's.'

'Wash your hands, love, your lunch is ready.'

'He's been telling us about vampires and how they can't go out in the daylight and how they don't like garlic . . .'

'Come on now, hurry up. It's turnip stew. Your favourite.'

'. . . and how they drink blood from people's necks, and fly around like bats and . . .'

'Come on. Have you washed your hands? It's ready.'

'Oh, good,' he said without much enthusiasm. 'How's Dawn today?'

'Not too good, love. Same as yesterday really.'

His mother slowly stirred the pot of constantly refluxing turnip stew. It bubbled thickly on the top of the stove. It was always on the go. Shurl, Firkin's mother, was not a very inventive cook. But

15

then again there wasn't a great deal of choice of raw materials in Middin.

'I'm just going in to see her.'

'It's nearly ready. Call your Dad.'

Firkin nearly answered 'What would you like me to call him?' but knew that his mother wouldn't notice. Right now her world revolved around the boiling pan of turnip stew and how best to distribute it to her family. Little else mattered beyond that. For the moment.

Firkin walked out of the other door and into the garden.

'Hello, Dad. Mum said to call you for lunch.'

'Eh. Oh. 'Bout time you showed up! Going to give me a hand? No, thought not. Bit of gardening's just what you need. Make a man of you that would.'

His father was always the same when he had been in the garden. The frustration of moving several tons of sticky black soil, which stubbornly refused to yield anything other than a thin skin of slimy mould, was frequently vented in Firkin's direction. Wyllf, Firkin's father, stubbornly clung to the firm belief that the stuff at the back of their hut was soil. It was on the ground and you walked on it. It wasn't carpet, so it *must* be soil. Although he did have his doubts. Sometimes he felt certain he would achieve greater botanical successes with an offcut of average quality, well-watered shag-pile floor covering.

'I'm just getting Dawn's present.'

'Take, take, take. That's all you do. How about a bit of sweat and toil over here? Oh, no. Not even once. When I was a kid we had to . . .'

His father continued in a similar manner while Firkin squelched across their patch of sticky goo. He'd heard it all before, how they don't build things to last anymore, or everything's in too much of a rush these days, or there's less meat in sausages nowadays. In the blackness of the mud, seemingly against all the odds, two snowdrops had managed to flower. They were beautiful. He felt somehow that he ought to find them symbolic, but he couldn't. Yet. He knew Dawn would love them. He reached down, picked them, and carefully carried them inside. Flowers for Dawn's birthday. He knew she would like them, but at the same time he

16

wanted to give her something more. If only he could make her better.

He knocked on her door and entered quietly.

'Hello, how are you feeling?'

'Bleaaugh!' she answered, eloquently.

'I brought you these. Happy Birthday,' he said and passed her the two tiny flowers. He felt very inadequate.

'Oh, Firkin, they're lovely. Thank you.'

He fingered his shirt and looked down at the bare floorboards.

'It's all I could get . . . I wanted to get you more . . . but . . . well . . . sorry,' he ended limply, shrugging his shoulders.

His little sister smiled weakly.

'It's alright,' she croaked, 'I understand.'

Firkin looked across at her sadly. He wanted so much to make her better, to stop her illness. He longed for the climbing-trees-Dawn, or the running-up-hills-Dawn, or even just a little of the laughing-hysterically-while-running-downhill-Dawn. He missed the fun he used to have with her.

He wished she could get better.

He wished he could make her better. All she needed was a few good meals and she'd be right as rain in no time. The whole of Middin needed a few good meals, come to that. They had so little and most of that went to the King. That King! That King!

Anger armwrestled melancholy out of the way and played merry hell with Firkin's emotions. It was all the King's fault. He hated the King. Images poured into his head. A fat bloated figure stuffed his face with grapes whilst everyone in the country starved. Huge stockpiles of food stood guarded jealously within impregnable fences. He hated the King. What did he do? Why was he here? Parasite!

Anger moved downstage leaving frustration and impotence to take the spotlight, their twin voices chorusing their favourite question.

'But what can you do about it?'

Firkin felt useless.

He knew what he wanted. He dreamed of a band of men, led by a shining knight, freeing the country from this tyranny. He dreamed of better times. But what could he do? What could he do?

17

He smiled weakly at his sister and walked out of the room. What could he do?

High in the lower foothills of the Talpa Mountains, the thief stared intently at his intended victim. He had been watching him for quite some time now. He crouched behind a rock and waited for the right moment. He had moved in from a long way away, dodging behind moss-covered rocks, then squirming through long grass on his belly, until he had reached his present spot. The final dash was always the worst. All the built-up tension and excitement would be released in one mad dash forward to snatch the treasure. But only when the time was right. Not yet. Not just yet.

His legs were beginning to ache from the crouching. He had to go soon. If only his victim would look the other way then maybe he could move, snatch, and away.

His victim stood and stared out across the valley. He was almost motionless.

The thief shifted uncomfortably. His victim turned and looked away. That was all he needed. Now! He stood and ran quickly across the small patch of heather, bent low, snatched the treasure and was running at full tilt before the victim had even realised the danger.

'Got it, got it!' cried the thief as he ran down the mountain. He looked back over his shoulder expecting to see a figure in hot pursuit. Nothing. He relaxed a little. Then became puzzled.

'Why isn't he chasing me?' he thought.

He stopped and turned to look up the mountain. This wasn't right. He always chased him. He stood for a moment then walked slowly back up the foothill. He peered round a boulder. The figure was still there, staring out over the valley. He hadn't moved.

He must have noticed me. Why isn't he chasing me? thought the thief.

He stood up and walked towards his victim.

'Why aren't you playing?'

'Eh?' said Firkin dreamily.

'I've got the treasure. I've won,' said Hogshead, tossing the shiny pebble up and down in his hand.

'Oh . . . well done,' Firkin replied distantly.

18

'What's up? You hate it when I win.'

'Sorry. I'm not in the mood to play.'

'Why?'

'It's Dawn. I hate to see her the way she is. I want to do something to help her but I don't know what.' He sat down heavily on a rock and hugged his knees.

Hogshead thought hard. 'What would Prince Chandon do?' he asked after a few minutes.

'This is serious!' snapped Firkin. 'My sister is ill along with most of the rest of the village and you're talking about fairy tales!'

'I only asked . . . I thought it might help us think . . . I mean he's always saving damsels-in-distress . . . and, well, I think your sister is pretty . . . er, distressed . . . and I'm sure she'd count as a damsel. I don't know what you actually have to be for proper damseldomness but I'm . . .'

'Shut up, will you . . . I'm thinking.'

'Oh.'

'Yes . . .'

Hogshead could almost hear Firkin's mental gears grinding. He was scheming.

'Yes. It just might work!' he said to himself. 'It just might. Ha!' He stood and ran off down the hill.

Hogshead watched him go. Then stood and yelled. 'Firkin? . . . Hey, wait for me!'

'But are you *sure* this'll work?'

'Of course I am,' answered Firkin in a hoarse whisper a few minutes later. 'Once the cart leaves here nobody looks into it.'

'How do you know?'

'Stands to reason . . . doesn't it?'

'What'll happen when the King finds out? He'll send out the Black Guards and we'll all be . . .' Hogshead's voice ended in a shrill whisper.

'The King will never notice 'cause I'm not going to take much. Besides, it's really ours anyway! C'mon.'

Firkin crept forward, keeping close to the back of the disused curing shed, and searched for the loose wooden panel that he knew should be there.

Thirteen years of enforced neglect had loosened many panels in the curing shed but Firkin only knew of this one at ground level. Most of the children in Middin had played in the curing shed at one time or another until it was declared out of bounds. The official reason was that it was 'unsafe and nobody, repeat *nobody*, is allowed in except to deliver tithe donations.' But, as with all things that are forbidden, this only made it all the more attractive to the children of Middin.

Carefully, Firkin slid the panel away and crawled through the hole into the dark. Hogshead followed, replacing the panel as he entered. The two boys waited for their eyes to adjust. Shafts of light beamed down from holes in the roof and motes of dust sparkled momentarily as they drifted casually through them. Rows and rows of hanging racks covered the walls and at the far end of the shed, the remains of the furnace could be seen. Most of it had been raided over the years for repairs to local huts.

Firkin and Hogshead had seen this all before and regarded it with little interest. Their eyes were on the cart in the centre of the shed.

A large cloth was drawn over the contents and secured firmly at the sides. The end was still open. Some of the tithe was still outstanding and was needed before the cart could set off.

Abruptly, a blast of bright light flooded the shed as the front doors opened and three figures walked in. Firkin recognised their silhouettes.

'. . . That's right,' said Angus the cart driver. 'Just put it on the back there. I hope they're clean this time!' He looked down the list and ticked the piece of parchment as he carried out his official duties.

The two other villagers placed their tithes under the heavy cloth and walked away grumbling. Angus looked down and counted off the ticks. Forty-three! he grumbled to himself, Why couldn't they store their turnips better than that? Ugh! He brushed away a couple of dozen of the tiny turnip-eating insects, crushing several as he did so, then went to fetch his horse.

As the door closed, and the padlock rattled against it, Firkin ran quickly forward. He rummaged under the cloth, pulled out a box and ran back.

'I don't like this,' whispered Hogshead, 'it's stealing!'

'Oh yeah . . . and what do you call tithes then?'

'Er . . . well . . .'

'How can taking something that's ours to start with, be stealing, eh? Come on.'

As Angus unlocked the door for the second time and entered the redundant curing shed with his tired old horse, two figures exited carrying more than they came in with.

Dawn's eyes widened in excitement and surprise as Firkin clamped his hand across her mouth and put his finger on his own lips. He signalled her to keep quiet. Carefully, he put the box on the bed and slowly released his hand.

Dawn looked at the box, then at Firkin and mouthed a silent, 'Wha . . . ?'

'Happy Birthday,' whispered Firkin and grinned to himself.

'But . . .'

'It's for you.'

'How . . . where . . . ?'

'Stop asking questions. I'll think you don't want it.'

'Oh, I do, I do, I do,' she clutched the box then dissolved in a fit of coughing.

'Come on then. Hurry up and open it,' urged Hogshead, looking nervously at the door. He had been unwilling to go through with this but now that he'd started, he was jolly well going to see it through. It had something to do with being hoisted by lambs' petards. Or was it sheep?

Dawn's face lit up with growing anticipation as she peered inside the box. Her small finger snaked over the side and poked inside a small pot. It withdrew with a cargo of frothy white stuff on the end.

'Is it?' she asked, her eyes wide with wondrous excitement.

Firkin shrugged.

'I think it is! Ooh Firkin!' she whispered and put her finger in her mouth.

It was.

Dawn grinned and her finger shot back into the pot. It was her favourite pudding. A local delicacy made from the milk of a local

21

rodent and some obscure herbs and heathers for flavouring. It was extremely rare because of the difficulty involved in gathering the milk. Dawn's finger carried a third scoopful of Lemming Mousse towards her broadly grinning mouth.

In the Conference Room, a few days later, the King of Rhyngill sat almost motionless. His studded black leather robes glistened blackly as he listened to his adviser, the Lord Snydewinder.

'Sire, would not it be advisable to make an example of them? Would not it be wise to crush this disobedience now? Nip it in the bud. Stamp it out!'

'You are certain they did it deliberately?'

'Yes, your Imperial Highness.'

'But a whole village?'

'It is necessary to maintain our control. If other villages hear that they can get away with it then they will all start. Where will it end? Our tithebarns will be emptied. We will starve!'

The King's robes creaked as he leaned forward.

'Well, my Lord Snydewinder, what do you suggest?'

'Burn the village!' came the shouted reply as Snydewinder slammed his fists on to the heavy oak table. 'Burn the lot of them!'

'Is there no other way?'

'We–we could ta–ta–tax them more!' exploded Burnurd, still flushed from his earlier success.

'Shut up!' yelled Snydewinder, landing a boot deftly. The huge guard scowled angrily.

'Snydewinder, how close are we to starving right now?'

'Could you be more specific, Sir?'

'What?'

'Well do you mean . . .'

'No, not that again. Tell me how much food we have in our tithebarns.'

'Including all the vegetables, Sire?'

'Everything?'

'Taking into account natural wastage and wilting?'

'Yes,' sighed the King wearily. 'Just answer me will you?'

'434 tons of vegetables made up from 34 tons of turnips.

27 tons of carrots, 14 tons each of twelve types of potatoes, 6 tons of . . .'

'Stop!' The King rolled his eyes wearily up to heaven.

'Sire?'

'Just tell me how long will all the food in the tithebarns – all the vegetables, all the livestock, all the chickens, EVERYTHING – how long will it last us?'

'All of us, Sire?'

'All the people in the castle.'

'Including the kitchen staff?'

'Yes.'

'Both of them?'

'Yes!' The King's voice echoed in the hard room.

Snydewinder went quiet and scribbled furiously on a piece of parchment. Burnurd mouthed silent obscenities from away out of direct sight. They mostly involved physical abuse and they all involved Snydewinder. After a few minutes the scribbling stopped and the Lord Chancellor looked up.

'Sire, I have it. All the food in our tithebarns, if consumed at our present rates, by the present company here, plus the kitchen staff (not present) will last approximately six hundred and forty-seven years eight months and two days, Sire.'

'WHAT?'

'Six hundre . . .'

'Yes, yes, I heard. I'm surprised that's all.'

'Well, if your Majesty requires more . . .'

'No . . . no . . . er . . . let me think.' It went very quiet. 'You are saying that we have enough food to last us over six hundred years and . . .'

'Six hundred and forty-two, Sire,' interrupted Snydewinder.

'. . . we've just raised the taxes again and you want me to burn a whole village because their tithe was incomplete!'

'It was a whole pot of Lemming Mousse, Sire,' corrected Snydewinder again.

'I know, I know.'

'One of your favourites, Sire.' And mine, he thought.

'Yes, I know but . . .'

'But you've got to do something about it, Sire. It is essential to keep order. As I have pointed out previously, once one village gets away with it who knows where it will end!'

'I will not order a whole village to be burned just because their tithe was a little light. We got it, didn't we?'

Snydewinder's one good eye smouldered, contrasting sharply with his black eyepatch.

'Are you getting soft, Sire?' he snapped.

'SOFT! How dare you say that?' roared the King. Burnurd smiled. He liked it when the King was angry with Snydewinder.

'Well, Sire, in the days of Your Predecessor, the village and the three nearest ones would have been torched if the tithe was even one carrot short! Will you go against your Father's old traditions?'

'We don't need the food. We've got tons of . . .'

'Your Father would never have said that!'

'I . . . we . . .' the King floundered. Snydewinder's ace card was working again. Klayth had never really known his Father, and Snydwinder knew it. The old King King Khardeen had left for battle thirteen years ago, along with all the other men strong enough, or willing enough, to fight in the war against Cranachan. He had left his son on the throne with the two bodyguards Burnurd and Maffew, and a skeleton kitchen staff. The men never came back.

Where they had gone remained a mystery.

Why the enemy never invaded remained a mystery.

This all left the burden of ruling firmly on Klayth's young shoulders.

He had to keep up appearances. He was the King.

He had to keep up the reign of terror. He was the King of Rhyngill.

He needed to rule with a rod of iron. That's what Kings of Rhyngill did!

Or so Snydewinder insisted.

'Show me that you are his son! Tithe defaulters need punishment! Now!' The shrill voice of the tall, thin, bony man shocked Klayth out of his reverie.

'What will you do?' shrieked Snydewinder.

'Burn 'em,' grinned Maffew.

'Yeah, burn,' nodded Burnurd.

'Yesss!' agreed Snydewinder staring wildly at the King.

24

'Burny, burny, burn,' giggled Maffew getting into the swing of things.

'Burny, burny, burn, b . . .'

The King slammed his fists on to the oak table and stood up, trembling with anger.

'No! No! No! I will not condone senseless burning!' His leather armour creaked wickedly.

Burnurd closed his mouth.

'What will you condone . . . Sire?' sneered Snydewinder, almost spitting the last word.

'You!' the King's pointing leather clad finger trembled inches away from Snydewinder's nose, 'you will issue a decree threatening to burn the village if their tithe is incomplete again. Threatening! . . . Do you understand?'

'I understand, Sire.'

'Good.'

'I just feel this a little weak considering . . .'

'What?' shouted the King. Burnurd fumbled with his armour almost shyly. Klayth could shout very loudly.

'. . . considering your Father's "Rod of Iron" policy, Sire.'

'I am the King! You – decree – now!' He thumped the table in time with the shouted words.

Snydewinder turned a shade redder, swallowed hard and said, 'Yes, Sire.' He left the King's chamber.

There are times, thought Klayth, when there is no choice but to pull rank, and order people about. And if that doesn't work, shout a lot.

Burnurd and Maffew stood quietly in the corner, unsure what to do and hoping that they were invisible.

'As for you two! . . . I am disgusted. "Burny, burny, burn." What were you thinking?!'

Maffew struggled to speak. 'Sorry . . .'

'Sorry . . . Sire,' agreed Burnurd a little more confidently.

'This meeting is now adjourned. Leave me alone.'

The room quickly fell silent. The King turned and creaked out from behind the table. He walked slowly towards the back of the Conference Room, past a tasteful arrangement of tournee lances and left through a tiny door tucked away behind the throne.

25

'Meeting adjourned,' he mumbled wearily to himself.

'Firkin's hungry for some food. Turn.
Want it now, hop, want it soon. Turn.
Pies for me. Hop.
Pies for you. Turn.
Ask the Pieman for some . . .'
Firkin stopped in mid hop and wobbled precariously.

Hogshead looked up from the white stones arranged in ten neat squares and squinted towards the source of the noise.

A small group of men jostled, pointed and raised their voices in the tones of the innocent wronged as they gathered to look at the Post. This was a tall, thin stick pushed firmly into the mud, and served as a remarkably efficient form of communication. Anyone wishing to send a message to the whole village would pin a note to the Post and then stamp on the ground to bring the people to read it. Of course, nowadays it was virtually redundant. So few people remained in Middin that communication was quicker by word of mouth. The Post was also the place where messages from outside were . . . well, posted.

Firkin put his foot down and took a step forward. Curiosity drew him towards the Post.

The group stood in a tight bunch and stared at a small yellowing piece of parchment as it flapped gently in the cool mountain breeze. It had appeared mysteriously during the night. Ominously, it wore a small patch of red wax and a blue ribbon. The seal of the King of Rhyngill.

Firkin caught snatches of conversation as they spun round his head.

'. . . I put all mine in . . .'
'. . . so unfair . . .'
He was too small to see the message.
'. . . not my fault. Mine was all there. You just ask the Missus . . .'
'. . . you try tellin' that to the Black Guards . . .'
'. . . or the King . . .'
Firkin squirmed through the tight mass of bodies.
'. . . cut yer 'ed off soon as look at yer . . .'

26

He stared at the decree and read quietly. Around him the debate raged.

'. . . but we've always paid in full . . .'

'. . . should we all suffer 'cos of one . . .'

'. . . what if the King counted wrong?'

'. . . no. He may be hard . . . but he's fair . . .'

'No, he's not. Is that the action of a fair King?'

'. . . it's only threatening to burn the village down.'

'. . . oh, and that makes it alright, does it? Just threatening?'

Firkin finished reading and turned quite pale. Nobody noticed him swallow hard, clench his fists and turn slowly away. The men continued to argue as he pushed his way through, out to the waiting Hogshead.

'Well?' he asked eagerly.

'Not very,' answered Firkin sickly.

'Eh? . . . what did it say?'

'He noticed.'

'Who . . . what?'

'The King . . . the tithe.'

'Ah . . . oops,' answered Hogshead.

Firkin walked dazedly towards his hut staring absently at the ground. In the space of a few minutes his whole world had been turned upside down, shaken by the ankles and thrown across the room. And it was all his fault. His minor misdemeanour was beginning to cause ripples in other people's lives. All his fault. He felt sick. His eyes misted over and filled with tears.

He was a criminal.

He harboured a guilty secret that affected the whole of the village.

He couldn't take any more . . .

Hogshead watched helplessly as Firkin wiped his eyes vacantly and ran away.

One of the last things you expect, in the middle of the night, is to be jolted rudely into consciousness by a strange hand, clamping your mouth shut and preventing your screams, and feeling your arm being pinned down into the bed, immobilised by some wild, crazed, maniac intruder.

It was the middle of the night and suddenly Hogshead was jolted rudely awake. He was pinned down with alarming efficiency, unable to move, unable to scream. His eyes stared into the face of the wild intruder, inches away from his own, as a wave of panic crashed over him, tossing him about like a Terrapin in a tsunami. Sweat broke out on his forehead, a cold flush sprinted arctically down his tingling spine, hundreds of questions about his imminent future jostled to the forefront of his mind in the hope of being answered. Thoughts involving long thin daggers, huge amounts of pain, torture and . . .

'Lie still, you fool!' came the barked whisper from his assailant. 'Stop wriggling!'

'Mmfflgh!' was the best he could do as a reply.

'. . . and keep quiet!'

'. . . !' he replied.

'Look, I didn't want to wake you, but I had to tell you face to face . . .' The hand released his mouth and the figure moved up into the moonlight streaming in at Hogshead's window. 'I couldn't just leave you to find the note in the morning. I can't carry on like this any longer. Not now.' Firkin fought to control the emotion in his voice.

'What are you doing jumping on me like that?'

'I'm telling you.'

'What?'

'I've got no choice. It's all got way out of hand. There's nothing left for me to do.'

'Eh . . . what?'

Firkin swallowed hard and carried on in a shaky whisper, 'There's only one answer. Only one way out of this. I've thought long and hard about it. Don't try to stop me. It's all my fault, I know. Oh . . .I hate to . . . go . . . like this. So much to tell her. So much I wanted to say. Before I . . . It's the coward's way out, I know. Alone in the dead of night. They'll say I did it for attention. But they'll stop me don't you see, I've got no choice. She'll be heartbroken, I know. I hate to make her cry. But there's no other way. Don't you see? I have no choice. No choice.' He stood and left quickly, holding back a quivering dam of tears. He paused in the doorway, turned back and whispered, 'Tell her I . . . I . . .' He turned and ran.

28

'Tell her what . . . why?'

The question was asked to a patch of moonlight where Firkin had been. Was Hogshead awake? Had Firkin really said all that? Why was it in the past tense? It had felt too vivid to be a dream. His arm ached.

Suddenly a thin, sharp thought snaked through the jungle of confused thoughts in his head. Did he mean what I think he meant? '. . . can't carry on . . . no choice . . . coward's way out . . . tell her I . . . I . . .' A peal of alarm bells rang out, drowning Firkin's final words.

He leapt out of bed, threw on his jacket and boots and ran over to Firkin's hut. In a few moments he was peering through the window at an empty bed and a tidy room. It was true. He was going to do it.

He had to find him. And quick. Firkin could not be left alone at a time like this. Hogshead looked about as he thought. Where would he have gone? Where!

Close to panic Hogshead ran as fast as he could.

He hoped he was right.

He hoped he could catch his friend . . .

Dawn rose slowly the next morning.

She struggled out of her room clutching a tiny scrap of paper that she had found under her pillow. Gallons of tears were poised just behind her eyes, waiting.

'Wyllf dear, have you seen Firkin this morning?' asked Shurl, washing up the breakfast dishes.

'No.'

Dawn stopped and listened at the door. Trying to calm herself. Trying not to believe it.

'He wasn't at breakfast and his bed is made.'

'Oh,' grunted Wyllf.

'It's very strange.'

'He's out at that Franck's again, I expect. Fillin' his head wi' rubbish no doubt.'

'He doesn't normally go without his breakfast though.'

'Shurl, I don't know where our son is. But I do know where he isn't. In t' garden 'elpin' me. He's never in t'garden 'elpin' me.'

Suddenly the door burst open and a plump red-faced woman whirlwinded into the kitchen.

'Is this a joke?' she shrieked waving a small tatty piece of paper. 'A joke, is it?'

'Hello, Mrs Hopwood. How are you today?' said Shurl.

'What does it mean? I've never read anything in such bad taste! A sick joke. Sick!'

'Good morning,' grunted Wylff.

'It'll end in trouble, you'll see!'

'What's she rabbitin' about?' demanded Wyllf.

Shurl shrugged her shoulders. 'Let her calm down, then she'll tell us.'

'If the Guards hear of this we'll be for it!'

'Mrs Hopwood. Calm down. Tell us what's the matter,' soothed Shurl as best she could.

'This!! Your son's leadin' my Billy astray!' she shouted, waving the piece of paper again.'

''Old on, we can't read it if you don't stop wavin' it about the place.'

Mrs Hopwood slammed the paper on to the table.

The three of them stared at it.

It was a short handwritten note.

What did it mean?

All it said was:

Dere Mum and Dad,

> *Gon to find Firkin*
> *Bak soone.*

Love,
> *Billy*

The three of them stared at each other in silence.

'Well?' shouted Mrs Hopwood. 'What's it mean?'

''Ow the bloody 'ell d'you expect me to know!' shouted Wyllf helpfully.

'Ooh, Language!' hissed Shurl.

'Well, she's always accusin' our Firkin o' doin' all sorts o' . . .'

30

'He's leading my Billy astray!' shrieked Mrs Hopwood.

'Leadin' your Billy my foot . . .'

Dawn had heard enough. They didn't care where Firkin or Hogshead were, just whose fault it was. She knew though. Firkin had gone. And she knew whose fault it was. She turned away from the door and struggled slowly back to her bed.

She clutched her note tightly. The last note Firkin had written.

A single tear rolled silently down her cheek as she thought about snowdrops.

There seemed to be a huge hole in the hut where Firkin should be. Her shoulders began to rock. She missed him so much already and he'd only been gone such a short time. It was such a shock. She sniffed as another tear escaped from her eyes. A thought rose unbidden through the surging emotions in the young girl's body. At any other time it would have made her feel wonderful. Right now it just made it all the more painful. In the last few moments, as he had written the note, Dawn had been uppermost in Firkin's desperate mind. Her bottom lip began to tremble.

Slowly, very, very quietly and with a certain sense of inevitability, Dawn broke.

Talpa Mountains

Fifteen years previously and 350 yards away from where Dawn lay sobbing, across a deserted valley high in the Talpa Mountains, was a heap of rags. A cold wind blew over the valley giving the heather and stumpy trees a look of frantic botanical excitement. The rags moved slightly.

A large, black, unidentifiable bird soared high over the nearby mountain ridge causing several small, yellowish rodents to scurry nervously for cover. The rags moved again, stirred by the cold wind.

With an immense stretch of the imagination and a leap of faith of biblical proportions it might have been possible, just, to believe that the heap of rags was, in fact, a tent. It was a tent that held itself upright in very much the same way that a drunken folk singer holds a melody: approximately, precariously and more by habit than any sense of perfect pitch.

For a moment the wind died, lending an eerie calm to the tiny Talpine valley. For a moment, the tent remained still until slowly, like the tentacle of an inquisitive octopus, a hand appeared and moved around the rocks. Its palm slapped regularly on the lichen-coated surface in a definite pattern. It searched.

Inches away, to its right, lay a small and curious contraption ingeniously fashioned from bits of wire and the bottoms of two green beer bottles. The hand touched it and in a flash had snatched the device off the rock, where it had been clumsily dropped the previous evening, and away out of sight. The wind blew again. With an enormous effort something inside the tent began to move and after a painful and arthritic struggle the tent seemed to disgorge, with difficulty, a small and immensely shabby man peering through what looked like a pair of dark green glasses. He scratched his head drowsily and yawned, blinking in the early sunlight. He thrust his hands deep into his tatty pockets and sighed a deep sigh. It was the sigh of an old and tired prospector who had

32

spent his life in the hopeless search for gold. He rummaged about in his pocket and pulled out all he had to eat. He looked miserably at the crust of dry bread, which felt like pumice stone, and thought longingly of bacon. Crispy fried bacon. And eggs. He looked around at the bleak valley and spat.

Looking up to heaven he shouted, 'One more day, that's all! One more. I've had enough!'

Success for the Prospector had always been just over the next hill, or just around that boulder, or there in that stream. Never at the end of his axe.

Except once.

It must have been getting on for twenty years ago when, out of the corner of his eye, he had seen it. In the mountains not far from here, he had actually struck gold. A seam of quartz had run diagonally across the face of a cliff gleaming and glinting silver-white at him as he had walked past. Until he stopped short. One silver-white glint wasn't. Silver-white that is. Keeping his feet exactly where they were, he leaned backwards. He looked at the silver-white glints and counted them off. Silver-white, silver-white, Gold! He memorised the position of the glinting auric spark, pulled out his axe and ran toward the huge cliff face. After a few moments searching he had found it. Thoughts raced through his head of a motherlode stretching miles into the cliff, of the tons of gold he could excavate, of the riches!

He held his breath, raised the axe, and chipped. A piece of gold came away from the cliff on a palm-sized piece of quartz. He stared in disbelief. He pinched himself, rubbed his eyes and swore once or twice, for effect. He looked again.

There, in his hand, was the element he had sought, the grail of his self-inflicted quest, the stuff of his dreams. He should be happy. Nay, ecstatic!

Deep down he was. He would have been a lot happier if there had just been a tiny bit more. Not much. He wasn't a greedy man. As it was, his strike, the sum total of his gold, would melt down nicely to make a ring, or two at a stretch. Just big enough for your average newly wed amoeba.

He turned over the quartz in his hand and ended his reverie.

Over the years this piece of gold, no bigger than the scale from a butterfly's wing, had become his mascot. He had struck gold once. He could do it again.

This thought had kept him going.

Until today.

The years had taken their toll. He was tired, fed up and right now he felt very, very old. Carefully, he placed his mascot deep into a tatty pocket in his shabby coat, collapsed the tent, shouldered his axe and pack for the last time and set off on his last day's prospecting.

Three pairs of oil-black eyes, set in yellowish faces, reflected six tiny sunsets. A silver haze of whiskers twitched nervously from each furry cheek.

Something was stirring inside them.

Something restless.

Behind them, a gentle rustling of heather heralded the arrival of four more yellowish rodents. Just behind them came two more, followed by another small group. And another, and . . .

They came from miles around, they were gathering on the cliff too. Something pulled them there. Something as insubstantial as smoke and as irresistible as lust. All those that heard the calling obeyed.

As the sun sparkled its last fiery photons of the day and sank below the far horizon, an old and tattered figure picked its way back into the valley. He found a suitable spot, unshouldered his pack and began to set up the ramshackle arrangement of sticks and moth-eaten sheeting that passed as his tent. Several hundred eyes looked down from far above, in unblinking rodent curiosity.

They kept vigil and watched as an ice-cold argent moon rolled silently skyward, and remained so all night. Waiting. And watching. The only motion was a host of tiny whiskers twitching feverishly and the constant cosmic rearrangement above their heads as the orbit engines powered the stellar bodies across the black satin sky.

The night passed quickly, finding nothing to hang around for.

As the rodents watched, and without any fanfare, a vague hint of orange slunk shyly over the horizon. A buzz of excitement rippled over the waiting throng. They shuffled their tiny paws restlessly. As one, they edged forward a few paces. The orange grew paler but somehow stronger. The cliff edge beckoned.

Without a word, or squeak of command and almost as one, they moved forward. A yellowish carpet rolled towards the sheer cliff edge, slowly at first, then gathered pace.

In the still, cold light of an undistinguished morning, high in the Talpa Mountains, countless lemmings stepped cheerfully off a cliff top into oblivion . . .

Whomph . . . zzzzip.

Inside his tent, the Prospector twitched in his sleep.

Whomph . . . zzzzip.

He grunted and rolled over.

Whomph . . . zzzzip.

With a start he opened his eyes and listened.

It was light. He sensed it was early. Just after dawn he would guess. He scratched his tatty beard and frowned. Something had disturbed him, he felt sure. But what?

Whomph . . . zzzzip.

Curiously, he edged forward and peered out of the raggy front flap. Everything looked normal. He poked his unkempt head out and looked around. A yellowish streak flashed past, inches away from his nose. He jumped and shot back inside, letting out a small yelp. He sat motionless for a moment, rubbed his eyes, put on his glasses and risked another look. Everything felt better now it had that familiar green tinge to it.

Nervously, he eased his head out again and looked up. A solitary crow croaked its morning cry. Nothing moved in the little valley.

He struggled stiffly out of his tent, stood and stretched away the aches of another night on the rocks. He yawned loudly. Then he opened his eyes. For a moment he didn't move. He stood blinking, his arms still outstretched, and tried to take in what he saw.

He had, in the past, seen mountains and valleys change colour overnight. So what he was staring at now was, in principle, nothing new. Both had quite often turned white at him, but that had only been snow. Small grassy valleys had turned silver at him occasion-

35

ally, but that had only been a particularly heavy dew. But never, not even once, had he heard of, or seen, a valley turn gold! It was a miracle. And all for him!

He looked skyward, laughed and cried out, 'Thank you.'

As if in reply, another nugget floated down toward him, landing on his tent with a 'Whomph . . . zzzzip'. A look of sheer bewilderment, turning to confusion, crossed his face as he watched the nugget slide down the roof of his tent, shake itself and scurry off at high speed with a squeak of relief.

He suddenly became suspicious. His brow furrowed in concentration and anger as he walked towards the gold and picked it up. Almost immediately, he dropped it again, fell to his knees and screamed, pounding the rocks with his fists in frustration.

In all his years of prospecting he had never come across gold like this.

Many people sought gold for many different reasons but never, he told himself, never, had he ever heard of anyone expressing an interest in gold for its warmth.

Or furriness.

It didn't take him very long to pack up his belongings. He shoved his raggy tent into his almost equally raggy backpack and, cursing for the fiftieth time, set off in a downward direction. Away from the mountains. He grumbled to himself as he walked. He pondered the unfairness of it all, he hated everything, everything! He kicked out at a medium-sized rock on the path in front of him after taking an instant dislike to it simply because it was there. He watched as it arced its way over a small ravine and bounced away down a pile of scree, raising piles of dust and a minor landslide. The Prospector, whose total of choice curses was now well into triple figures, kicked another rock. He watched it go and thought of lemmings.

'Serves them right!' he shouted to no one. 'Hate the nasty little things! Jumpin' off the cliff on me like that. Hate 'em! Hate 'em!'

He had spent the majority of his life in the Talpa Mountains searching for gold. He had almost begun to regard the mountains as friends, but now . . . after throwing hundreds of financially useless rodents at him! That was the last straw. The end of a beautiful, albeit one-sided, relationship.

36

He only came here to find gold and get rich.

He waved two fingers at the whole mountain range in a gesture of frustration, helped his total of curses well on its way to four figures, turned and miserably continued in a downward direction.

Angrily he kicked out at another stone and let out a yell. He looked at his boot and cursed. A red and throbbing toe grinned at him from the end of his boot.

It was turning out to be 'one of those mornings'. In fact thinking about it, it made 'one of those mornings' look like a public holiday.

'And they don't make animal skins as good as they could either! I could do better!'

He swore again and hobbled on, grumbling.

Suddenly, he froze. His eyes went cloudy and swam like listless turtles behind the green glass. His hand twitched occasionally. Something strange was happening inside his head. His thought processes were being rerouted. It was as if a malevolent gremlin had invaded a telephone exchange and was ripping out handfuls of coloured wire only to shove them randomly into other holes. Spraks flew. Some fuses shorted, others teetered on the edge of overload. The gremlin shrieked wildly as dozens of wires were crosspatched with gay random abandon.

There was a flash of blinding blue-white light, a peal of neuronal thunder and a faint smell of ozone. The gremlin had crosspatched one too many times. A whole new routing network had appeared. Had this been a cartoon the previous two paragraphs could easily have been replaced by a small scrappy drawing of a light bulb hovering nonchalantly above the Prospector's head.

The Prospector smiled and turned to go back to the valley. He smiled the smile of a man who suddenly knew what he was doing.

Virtually all his life he had wanted to be rich. He knew that people bought gold, therefore having gold made you rich. So had been placed around his mind's eye the blinkers that had brought him to the mountains. The premise 'I want to be rich' had been transmuted to 'I need gold.'

But a moment ago all that had changed.

His thought processes had gone something like this:

'For centuries people have been making goatskin coats, moleskin trousers, even snakeskin handbags. People *like* things made from other animals and, crucially, people *buy* things made from other animals. Why can't I add lemming skin to the lucrative fur trade? Why not indeed!'

The more he thought about it, the more he liked it.

He mulled over all the advantages:

1 Easy availability, they came to you.
2 Minimum energy requirement for harvesting. No capital expenditure required for the expensive trapping implements. Just pick the little blighters up!
3 Absolutely no hassle from animal-rights activists. If lemmings insist on topping themselves, who am I to stand in their way? It's the way Nature intends it!
4 It's not a bad little valley, really.

So were formed in his head, in those few seconds, the seeds that would rapidly grow to form the first Lemming Skin Trading Co.

The germination, however, took somewhat longer. Four weeks longer actually. During that time, the Prospector had skinned, cleaned and cured literally hundreds of small yellowish rodents. He'd built a small curing oven that could take thirty or forty pelts at a time and had even started to use some of them. The first recorded use of a lemming skin was by the Prospector, in OG 1023, to sew a patch on to the toe of his boot.

He grinned quietly to himself as he passed Inspiration Ravine and kicked a stone into it for old time's sake. The last few weeks had been the busiest of his life. His lemming-skin rucksack carried only a small percentage of the work he had done. The rest was hidden in a small cave in the cliff.

He walked down the mountain with a feeling of accomplishment. He was not only immensely proud of what he'd achieved, taking an idea, working on it, and coming up with an end product – a brilliant end product even if he did say so himself – he was also scared witless. Right now, on his shoulders lay the burden of launching lemming skin on an unsuspecting world.

This thought had been with him for the last few weeks and so he'd tried to think of a short, snappy name to capture and fire people's imagination. His favourite at first had been the Talpa Export Skin Trading Company Limited, but he wasn't very happy about the acronym. He tried shortening it to Talpa Wear and even considered holding a series of parties in people's homes as a promotion, but in the end he settled on The Lemming Skin Trading Co. Ltd. You knew where you were with a name like that.

He needn't have worried. In a matter of months lemming skin had been adapted for, and tailored into, hundreds of different garments and their essential accessories. Lemming was the height of fashion. Outlets sprang into being all over the known world, supplying warm underwear for the terrified tribesmen of the fearfully icy wastes of the Angstarktik; battle bikinis for the Raft-People of the Eastern Tepid Seas; padded knee protectors for the Co-operative Monks of the Meanlayla Mountains; and hard-wearing, soft-soled boots for the Dancing Dervishes of Yeehpa! Yeehpa! to name but a few. Anyone who was anyone had something lemming. Even people who weren't anyone had something. Everyone wanted something. Prices rose and, like the cliff-diving troopers in the Northern Wastes of Thkk resplendent in their lemming skin fezes and ceremonial kites, the money tumbled in.

Soon people moved into the valley and a small village coalesced in readiness for the second season. The Prospector had employees. He was happier than he'd ever been. He had a permanent home, a decent bed and a purpose in life.

Finally, after decades of trying, he had achieved something.

He had arrived.

It was a clear summer evening in the Talpa Mountains and the Prospector was sitting in his favourite place. He was high on a rocky outcrop, facing the cliff, and he was looking out over the valley and the people in it. He took another sip of his favourite new cocktail, The Twisted Lemming*. Just a few more minutes, he told himself, then he'd go down.

* A local spirit-based cocktail with up to thirty naturally occurring 'botanical' ingredients, including juniper berries, coriander, quinine and an alarmingly large amount of alcohol, served on ice with a twist of lemon. Its reputation for inducing rapid and almost total inebriation among those unfamiliar with its easy drinkability was legendary among the locals. It should be stored in a cool, dark place, preferably under oil.

Far below him in the tiny, freshly painted village, huddling under the shadow of the huge cliff, the excitement continued to mount. The whole place felt like a stage, set and ready for the first curtain to rise on its first night. But the action eagerly awaited here had a distinctly downward direction. The preparations had been made, the ovens in the curing sheds fired up, everything had been checked at least three times, now all anyone could do was wait, staring fixedly at the cliff-top horizon.

Everyone, that is, except for the tall, thin, black-clad figure walking slowly around the village. His eyes swivelled silently in their sockets, peering round corners, under covers, through open doors. Searching for information. Gathering. Collecting.

Had anyone been watching him earlier in the evening they may have been curious to see him take out of his pocket a small brass device, with precisely graduated vernier scales and a tiny eye-piece. Curiosity would have grown as he had raised the sextant and looked along the cliff, paused, consulted a small compass and star chart, then written something in a small black book. The onlooker may have been left with an uneasy feeling had he seen the grin of satisfaction and barely disguised greed as the tall, thin man had rubbed his black leather gauntlets together.

That had been several hours ago and now the first glimmers of dawn's cold light were edging almost shyly over the horizon. The Prospector and the villagers waited in the valley, their breath hushed in excitement, their attention transfixed by the cliff edge far above them. The scene had an almost religious feel to it, a crowd awaiting the second coming. But this crowd's motive was far from holy.

Suddenly a hand shot forward and pointed. People gasped and watched as a tiny yellowish rodent tumbled gently earthwards. Then another followed, its tiny paws flailing uselessly against the rushing air. Then another.

Then . . . Whomph . . . zzzip!

It had begun.

With the attention of the villagers firmly fixed on the tumbling cascade of rodents, the tall, thin figure walked quietly away and looted a small warehouse.

*

The next day, thirty-eight miles beyond the Talpa Mountains, high in the Royal Sector of the Imperial Palace Fortress of Cranachan, a tall, thin figure rushed down a long corridor. His footsteps echoed briefly as he flashed past a section of bare wall, then were subdued again as the miles of tapestry soaked up the sound. Acres of brightly coloured cloth depicted past cultural events, initiated by earlier rulers to cement larger inter-kingdomnal relations. The sieges, battles and sackings of days gone by passed unheeded as the young man clutched tightly at the bundle of yellowish garments and ran on. A wild glint smouldered deep in his eyes.

This was the Chief of Cranachan Internal Affairs. He was the youngest ever holder of his post and had achieved this station by utilising the old-fashioned and time-honoured expedients of hard work, bribery, blackmail and sheer greed. Strangely enough, on accepting this role he had not received a thorough job description, a grave error on the part of the personnel department. By keeping the premise 'A vague definition is a flexible definition' firmly entrenched in every waking thought, he had swiftly and ruthlessly set about expanding his power base. Any position of power, however small, not firmly nailed down was mercilessly incorporated into his rapidly expanding empire. Unsuspecting chairmen would be unseated, heads would be removed with almost surgical precision, nobody was entirely safe. And he was always on the look out for more.

He smirked again to himself as he peered slyly at the clothing he carried. Ahead of him two huge Imperial Guards stood immobile, their axes blocking the massive oak double doors. They fingered the shafts nervously as the black-clad figure careered towards the door, and the meeting progressing inside. They were dis-courteously swept aside with a flick of a gauntlet as the Chief of Internal Affairs burst into the Commercial Chambers like a small, but deadly, whirlwind.

The King looked up from the high chair at the end of the weighty oak table. The three other heads turned and stared at the slightly breathless figure.

'Fisk, you're late!' boomed His Imperial Highness the King of Cranachan.

41

'Yes, Sire, may I offer my most profane and obscene apologies and spit upon the graves of all who walk in your Royal footsteps,' he answered in the centuries-old formula.

'You'd better have a damn good reason.'

'Yes, Sire. Of course, Sire.' His voice was remarkably calm. Inside his guts were a bucket of eels being shown jelly and vinegar.

'Take your seat, we will come to you later.'

'Yes, Sire.'

The King turned and addressed the rotund man on his left. His mouth was still agape and his heavy brow glistened with a film of perspiration.

'Gudgeon,' yelled the King, 'do continue, we haven't all day!'

The Scribe of Trade and Industry closed his mouth, swallowed hard and continued, dabbing his brow as he spoke.

'Er . . . ahem. As I was saying, before I was so rudely interrupted,' Gudgeon glared hard at Fisk as he noisily shuffled papers and settled down, 'we need a full two years, but without proper support the Talpa Mountain Steppe scheme will fail and our crop of high-altitude maize will fall far short of our estimated . . .'

'I'm sick of hearing your whingeing. We don't need to grow our own!' thundered the Head of Security and Wars.

'Oh, and what do you suggest then?' shouted Gudgeon, turning to look at the Right Horrible Khah Nij.

'You know damn well. Cry "Havoc!" and count the spoils of War!' came the snarled reply.

'Why can't you try a more peacable solution?'

'Peace? I like peace,' answered Khah Nij, 'a piece of this Kingdom, a piece of that Kingdom. Ha, ha, ha!' The Head of Security and Wars threw back his tightly cropped head and laughed loud.

Gudgeon scowled angrily. Fisk watched and grinned a power-hungry grin.

'Frundle, what do you say?' pleaded Gudgeon. 'I can get no sense from this madman.'

The Lord Chancellor of Cranachan opened a large book in front of him and considered the figures. He stroked the side of his long nose and concentrated hard.

42

'C'mon, Frundle, what do you say?' repeated Gudgeon, wiping his brow.

The Lord Chancellor looked up over the half-moon glasses perched precariously on the end of his nose.

'Two years?'

'That's what I said earlier,' answered Gudgeon with exasperation.

'Very well, you may tell the farmers they can have the money . . .'

The Scribe of Trade and Industry breathed a heavy sigh of relief. 'Thank you.'

Khah Nij scowled angrily.

'. . . providing,' continued Frundle, 'that the work is carried out and the Steppes are producing crops within two years. Otherwise our Right Horrible Friend here may . . . er . . . take his own steps.'

Gudgeon swallowed hard as Khah Nij made a gesture with his finger across his throat, and grinned.

'So, that's decided,' declared the King. 'Any other business?'

This was the moment that the Chief of Cranachan Internal Affairs had been waiting for. Quietly he raised his black-gloved hand.

'Fisk, you may speak,' shouted the King, and then added quietly, 'May I remind you, this had better be good.'

'Thank you, Sire, I had not forgotten.'

He picked up a pair of yellowish trousers that lay by his side on the table. They shone with the lustre of a fur coat. He cleared his throat. Mostly for effect.

'My Liege, members of the Council, I trust you know what these are?'

Silence.

'And these?' he held up a pair of gloves made from the same material.

'And this?' A shirt.

'This?' A hat.

'These?' A pair of slippers.

'This? These? One of these?' Soon a large pile of yellowish garments lay on the table.

43

Khah Nij drummed his fingers on the table in obvious irritation. 'So what?' he shouted.

'What,' answered Fisk calmly, 'do they have in common?'

'They're yellow,' answered the Head of Security and Wars derisively. 'Do we have to listen to this rubbish?'

'They're all made from lemming skin,' answered Gudgeon. 'I've heard of this but I've never seen any. Where did you get it?'

'Let's just say I acquired it. But does anyone know where it comes from?' said Fisk smugly.

'Lemmings,' shouted Khah Nij, dripping derision.

'Just over the eastern border in Rhyngill,' replied Gudgeon quickly to save face.

'That is where it is cured and fashioned into garments, correct. But I ask again. Where does it come from? Where does it *grow*?'

'Fisk,' shouted the King, 'we all know it grows on the backs of lemmings. This is not a natural history lesson, and what it's got to do with Internal Affairs is not immediately apparent. So I would be grateful if you would share with us the significance of the point you are failing to make, as I am rapidly losing my patience!'

'With all due respect, Sire, it is an Internal Affair.'

Fisk's comment produced a thick silence and four baffled faces. He had them.

'I shall explain. These garments are made from the skins of lemmings that, for reasons best known to themselves, jump off cliffs in huge numbers. Their favourite cliff is situated just over the border near a tiny village in Rhyngill. All the lemming skin is cured there. The money is rolling in. Khah, have you checked on the status of our eastward border recently?'

'No, it needs little supervision. It is a natural border. No army could climb those cliffs!'

'Gudgeon,' asked Fisk, 'what is the status of our export agreements to Rhyngill for livestock?'

Gudgeon looked puzzled. 'None,' he replied.

'Frundle,' asked Fisk, 'is not the unauthorised exporting of Cranachan-grown livestock to Rhyngill tantamount to rustling and punishable by death?'

Khah Nij's eyes lit up.

'Yes. Am I to understand from this that the lemmings, from

44

which all these garments are made, and which bring in so much money, do not live in Rhyngill?'

'Well put, Lord Chancellor. They live in the Cranachan region of the Talpa Mountains. By rights, all the lemming skin grown in that region, and illegally removed from Cranachanian land, is still our property. Therefore all the monies raised due to its sale is also ours. Gentlemen, they're stealing our money!' There then followed a few moments' silence as they took in what Fisk had just said.

'A serious problem, Fisk,' said the King, finally, with his hand on his chin. 'What do you propose to do about it?'

'Well, Sire, I have an idea . . .'

It was a warm night in the town and the streets were busy. People bustled and milled about in the way that people normally bustle and mill about, only a little more watchfully. There were two types of watchfulness adopted by the people in Fort Knumm, as they bustled and milled about. There was the type of watchfulness of people who watched for unwanted thieving hands removing large proportions of their wealth, and then there was the type of watchfulness of people watching for people who weren't watching for unwanted thieving hands removing large proportions of their wealth. The latter were normally the people with the unwanted thieving hands. Although they saw their hands more as tools for facilitating the swift and fair redistribution of wealth. In their direction.

Way above, a full moon glowed over shabby roof tops and millions of stars watched almost unblinkingly, although not quite as warily as the people below. It was nearing autumn in OG 1024 but to most of the residents of 'The Fort' small details of season or year didn't matter. To them details like nature, the changing of the seasons, day and night were more or less irrelevant. If you can't see what the hand of Nature does to the flora and fauna over a year then who cares if it's spring or winter? It wasn't really that the residents and visitors were anti-Nature, simply that there wasn't enough in Fort Knumm to really bother about.

Don't get me wrong, there was other wildlife in the Fort than people. The streets were littered with a host of stray cats, rats and

45

the odd mangy dog teetering on the brink of rabid depravity. People kept small menageries and a few pigs in their squalid back yards out of a real and devoted sense of haute cuisine. Most of the buildings played host to a small colony or two of woodlice and several types of cockroach. But by observing all of these creatures' everyday habits it would be impossible to gain any accurate idea of seasonal variation.

Woodlice, for example, are not known for their annual long-distance spring migrations.

For the residents of Fort Knumm, day and night were almost equally unimportant. The buildings leaned out at the tops so far and were jammed so close to each other that the sky had become the smallest of slits, that shed little light into the murk below. Even at midday on the brightest of sunny days only the bravest or most foolhardy of photons would dare venture into the world beneath the rooftops. And then only in packs. The people of Fort Knumm lived in an almost permanent twilight and without the sun and moon to dictate time, life continued at full pace virtually twenty-four hours a day.

It was a busy town for passing traders and amongst one of the very, very few that returned regularly, and voluntarily, was a certain Vlad Langschwein, Esquire. Nobody really knew where his interests lay but once a month, regular as clockwork, he would turn up for a good night out. He'd been doing it for years. At least as long as anyone could remember.

Tonight, for outside Fort Knumm it was quite obviously night, the hunched figure sidled furtively through the back streets, past hundreds of open doors, searching for the one he wanted. He instinctively kept to the shadows and shied away from any really bright lights. Eventually a garishly pink, heart-shaped frame caught his attention and he stepped off the murky street, through the open door, into the even murkier interior of 'Daisy and Maisy's Plesure Parlor'. Vlad walked in on to the ankle-deep carpet, fumbled for the small handbell and signalled his presence. Pictures looked out of the pink darkness and showed scantily-clad female bodies cavorting in numerous poses designed to show their voluptuous nature to full frontal advantage. Vlad licked his cold lips in appreciative anticipation. The patter of sharp stilettos rattled into earshot and a young woman appeared, panting gently in what she hoped was a sultry and enticing manner.

'Yeh, c'n I 'elp yer?'

Vlad, ignoring the accent as best he could, leaned forward and whispered, 'Goot Eeeevenink, issss Maisssy, er, available?'

Five days of furious cutting, slicing, cleaning and placing in the curing ovens were coming rapidly to an end. The little group of villagers had worked virtually non-stop to prepare the lemming skins as fast as possible. The whole place was a mess. It would probably take another five days to clear it all up again. If they were lucky.

Right now though, that was one of the last things on the villagers' minds. All eyes were focused on one point. And that was rapidly approaching – the tender furry underbelly of the last lemming of the season.

The Prospector had the self-appointed, honourable duty of dispatching this final rodent and he was revelling in it. He toyed with his captive and enthralled audience, juggling with the knife, pretending to cut his finger off, feigning regret at the passing of another furry life into the great wheel in the sky. And the audience loved it.

Suddenly a cheer erupted as the Prospector completed the last cut and held the glistening yellowish skin high in the air. It was all very primeval. The work was over and everyone knew it. The crowd broke ranks and people scurried everywhere, rapidly moving tables, clearing spaces and setting out a variety of multi-coloured dips with long strips of vegetables beside them. A party miraculously coalesced.

A huge bowl was hauled unsteadily out of one of the nearer huts and placed carefully on a long trestle table. Glasses were swiftly filled for everyone. The Prospector made a small speech and each village toasted his neighbour and their good fortune with brimming glasses of Twisted Lemming. The party had begun.

A whole team, a whole village, had simultaneously let their hair down at the end of a – literally – bloody hard week, and was now collectively enjoying its metaphorical swish over equally meta-phorical bare shoulders. It was going well. Within a very short

47

space of time nobody was entirely sober. The musicians' bum notes passed unheeded as numerous barrels of foaming beer were broached. Not for the first time, the Prospector sat back in his chair and grinned. He was quite simply a very proud and happy man. The skins had been skinned and placed in the curing ovens, the beer had been opened and was flowing freely down all but the most puritanical of throats, everyone was having a great party. What, he asked himself, could possibly be wrong with that?

Almost immediately, with the sense of timing that so often accompanies such fate-teasing questions, the Prospector was made to wish he hadn't asked. In the same tradition that was begun by a malevolent iceberg and an 'unsinkable' ship, his unguarded and self-congratulatory thoughts had somehow tipped the delicate balance of fate far into the opposition's court. The Prospector's bearded smile dropped, like an avalanche on a sunny day, as an awestruck silence oozed thickly over the revelling crowd. The music spluttered into silence, the beer stopped flowing and the revellers stopped revelling. The villagers turned to face the oncoming threat and slowly, like a single ripple on a giant oil slick, they spread out from the advancing centre. A group of four armour-clad horsemen fingered their weapons significantly as they moved slowly and menacingly through the crowd. Metal studs sparkled on the riders' masks and their horses' faces. The semi-circle of people grew in diameter until inevitably, like an overstretched elastic band, it gave way. The band of riders advanced until they stopped before a low trestle table and a small old man sitting on the other side. The solitary figure of the Prospector sat and faced the faceless riders towering above him. Something was happening and he had the distinct feeling that he was rapidly going to wish that it hadn't.

A gauntleted hand reached down and thrust a roll of parchment in front of him. The mouth of the masked face that was attached to the hand opened and barked, 'You have one day!' The leather gauntlet withdrew.

The words echoed around the valley with ominous finality. The group of horsemen turned with easy military precision and left in a black and brooding murderous silence.

48

The Prospector stared at the roll of parchment sitting innocently before him, and felt suddenly and rather alarmingly sick.

The pink satin sheets of the heart-shaped bed rustled sensuously as Maisy rolled back the top covers. She smiled in a vacantly voluptuous manner and fumbled coyly with the top buttons of her blouse. It was an exercise in professionally amateur seduction.

Vlad opened the dark curtains and looked out at the cold silver moon hanging full over Fort Knumm. Moonlight flooded in and lit his high forehead, emphasising its thin and receding hair line. His skin had a pale blue hue, contrasting strongly with the high collar of the long black cloak, hanging like a pair of tired leather wings from his hunched shoulders. He turned slowly, his hands steepled in front of him, long grey nail touching long grey nail. The gaze from his pale watery eyes slid out of murky eye sockets and slid over Maisy's young, tender body. An eyebrow raised itself in silent admiration.

Maisy stood demurely in front of the bed and attempted to look enticingly virginal. It had taken her a lot of practice. She slipped a silky strap over her bare shoulder and pouted with the calculated degree of moist, waiting lips that turned grown men into desperate dribbling wrecks. A woodlouse trundled across the carpet on some nocturnal journey, the destination of which was known only to itself. It crunched quietly under Vlad's shoe as he stepped forward to seize Maisy's bare shoulders. Long grey fingernails sank into her tender flesh as his grip tightened. Maisy shuddered in revulsion.

'My, your hands are cold.'

'Yessss, not ssso bad for holdink you vith,' whispered Vlad grinning in the moonlight.

He picked up the young woman easily and carried her over to the bed. She sank into the deep warm feather mattress. Her panting changed up a carefully calculated gear. She was a real pro.

Vlad unfastened a small clip at his neck and threw off his cloak with a flourish. He stood in front of Maisy, outlined in the cold moonlight wearing nothing but a wicked grin, a full evening suit and spats. A handkerchief waved neatly from his breast pocket. He leaned forward and stared a subterranean stare into Maisy's wide brown eyes.

'My, what big eyes you've got!'

'Yesss, not ssso bad for sssseeink you vith.'

Vlad brushed the girl's hair away from her neck and licked his cold grey lips in evil anticipation.

'My, what big teeth you've . . . uh-oh!'

The cold blue of the moonlight glinted on the two razor-sharp teeth that emerged from behind the dead-fish smile of the creature that held her immobile.

'Relaxssss mein darlink, thissss von't hurt a bit.'

For Maisy, as for hundreds of others of her profession, it had suddenly become too late . . .

The party atmosphere lay shrivelled and dead on the floor like a month-old balloon. A pall of thick silence hung over the village, turning a celebration to a wake. The Prospector shook his head slowly and worriedly passed the roll of parchment on. At first he had hoped that it might be a joke, and had read on, half-expecting a witty punchline. It didn't come. Instead the signature and seal of King Grimzyn of Cranachan stared incontrovertibly back at him. As he had finished reading, his lip curled back and he started to giggle wildly. He fought the reality of it. Fake, must be, mustn't it? He picked at the seal and his fingers dug into the red wax. The signature stubbornly refused to smudge. It hit him. It was real. He stopped, his face fell, the watching villagers stood and fidgeted nervously. He couldn't speak. He couldn't believe it.

All he could see in his mind's eye was his future stuck in a stomach-wrenching nosedive, the joy-stick jammed, the engines screaming and the ground, huge and horribly solid, accelerating towards him. His trembling hands reached out against the acceleration and gripped the joy-stick with white-knuckled terror. Screaming wildly inside silent synapses, he pulled back hard. The aileron lift of inspiration fought with the tug of depressive panic. He pulled again. Harder. The ground ahead moved imperceptibly down. Again and hold. His teeth bit hard together, the muscles on his jaw bulging with the effort. Slowly, against the odds, the sound of straining metal ringing in his mind's ears, he pulled out and levelled off. A tiny patch of clear blue genius shone out above him,

50

gleaming against the dark clouds of doom. He set his jaw, aimed for the centre and accelerated for it.

'Oh no they don't!' he shouted. 'No way!'

The villagers, as one, looked in bewilderment at the old Prospector as he shouted angrily to himself.

'No way. Not a chance. Who the hell do they think they are? My lemming skins. I found them. Mine! Not theirs!'

In a state of intense agitation, he stood, placed his bottle-green glasses on the end of his nose, and rushed off towards the curing shed.

'Don't just stand there!' he yelled over his shoulder, 'C'mon there's work to do!'

Far away, in one of the countless back streets of Fort Knumm, a pale hunched figure walked slowly through the moonlight shadows. He kicked out at a dog as it lurched in front of him and cursed in frustration and loathing as he missed. He pulled his long black cloak tighter around himself and stared up at the moon.

Der moon, he thought to himself. I follow der moon. Vonsse a month der urgesss ssstart, und vonsse a month I follow. Der sssame think every time. Oh a different girl, ja, but der sssame think happensss. An exssstasssy of fumblink, der qvuick nibble den a momentsss pleasssure ass I get dat varm sssticky feelink . . . den vhat? 'Ssssorry darlink, mussst fly.' Vhat haff I got to sshow for it? Oh der musst be more to life dan disss . . . vell okay ssso maybe I'm not sstrictly alive in der true sssensse of der word but whossse counting? It'sss der principle of the think, you know, qvuality of lif . . . er . . . er undeath.

Vlad's stomach rumbled in the dead of the night. He needed something solid. He walked disconsolately on towards the blinking neon lights of a tiny back-street cafe.

Several streets away Maisy, one of an elite band of professionals known collectively as the Fort Knumm Hand Maidens, tossed fitfully in a shallow sleep. The pink sheets rustled gently as she moved from side to side. Two spots of dried blood clung to her neck, a scabby souvenir from her latest nocturnal visitor.

In the morning she would feel a little more tired than usual, slightly more hazy, a tiny bit anaemic, and very, very hungry. But that would soon pass.

She would, like all the others, remember nothing of Vlad Langschwein.

Early the next morning Vice-Captain Barak of the Cranachan Imperial Guard (F Division) was sitting high on his horse, who was in turn standing high on the eastern border overlooking the Rhyngill Sector. Barak sniffed the fresh Talpine air and coughed noisily, the horse chewed on another mouthful of sparse grass. 'Troop,' shouted Barak, shattering the silence, 'What've I told you about smokin' on duty? Put it out!'

Corporal Troop looked around bewildered.

'Are you deaf?' barked Barak. 'Out. Now!'

'But Sir, I'm not smoking.'

'Well somebody is and it's not me. I'd know if it was me wouldn't I, Troop?' He turned and surveyed F Division of the Imperial Guard.

'Yes Sir,' answered Troop. That was the Vice-Captain for you, thought Troop, such an incisive mind.

'OK men,' shouted Barak, 'Own up now an' I'll make it easy. You know the rules. Which one of you is smokin' on duty?'

He stared at each one of them hoping to catch a finger of smoke drifting up from a hastily hidden cigarette. Silence.

'You're only makin' it worse for yourselves.'

Silence. F Division swallowed nervously.

'C'mon confess,' Barak was rapidly losing what little patience he normally had, 'confess or I might just 'ave to get 'eavy. Knowworrimean?'

Nervously a hand rose from the back of the division. Barak dismounted and stomped forward menacingly. F Division parted. After years of serving and cringing under this particularly short, balding Vice-Captain they knew how to avoid a damn good 'Baraking.'

'Ah. Private Fossett,' whispered Barak in a voice that would melt granite. 'Am I to take it that your raised hand is a request for lavatorial relief or,' he took a deep breath, looked up into

52

Fossett's face and yelled, 'ARE YOU GOIN' TO TELL ME WHO IS SMOKIN'? EH?'

Fossett smoothed back his ruffled hair and whispered, 'Yes.'

'YES . . . WHAT!' continued Barak, his face turning red and his barrel chest inches away from the trembling private's stomach.

'Yes . . . er Sir.'

'What are you trying to say? Think carefully now before you answer. I MAY be a tad ANGRY!' Barak's face obligingly turned a tasteful shade of crimson to illustrate the point.

'Yes Sir.'

'I'm all ears, Private . . . and if you don't tell me now, THAT'S ALL YOU WILL BE!' The Vice-Captain smiled a crocodile smile as he caressed his freshly drawn knife.

'It's . . .' quaked Fossett. 'It's . . . none of us, Sir.'

'What? Don't make it worse. I can smell smoke and if I can smell smoke then SOMEBODY IS SMOKING. You don't get palls of smoke idly driftin' about in the mountains for no reason. You're not tellin' me that they go hikin' about in the mountains this early in the mornin' just to get a breath of fresh air. Now, Fossett . . .'

The quaking private gulped what he sensed would probably be his last gulp.

'. . . I'll ask you once more, and I'll ask you calmly. WHO IS SMOKIN'?'

'N . . . N . . . N . . . None of us . . .'

Vice-Captain Barak turned a shade of red that, had he been a peony, would have certainly won first prize at any flower show. He reached up and shook Fossett warmly by the throat.

'SIR! He's right, Sir,' shouted Troop pointing out over the cliff.

'Sir. Look. Sir.'

Still clutching the choking private he turned and looked. A pall of smoke hung over the tiny village in the valley far below.

Something was burning.

'Oh Shi . . .' Barak released his grip, Fossett instantly forgotten, and remounted his silently grazing horse.

'Follow me, men,' he shouted as he galloped off and descended the narrow, almost invisible, pathway leading down over the sheer cliff border.

Fossett crawled limply along the cliff top and wished he'd learnt the art of keeping his mouth shut.

'What d'you mean "there ain't any"?' barked Vice-Captain Barak a few minutes later as he stood in the tiny, smoke-swathed village.

'None . . . all gone. Whoof.' The Prospector made a gesture with his hands as if something had just exploded.

'What d'you mean, 'Whoof'? We're talking lemmings, not dogs.'

'Whoof, as in accidentally spill a large quantity of highly inflammable liquid over them, carelessly drop in a burning stick and . . . Whoof! Spontaneous combustion. It really is most regrettable.'

'But what about the message on the roll of parchment? Yesterday . . .? Don't tell me. Let me guess . . . Whoof?'

The Prospector nodded sagely through his bottle-green glasses.

Barak was starting to panic. Things weren't going right.

'But you can't 'ave done that. I've got orders. An' orders is orders.' A pathetic note of pleading crept into his voice.

The Prospector looked pityingly at the top of the Vice-Captain's head.

Inside he was rubbing his hands, it was all going perfectly.

'What, precisely, are your orders?' he asked.

Barak looked up from the ground in front of him, having urged it to open and swallow him to no avail. His eyes glazed over as he appeared to begin to read the inside of his head.

'Acquire and return all end products arising from all illegally imported livestock brackets rodent close brackets.'

The Prospector smiled. 'Well that's alright. Why didn't you say?'

'What d'you mean?' asked Barak desperately.

'I mean you've got nothing to worry about. If you just wait a couple of hours, maybe three, possibly four – you know, till the fire's cooled down – you can take it. Take it all.'

Barak's face brightened. 'What, just like that? Without a fight?'

'Clearly,' smiled the Prospector in mock defeat, 'we are grossly outnumbered. Rather than face bloodshed and almost certain slaughter at your hands, I will concede to a gentlemanly defeat at the hands of a superior force.'

Barak's chest swelled as he nodded his agreement. 'Accepted. So glad you saw sense. Wise decision.'

'While you await the final cooling of the fire, may I offer you the hospitality of our humble village?'

'Well . . . I . . .'

'Fancy a drink Vice-Captain?'

'Well . . . ahem . . . I wouldn't normally but . . . er . . . under the circumstances . . .'

'And for the men?'

'I don't really see as it'll do any harm. Most kind!'

The Prospector's arm snaked around the Vice-Captain's shoulder as he led him away to a long and very comprehensive introduction to the local cocktail.

The next day, back in Cranachan, Barak felt like death warmed up. To say that he had a headache, would be like saying that a fully fledged tropical hurricane ripping its way through tiny coastal villages and completely destroying anything within a ten-mile radius of its epicentre is a minor inconvenience. He was also exhausted after riding the worst part of the night to get back. It shouldn't have taken anywhere near as long as it did, even if they had been riding backwards, but on the way back Fossett had declared that he recognised where they were and that if you go down over there, behind that hill, through a small valley, then just the other side is that outcrop where we can see the Palace from. It'll save miles. Unfortunately, in their collectively drunken state it had sounded a remarkably good idea. A far better idea than it actually turned out to be. Within minutes they were lost; within hours they were completely lost and, worse, the drink was beginning to wear off. Eventually, after rattling around the mountains for hours and sobering up to only mild intoxication, Troop did in fact recognise where they were and led them back to the Palace, with Fossett struggling along behind under the weight of the several saddlebags full of lemming produce.

That had been yesterday. Right now, after far too few hours' sleep and still requiring several hundred cups of strong black coffee, Vice-Captain Barak of the Cranachan Imperial Guard (F Division) knocked sheepishly on the pair of huge oak doors. The doors that led into the Commercial Chambers. He counted to three, pushed the huge brass rings and slithered in, followed by the rest of F Division. It wasn't often that F Division had an audience with King Grimzyn in person. Face to face. And all of them wished that it wasn't happening today.

If it went the way Barak dreaded then it would almost certainly be their last.

'Your Highness. Gentlemen of the Cabinet,' whispered Barak through the sort of mental and physical fog that made a fortnight's trepanning seem like fun. 'It is my duty to report that our mission is, ahem, accomplished.' This last word was whispered even quietly more than the rest of the sentence. The men of F Division, as one, placed their cargo carefully onto the shiny marble floor. A small, hazy black cloud floated ominously out of the saddlebags.

'All end products arising from all illegally imported livestock brackets rodent close brackets acquired and returned, Sire.' He saluted limply to the King, then the Head of Security and Wars. Millions of metaphorical caterpillars simultaneously turned into butterflies somewhere very close to Barak's lower intestine. It made him feel incredibly sick.

'Excellent,' said the King and leant forward to get a closer look.

'Any resistance?' barked the Right Horrible Khan Nij.

'None, Sir.' Barak swallowed thickly.

'Not even a teensy-weensy bijou scufflette?'

'None, Sir.' Barak stared at a point three inches above the Head of War's head. Externally only the slightest hint of terror showed, a vein pulsing rhythmically on Barak's forehead. If he could have turned back time, then he would have returned to that moment, earlier this morning, when Troop had suggested, "Just a passing observation, Sir, but don't you think that perhaps the orders we had referred to *intact* products arising from all illegally imported livestock brackets rodent close brackets, sir? Sir? Are you feeling alright, Sir? You've gone all pale." At least then something might have distracted Troop, or injured him, or killed him, or something; the passing observation would not have been made and Barak would be standing in front of the Council of Cranachan, blissfully unaware of the monumental difference between what the Council expected the contents of the saddlebags to be, and the dreadful reality about to be uncovered.

Khah Nij was delighted with Barak's easy victory. 'It would seem, your Highness, that those squalid little creatures that infest Rhyngill have recognised a superior fighting force at long last!' His eyes swivelled sideways towards Barak as he whispered, 'Well done, old chap. Could be a good reward in this for you.'

Barak screamed and ran wildly out of the chamber, his arms flailing madly above his head. At least his mind did. Actually, all he did was swallow slowly and extremely nervously. The way a man would had he just been informed that there were several pounds of TNT hidden, somewhere, in his trousers.

The vein on his forehead pulsed with a slightly more vigorous tempo.

The Chief of Internal Affairs gently, and greedily, rubbed his hands together.

'Sire,' he began, in the tone of voice used by people when they think they are about to make an historic speech, 'inside these humble saddlebags, that lie here before us, is the entire year's supply of lemming skin, returned to its rightful owners. We are privy to witness the fact that, as of here and now, from this moment in time, henceforth, Cranachan holds the key to the forces of supply and demand. We now control the whole of the market for the whole of the known world . . .'

'Er . . . forgive me for asking,' queried Gudgeon, the Scribe for Trade and Industry, 'but there doesn't really seem to be an awful lot there.'

Fisk had now worked up into a full head of speechifying and failed to hear Gudgeon's question.

' . . . thus allowing us to set up a complete and total monopoly on lemming skin. A monopoly in which we set the prices, where we control the . . .'

'A whole year . . . in there?' pondered Frundle, quietly scratching the side of his nose.

' . . . where we rule the roost, allowing us to raise our revenue and fuel our war machine . . .'

' . . . in five bags?'

'. . . giving us the financial freedom to redecorate the Palace and all the surrounding . . .'

Everyone in the room was trying to ignore the raving Fisk.

'I must admit,' said the King to Frundle, 'I did expect a little more, er, volume.'

Fisk was still oblivious to the rapidly germinating seeds of doubt around him.

'. . . and capital to invest in any civil engineering or agriculture scheme we can dream up, for now and for generations of Cranachanians to come!' Fisk looked around, waiting for his applause. All eyes were on the five dust-blackened saddlebags dumped unceremoniously before them.

'Barak, old chap,' began Khah Nij gently, 'would you like to be ever so kind and open one of those bags for us?'

Nonononono, he thought. 'Yip,' he squeaked. Beads of sweat burst onto his brow, his vein added another few beats per minute. He bent down and began fumbling with the clasps.

'Barak,' called the King, beckoning with a long imperious finger, 'Open it here.'

With the speed of a man that has the feeling he is approaching almost certain death, he moved nervously forward.

A small cloud of fine black dust billowed out of the saddlebag as he placed it on the table in front of the King. Barak grinned a doomed grin. He fumbled slowly with the clasps again, attempting to postpone the inevitable, hoping that by some miracle the ashes had recongealed into bright, gleaming skins.

'Barak. Open!' insisted the King.

The Vice-Captain swallowed hard, took a deep breath, held it, then upended the saddlebag at the King's request. Clouds of dense black dust exploded to fill the room, instantly blocking out the light. It was as if the Council Chamber had suddenly been transplanted on to the top of the smokiest of fumaroles in the midst of a particularly splendid fume. Clouds of black danced and swirled with lung-choking abandon and eye-watering madness. And from somewhere in the silent maelstrom the small and apologetic voice of Vice-Captain Barak of the Cranachan Imperial Guard (F Division) Retired, whimpered, 'Your Highness . . . I can explain . . .'

Under the cover of a cloudly night in OG 1024, a small wooden cart rattled its way down one of the foothills of the Talpa Mountains. The Prospector grinned to himself as he thought of Vice-Captain Barak's face.

'Whoof!' he whispered quietly and chuckled.

He pulled on the reins, steered the pony slightly to the left and continued down the indistinct track out of Middin. The heavily laden cart creaked gently, as if it also knew that it alone held the entire year's lemming skin harvest.

Good job I remembered that cave, thought the Prospector for the several hundredth time. Then, I wonder what price we'll get for this lot.

He pulled the reins again, steering the cart carefully between two rocks, and trundled away into the cover of the deep, dark night.

Vlad

Firkin's nerves were as taut as steel cables as he crept through the narrow gorge, past the sleeping creature. His whole body was quivering. One more shock, just the tiniest fright would send his spirit crashing down a scree-ridden slope of panic, into a dark ravine of terror.

It could be worse, he told himself, in an attempt at self-reassurance.

It could still be night time. It could still be dark. Things could still be moving up behind me. Things with long bony fingers and huge slavering mouths hanging open in anticipation and hunger and . . .

STOP! Concentrate! Wait for the snore. Step. Snore. Step. Beads of sweat stood out on his forehead with the effort of concentration.

He was so close to hysteria that he was almost sharing its shoes and socks.

He had left Middin the previous night full of courage, bolstered by adrenalin and blind lunacy. The first few hours had been fine as he had picked his way down the one track out of Middin. His main concern was stumbling or twisting his ankle on an unseen stone. As he had descended further, on to unfamiliar ground, his senses had sharpened so that he became aware of hundreds of tiny nocturnal movements and sounds. His imagination had started to play tricks on him, changing innocent tree trunks into hideous gargoyles or vicious and malevolent dragons, waiting in the shadows, harbouring murder thoughts. He'd tried to see more clearly by looking out of the edge of his eyes but things still remained grey and fuzzy.

After a few hours in the thick black night, he became uncomfortably aware of breathing close to him. Deep rasping breathing in the still night air. It was close. Too close for comfort. With a struggle he contained his panic. He stopped walking, held his breath and listened. His pulse pounded noisily in his temples. All around was thick silence. His lungs felt ready to explode with the pressure. Silence. He let his breath out slowly expecting his rib cage to collapse with the strain. He broke out in a cold sweat as the breathing started again. He stopped. It stopped. His mind raced. He could see nothing. He could hear nothing. He took another breath. He heard another breath and . . . Suddenly the panic evaporated. He nearly laughed out loud in sheer relief as he listened to his breath, loud in the still night air.

His spirit lifted slightly as he set off again.

His progress continued well for a few more hours despite the dark, until he heard footsteps. Footsteps getting louder. He kept walking. The footsteps got louder. And louder.

'My footsteps,' he told himself. 'They're my footsteps, that's what.'

So, to categorically prove it to himself, quite matter-of-factly he stopped and listened. Silence. A reassuringly deep, dark silence. Except for the patter of footsteps pounding towards him.

Icicles of fear shot up his spine and the hairs on the back of his neck bristled in porcupine terror. He dived noisily into the undergrowth, remained still and listened. He could see nothing. The footsteps grew louder. 'It's heard me. It's in the trees,' he thought, close to panic. The steps grew louder and louder. 'It's coming!'

He lay in unmoving agony, badly contorted, where he had landed in the bush, three milligrams of adrenalin away from total catalepsy. He dared not move. He dared not breathe. The steps came nearer and nearer, growing louder and louder and . . . continued past.

He listened until his ears hurt.

He lay motionless for what seemed like an eternity then he let out his breath and relaxed to a state of mere frigid terror. The footsteps hadn't stopped. Maybe it wasn't after him, or maybe it was waiting. He lay still for another few minutes, until he'd settled down to a mild panic, then stood up as quietly as possible. His eyes strained in the gloom, looking for any sign of the owner of the footsteps. After satisfying himself all was clear, and at first incredibly reluctantly, he continued on.

That had all been hours ago. Since then the sun had come up. The sky was clear, the birds were singing. The occasional cricket chirped and Firkin, the brave adventurer on his noble mission, was terrified again.

He'd rounded a corner in the path and stopped dead. At the side of the path was a small sturdy boot and inside that was probably a small sturdy foot. Firkin felt sure the foot was attached to a body, and more than likely another foot. But the rest of it, whatever it was, was hidden in the tall grass, close to the path, as it lay snoring loudly in the fresh morning air. Firkin listened to the regular snores and carefully considered his present predicament.

He looked around him. The path at this point ran through a steep narrow gorge. The high sides and mossy handholds made climbing round impossible for all but the most experienced climber. He could walk back up the path and find a way round but, without a compass and map, he could easily lose direction and never find the path again. There was only one choice. Well, two, but going back to Middin, a sick sister and a host of questions from a pair of almost certainly irate parents, was not an option he relished. Reluctantly, and with a rapidly rising adrenalin titre, the decision to press on forward, past the sleeping creature, was made.

If he timed his steps right, just as it snored, he could move very quietly. Snore. Step . . . Snore. Step . . .

He gritted his teeth and stepped forward on tippy toes. Tension was rising again and every muscle ached. Snore. Step. He daren't look at the body, in the grass, away to his left. Snore. Step. He kept moving almost soundlessly, the snores masking any slight noise he did make. Snore. Step.

Firkin's was as tense and nervous as a headache in a pharmacy as he crept through the narrow gorge past the sleeping creature. His whole body was quivering, one more shock, just the tiniest fright . . .

Suddenly the sky erupted in a cacophony of flapping wings and leaves as a wood pigeon crashed out of the trees. Firkin froze completely. His adrenal medulla kicked into overdrive.

The sleeper awoke with a start, twitched in shock, sat bolt upright and yelled, 'Firk . . .' Firkin collapsed . . .

Hogshead stood up, confused and hugely relieved that his worst thoughts were unfounded. He walked over to Firkin's crumpled body.

OG 1025 continued to trundle by uneventfully in the mountain kingdom of Cranachan. Well, uneventful is a relative term and life under a tyranny as . . . er, tyrannical as that headed by King Grimzyn and his evil cohorts was, to any society approaching normality, far from uneventful.

In the few months since Fisk, the Chief of Internal Affairs, had reluctantly accepted Vice-Captain Barak's apologies and willingly accepted his letter of resignation, a lot of 'unevents' had happened inside Cranachan. Forty-three petty criminals had been put to death for a range of minor crimes, such as actual physical abuse, hurling rabid animals without due care and attention, and littering. King Grimzyn had initiated a kingdomwide clampdown on littering, in the belief that having clean streets would encourage rich tourists to visit, and so save him the time and trouble of going out of his way to remove as much of their wealth as possible while staying in a foreign kingdom. Far easier on your home patch. Remarkably, rich tourists actually seemed to believe the brochure which told them that Cranachan 'is one of the safest kingdoms for the casual visitor. Local residents can provide a colourful evening's street entertainment, providing exciting displays of knife throwing, swordsmanship and the art of the hatchet. Murder mystery weekends can easily be arranged; you can, of course, provide your own victim. Payment can be made throughout Cranachan using access to your cash and jewellery. Come to Cranachan and you'll never want to leave.'

Several small uprisings had been nipped in the bud, resulting in the arrest and immediate imprisonment, or death, of all the perpetrators and a few 'innocent' bystanders. Although, once again, 'innocent' in Cranachan would probably mean 'guilty' everywhere else.

Somehow in the midst of this chaos, Gudgeon had made a very interesting discovery.

Life was about to change dramatically for Crananchan, Rhyngill, and not least for the Chief of Internal Affairs.

Fisk knocked on the huge oak doors to the Commercial Chambers and waited, under the watchful gaze of the two guards, wielding their axes with the easy professionalism of men born to the job. Fisk quivered gently in his boots. An echoed bark resonated from within the chambers. He swallowed hard, pushed the doors and strode in. His footsteps echoed under the watchful gaze of the assembled council. He strode forward across the shiny marble floor, stopped and bowed low.

'My liege, I am summoned. I am your humble servant.'

'Creep,' muttered Gudgeon under his breath.

'What is this?' yelled the King, holding up a yellowish garment. Fisk looked around nervously. The answer was obvious. Was it the right one? He said it anyway.

'A pair of trousers, your Royal Altitude.'

The King winced. Fisk felt very uncomfortable.

'Yes,' replied the King, through clenched teeth, 'as far as that goes you are correct. However, I ask again, what is this?'

Fisk shuffled uncomfortably as a very similar conversation flashed into his mind from several months ago. Something told him that this time it wouldn't have quite the same conclusion.

'Er, do you perhaps mean, "what is it made from?"'

The King nodded imperiously and bared his teeth. Fisk was suddenly reminded of a picture he had seen as a child. It was of a huge lion, jaws wide and salivating, eyes gleaming with the anticipation of ripping the head off the tiny mammal pinned down under his two huge paws. Suddenly, and all too clearly, Fisk knew how that mammal felt.

'I believe, your Royal Lio . . . Highness, that the garment held by you, in your hand,' Fisk was flapping, 'is made from the skin of several l . . . l . . . lemmings.'

'Correct.'

'But, Sire . . . forgive my apparent stupidity, but did I not initially present that garment to you several months ago, in a very similar manner? Oh, er, not that I'm criticising your presentation style at all, it's not even a thought that had crossed my mind. Didn't even like to mention it really, come to that.' He ended limply and smiled a pathetically cheesey smile, born from an emotion closer to intense fear than happiness.

'It is the same garment.'

'Ah, I see.' He didn't. 'But why are you showing it to me?'

'Because of these.' The King reached behind him and pulled out a pair of almost identical trousers. These, however, were slightly better made, had studs reinforcing all the major strain points and were less faded. In short, they looked like the tailor had had at least a year to practise since making the first pair.

'Oh. You've got a new pair. How, er, nice. Where did you get them from?' asked Fisk, feeling that he didn't really want to know the answer.

'I bought them in a market in Rhyngill,' said Gudgeon smugly.

'They must be from last year,' countered Fisk, beginning to feel angry.

The King beckoned Fisk closer, turned the trousers inside out and revealed a small white tab sewn into one of the seams. The writing on it said, 'Made in Rhyngill from 100% pure lemming skin. Harvested in OG 1024.'

Fisk's jaw dropped open.

'. . . ?' he said, staring limply at the two pair of trousers before him.

'It was a very busy market,' continued Gudgeon, twisting the knife, 'A wide range of stuff there. So I bought this, and this, a couple of these, these, this, one of them, this . . .'

Yellowish items cascaded out of a large bag until a huge heap lay on the table in front of Gudgeon.

'It would seem,' came the voice of Gudgeon round the sizeable heap, 'that the lemming skin trade in Rhyngill is alive and well and, judging by the prices they're charging, very, very profitable.'

Fisk composed himself and prepared to speak. 'But . . .' Words failed him.

The King slammed his fists on the table and rocketed skywards. His crown wobbled dangerously on his head.

'Yes. 'But . . .' But how? But why? But what are you going to do about it?'

'. . .' replied Fisk, choking as fear wrung his vocal chords like a dirty rag.

'Go away and do something,' growled the King.

Fisk struggled to maintain his balance as he bowed long and low and backed feebly away towards the door. His head spun with panic and a million questions.

'Leave it to me, Sire,' he somehow managed to croak as he backed through the huge oak doorway. 'I'll . . . I'll . . . er, think of something.'

King Grimzyn, barely controlling the seething anger within, sneered a sneer that would freeze liquid nitrogen. Crystals of pure terror precipitated in Fisk's blood and lodged in his already arctic heart. He felt pale and drained, like the discarded, shrivelled skin of some ice-bound lizard.

In the same way that afterimages lodge on retinas exposed to bright light, a feeling lodged in Fisk's cold soul. The icy blast of King Grimzyn's fury became the glacial terror within a condemned man. Fisk suddenly saw himself standing at the base of a several-hundred-foot ice wall, looking up at the trembling tons of ice waiting for the chance to crush him into icy oblivion.

He closed his eyes and shook with sheer terror.

'Are we there yet?'

'What?'

'Are we there yet?'

'No!'

'Oh.'

Silence fell, once again, between the two boys as they continued trudging through the forest. Around them towered the tallest trees they had ever seen, making them feel very small indeed.

'I'm hungry!'

'What?'

'I'm hungry, and my legs are tired. My shoulders are aching, my feet are hot, I'm thirsty and . . .'

'Shut up, will you!' snapped Firkin. He was still angry about Hogshead terrifying him in the gorge. And Hogshead was upset about Firkin upsetting him in Middin. Luckily, it hadn't taken Firkin long to recover from the shock of being scared out of his wits but there was now a strained and wary look in his eyes.

'But . . .'

'Be quiet! There's nothing I can do about it. It's not my fault that you didn't bring anything with you. Is it? Now come on. It can't be that much further.'

'I get hungry when I'm scared an' last night night was dark an' I was scared an', an', an', I'm hungry. So there.'

'Shut up.'

'That's not nice.'

'Shut up! Shut up! Shut up!'

Hogshead pulled a hideous face at the back of Firkin's head and carried on through the forest.

It was getting late and they'd been walking through the trees for hours. He hadn't thought a forest could be so big. He hadn't thought it would be so far to town. In a nutshell, he just hadn't thought. Neither, unfortunately for both of them, had Firkin.

Leaving Middin on his crusade had seemed like such a good idea last night; or was it the night before? Already it seemed so far away and so long ago.

During the late afternoon and early evening the foliage had changed from dense dark pinewoods to a more open and varied woodland, with bushes huddling between huge old oaks and ash. The path had become more uneven and now gave a definite impression of underuse and even dereliction in places.

The light began to fade, turning the greens to a mucky grey. Firkin started to have difficulty seeing where he was putting his feet. He stumbled on roots snaking across the path. He splashed in puddles. The dark closed in. Soon the only way he could see was to look out of the corner of his eyes.

'Alright,' said Firkin finally, 'it's time to light the lanterns.'

'Oh, good,' said Hogshead expectantly. 'My shins are bruised to bits.'

'Well, come on, hurry up. I can't see a thing.'

'What?'

'Come on, get them out. You know what to do.'

'Me?'

'Yes.'

'Er . . .' Hogshead took a deep breath in the rapidly congealing gloom. 'I haven't got them. Have you got them?'

'Oh dear,' said Firkin embarrassedly as it dawned on him that they were lampless. 'Oh dear, oh dear,' he said as the last photon of the day winked at him from behind a tree and headed home for bed. He blinked rapidly. It made no difference. Darkness had settled down for another long night and right now he could see about as much as an eel in a tin of matt-black paint. In a box. With the lid on.

In a cottage, in a clearing in the same huge forest, a gaunt figure was feeling very, very gloomy. He was, not to put too fine a point on it, bored witless. He looked up from the pack of cards, spread out in front of him on the table, and stared at the rusting range lurking in the far corner of the room. It was in a sorry state. Years, possibly decades, had come and gone since the cast iron had last been blacked and it was probably just as long since anything had been cooked on it. Actually, that isn't strictly true. Things were still cooked on top of the range but not using coal, or even the range. Nowadays he used self-contained vats of boiling fat and a glass-fronted thing that went *ping*!

A heavy sigh whistled out between his two pointed teeth as he gathered up the cards, and continued to play, in the small pool of candle-light.

'Patienssse! Patienssse!' he thought, 'I'm sssssick of it. I really could do mit ein gut game of . . . of . . . vell, anythink, asss long asss its cardsssss!!'

A few minutes later, after losing again, he stood up, trudged over to the wall and flicked a switch.

'Oh dear, oh dear,' whispered Firkin again, feeling very lost and very hungry. He could hear things moving in the undergrowth and tried, desperately, to ignore them. The memory of last night was still too real for comfort. He ducked, suddenly, as a pair of leathery wings flapped past his head and disappeared into the solid blackness. An owl hooted, much too loud and much too close. His senses sharpened and his imagination amplified every sound his ears snatched from the gloom. The tiniest insects' wing beats became squadrons of marauding dragons, with flaming nostrils, hell-bent on acres of destruction. The rustle of shrews in long grass became an advancing pack of hunger-crazed hyenas, out for blood. His blood. His eyes were wide open, straining into the tar-pit black.

'Can you see something over there?' whispered Hogshead.

'Where?'

'Over there.'

'I can't see where you're pointing.'

'Over *there*.'

'Where?'

Hogshead fumbled about in the dark and eventually found Firkin's hand. Using this, he pointed.

'Over there . . . can you see it?'

'What?'

'Don't you think its a bit lighter over there?'

Firkin's eyes strained harder into the optical vacuum.

'Er, you could be right!'

'It's lighter isn't it?'

'. . . Could be.'

'What is it?'

'Dunno. Lights, I'd guess. Let's go and have a look.'

'Should we?' said Hogshead doubtfully.

'Why not?'

'Well . . . why?'

'Because I'm not staying out here, in the dark again, if there's someone with a light on over there.' He pointed uselessly. 'Come on.'

Firkin moved forward gingerly, taking every step with care, not knowing what he was about to stand on. Or in.

Invisible branches scratched them and caught at their clothes. Dense knots of criss-crossed twigs blocked their progress, forcing them to stumble into each other. Black ivy snaked around their ankles.

Progress was slow but eventually, hot, sticky and panting, they stood within feet of the edge of a clearing. In the clearing was the source of the light. Their hearts pounded in fear and exertion as they stepped quietly out from the blackness.

The shock was incredible.

The stood with their mouths open in sheer disbelief and blinked in the dazzling light as it flashed red, then white.

'D . . . d . . . do you see what I see?' whispered Firkin, transfixed.

'Er . . . what do you see?'

'Something . . . that . . . shouldn't . . . be here.'

'Yes.' Hogshead's jaw fell open limply. Red then white.

'Something I thought was a fairy tale.'

'Huh.'

'Oh.'

The stood and stared across the dazzling clearing. Sharp black shadows stretched away from their ankles back into the trees. The clearing flashed red, then white.

'I think I've gone mad.'

'Me too.'

'Daddy, there's the bell again.'

'What? Oh, OK,' said Val Jambon looking up, through a cloud of flour, as he enthusiastically rolled out the pastry.

'You'd better hurry up. He'll get angry.'

'Yes, I know. Fetch me those buns will you?'

'These nice sticky ones?' asked the little girl, prodding them playfully.

'Yes – ooh, don't do that dearie.'

'This one's a rejeck. It's got a hole in. Look. Can I have it?' she said, grinning up at her father, putting her head to one side and her toes a bit closer together for added effect.

'Yes, yes, Courgette, you naughty girl. Now put two on to a plate, will you?'

'Yeff,' she said from behind the rest of her enormous and very sticky bun.

Soon the tray was prepared, two sticky buns, a glass of orange juice and a pair of special chocolate biscuits. The Cook picked it up, headed for the door, and started on the long journey upstairs.

Eventually, after several flights of long winding staircases and many hundreds of yards of empty corridors, the Cook arrived. He knocked smartly on the door, pushed it open, and entered the room.

After the bleak and empty corridors outside, it was always a shock to see the bright colours in this room. And the carpet.

70

Nowhere else had carpet. Not nice, deep, comfy, red carpet like this, covered in dozens of big, soggy cushions. He placed the supper tray carefully on the little table in the centre of the room and looked around again. There were lots of little paper birds lying everywhere, a scatter of tiddlywinks in a corner, a ludo board, a cuddly penguin, at least half a dozen books and, sat high on one of the cushions, a small soggy bear. The phrase 'well-loved' is a good place to start from when describing this little bear. Once upon a time he would have been entirely covered in fur. An awful lot of that had been rubbed off in the years of enthusiastic cuddling and not so gentle affection he had enjoyed since then. His nose didn't have a great deal of fluff in it any more and some of his seams were wearing alarmingly thin. But he was a happy bear. He was lucky. He had both eyes and his ears were still in place. Just.

The Cook turned, closed the door, and, his task complete, headed off back downstairs.

The little bear sat on top of a heap of cushions, his head on his balding chest, and waited to be played with.

Hogshead's ear was stinging. Surprisingly, this made him feel very happy. He flashed red and white in the forest clearing.

Having an earlobe that pulsed with angry pain didn't normally make him happy. He wasn't that sort of chap. But now, right now, here in a clearing in the middle of a huge forest, miles from home, there was little that could have made him happier. Except, perhaps, for a hot plate of steaming stew, a nice hot bath, a freshly made bed, several really good story books, a pot of tea, half a dozen assorted mince pies. And not being here, in a clearing in the middle of a huge forest, miles from home, with a sore ear.

His stinging ear was reassuring. It proved to him that:

(a) he was alive,
(b) Firkin was alive,
(c) some parts of his brain were still functioning, relatively, normally,
(d) the rules of cause and effect still applied,
(e) he might not, after all, be hallucinating wildly, and

(f)   something very, very strange indeed was, in actual fact, facing them from the other side of the clearing.

'Firkin,' he whispered, 'what did I just do then?'

'You pinched me,' came the monotonal reply.

So far so good, thought Hogshead.

'And what did you do, then?' he asked out loud.

'I hit you,' replied Firkin, staring straight ahead, 'probably on the ear.'

Hogshead was very pleased. He'd now double checked (a) to (e). He took a deep breath and flashed red then white.

Time to test (f), he thought. He almost hoped he was wrong.

'Firkin,' he whispered.

'Yuhhh,' came the absent reply as Firkin flashed red then white.

'What can you see? In this clearing. I mean, precisely, what can you see?'

Firkin appeared to struggle. 'Er . . . over there?'

'Yes.' Red then white.

'. . . The other side of the clearing?'

'Yes.'

'You mean that tiny little cottage?'

Hogshead knew that Firkin could see it too.

'Yes . . . that tiny little cottage.'

Right, thought Hogshead, now for the crunch question.

'Firkin, now think carefully before you answer this, do you happen to notice anything, just a teensy-weensy bit, well, odd about that tiny little cottage?'

Firkin didn't have to think hard about the answer. It had hit him as soon as they had set foot in the clearing. 'Well, you don't normally run into cottages that have windows made of . . . of . . .' Firkin couldn't handle it. He stood, stuttering like a needle in a faulty groove, until Hogshead supplied the essential word.

'. . . sugar,' he whispered.

'Yes.'

'. . . and marzipan doors . . .'

'Ye . . .'

'. . . and icing roofs . . .'

'Y . . .'

72

'. . . or gingerbread walls.'

Firkin stood with a strange grin on his face. He flashed red then white. 'You can see it too,' he said. 'Ha, ha, ha – what a relief! Ha. I thought I was . . . ha . . . going mad . . . Quite . . . quite . . . mad. I mean . . . ha . . . fancy thinking a cottage was made out of . . . ha . . . gin . . . gin . . . gin . . . ridiculous . . . I mean, what happens when it rains? . . . Ha . . . Ha . . . It's not real . . . fairy story . . . fantasy . . . it's not real at all, it's . . .' He stopped and turned to Hogshead for the first time since entering the clearing. His face went deadly serious. They both flashed red and white simultaneously. 'It's *not* real, is it?' There was pleading in his eyes. He gripped Hogshead's shoulders tightly.

Hogshead wasn't sure. Firkin had just agreed that he could see what Hogshead could see. But there was still something that didn't add up. Something definitely not right about it. Red then white.

Hogshead had a very small, but nonetheless real feeling that this cottage was not quite your normal, run-of-the-mill, recently refurbished, highly desirable gingerbread residence. At the moment, though, the reason for this suspicion, somehow, escaped him.

'Tell me it's *not* real,' repeated Firkin. 'It can't be. It's just one of those things that Franck told us about. One of his daft stories.' Red then white.

Hogshead pictured, in his mind, the image that Franck had created for them. Suddenly, it clicked.

'Firkin, think carefully before you answer. Do you remember, in the stories that Franck told us, anything ever being mentioned, even slightly, about that huge red neon sign over the door flashing on and off?'

'Er, you mean the one that says "EAT AT VLAD'S"?'

'Yes.'

'Well now that you come to mention it . . .'

'. . . And the sign saying "ASK ABOUT THE SPECIALS"?'

'. . . erm . . .'

'. . . and "STAY FOR THE MEAL OF YOUR LIFE"?'

'Actually . . . no.'

A thin wisp of aromatic air floated out of the cottage and across the clearing. It almost appeared to know where it was heading. A sentient smell. Red then white. 'Weird, isn't it?' continued Hogshead. 'It's not like Franck to miss out on a detail like that. You would have expected him to have told us that bit. He knows how much I like food.'

He sniffed the air. Aromatic fingers shot up his nose and began teasing his olfactory receptors. Unknowingly, he took a red step forward, then a white one.

'It smells wonderful . . .' His stomach rumbled in agreement.

The fingers pulled. They snatched at Firkin's nose. Yielding, he took a step forward.

'. . . and I'm starving.'

'There's probably nothing else for miles around . . .'

Firkin's stomach rumbled for effect.

'. . . and there's nothing in the bag . . .'

'. . . and we have walked a long way today . . .'

They walked dreamily across the clearing, all suspicious thought forgotten, flashing red and white as they went.

Ahead of them, silently on well-greased hinges, the door of the cottage swung open.

'. . . we really could do with a rest . . .'

'. . . and a bite to eat . . .'

'. . . after you, Sir.' Firkin bowed low at the open door.

'Oh, thank you.'

They stepped over the rush mat, embroidered with the word *Wilkommen*, into the – almost – deserted cottage.

The Chief of Internal Affairs' quarters were a mess. A lot of work had passed over his desk in the few days since his meeting with King Grimzyn. Fisk had worked like a man who knew there would be no tomorrow. If he didn't find a solution soon, he might well be right, for himself at least. One barked order from King Grimzyn and OG 1025 would be the last year Fisk would see. This lemming problem was getting out of hand. He had to think of an answer. He either needed a solution soon or a passport to somewhere very far away. He looked despairingly at the mess in front of him.

Maps of Cranachan's eastern border were piled high on top of documents of ownership, importation agreements and internal memos specifying the precise positioning of the border. The whole room looked like the result of a limited nuclear strike on a very busy barrister's office. One with a particular interest in border disputes.

Fisk had looked at every inch of every map of the border, through a powerful magnifying glass, and not once did the border deviate from its cliff-edge position. Trying a different tack, he'd pored over hundreds of legal documents, searching for a loophole that would allow him to bring into question the legal validity of the original placing of the border. Nothing. The floor was littered with screwed up pieces of parchment, hurled there in frustration.

No matter which way he looked at it, and he had tried an awful lot of different ways, he could only conclude that once the lemmings crossed the border into Rhyngill, there was no way that Cranachan could have any sort of claim on them, let alone get them back, legally. Surprisingly, despite his ruthlessly heartless and greedy nature, Fisk liked things to be legal. Not necessarily entirely legal, but with just the right amount of non-illegality to allow him to get his own way without causing himself too much of a problem.

It was mainly for this reason, as well as the risk and expense involved, of course, that he didn't approve of the idea (Khah Nij's idea actually) of storming into Rhyngill on an annual basis and stealing the skins *en masse*. Besides, that was hard work and was sadly lacking in the finesse department. No, there had to be a better way.

In a gesture of frustration, his black-gauntleted hand flexed and flicked another ball of parchment over the edge of the table, into oblivion. He watched it arc away, spinning gracefully, until it disappeared over the table's artificial horizon. He stood up and looked at the waste-parchment basket. Not one had landed in there. All had overshot their mark. Grumbling to himself he pulled the table back a few feet, sat down and launched off another volley of yellowing parchment spheres. He stood up to assess his accuracy, smirking in satisfaction to see that five out of eight had hit their mark and that the other three were at least well within range. He sat down again and chewed the end of his quill thoughtfully.

Suddenly, he reached out, grabbed a fresh piece of parchment, screwed it up into a tight ball and flicked it after the others. Almost nervously he stood and peered over the edge of the table . Direct hit! He shouted with joy and ran out of the room, knocking over his chair in the mad dash.

He had it. Problem solved!

It has been said that the way to a man's heart is via his stomach. Well, the way to a man's stomach is certainly via his nose. Just ask any endoscopist.

This definitely held true for Firkin and Hogshead. They had both been captured by the mysteriously seductive aroma emanating from the tiny cottage and had followed its nostril-quivering gradient as obediently as bees to a buddleia. Their stomachs rumbled seismically, in an attempt to grab someone's attention, as the two boys sat on red sugar-chairs bolted firmly to the icing floor.

The illusion of homely cottaginess had been left, along with a few twigs and the odd greenfly, firmly on the far side of the threshold. The interior could almost have been from a different planet. The two boys had never seen anything like it and, strangely, didn't feel out of place.*

The interior of the cottage was decorated in garish, attention-seeking colours, perfectly suited for the clientele for which it had been so meticulously designed to cater. The gingerbread walls were coloured red with cochineal and hung with brightly coloured, glossy pictures of hamburgers, cheeseburgers and mixed grills nestling amongst cardboard containers of anaemic fries. Jelly oak beams held up the shortbread ceiling. Candyfloss striplights were connected by liquorice wires. A sherbet fountain cascaded gently

---

* For years it has been known that, given a free choice, children will eat the greasiest, most fattening convenience foods available, washed down with gallons of tooth-rotting, high-sugar drinks. Also, given a free choice of environments in which to practise such consumptive habits, they will invariably head for the most brightly and tastelessly decorated available to them. Psychologists have speculated long and hard about the reason for this and most concur that it is 'That these environments fulfil a longing to return to an environment and way of life held within the deep subconsious of the collective memory.' Others believe that it is entirely due to the fact that they are too young to get into pubs.

76

in the far corner and jelly fish swam in a tank under the counter. The boys stared intently at the rice-paper menu. Hogshead was dribbling.

'Ooh . . . with cheese!' He waved his upturned, clenched fists close to his ears and grinned wildly.

They were amazed at how comprehensive the menu was. They were almost spoilt for choice.

'. . . and tomato sauce . . .'

Firkin looked up.

'I wonder where the waiter is.'

'. . . ooh, ice-cream . . .'

'I can't see anyone.'

'. . . chocolate fudge cake . . .'

Firkin looked around at the half-dozen other identical sugar tables, with red sugar-chairs. They were all arranged neatly and set ready with knives and forks, condiments, tomato sauce, chocolate sauce, sugar lumps . . . in fact everything needed for a full meal.

Except for people.

He looked back at his menu and tried to make a decision. The choice was exhausting.

'Goot eeveninck gentillmen.'

Firkin and Hogshead jumped.

'Vellcome to mein ressstaurant.'

'W . . . wha . . . who?'

'I am der owner of dis essstablissshment, Herr Vlad Langs-chwein.' With that he gave a long low bow and remained standing at their table with an air of expectancy, tinged with not a little excitement.

He was not a very tall figure and stood slightly hunched at the shoulders. He wore a black suit with a white wing-collar shirt and a badly tied bow tie sitting unceremoniously at his wrinkly neck. A towel, hung grubbily over his left arm, completed the picture of shabby subservience. Except, of course, for the peculiar grey-blue tinge to his skin.

He bent slightly closer to Firkin and stared at him from pale watery eyes.

'Vhat may I sssserve you vith?' he hissed. 'A sssmall ssside ssalad perhapsssss? Ssss Sssss Sssssss.' His shoulders twitched slightly as he laughed at his private joke.

77

'Erm, ahem, we h . . . haven't decided yet,' answered Firkin, fingering his neck, which suddenly felt strangely uncomfortable.

'May I asssissst you in your sssselection?'

'What would you recommend, Mr Langschwein?' asked Hogshead cheerfully. The prospect of a good feed had considerably brightened his spirits.

'Pleassse, pleassse, call me Vlad. It'ssss ssso much friendlier sssomehow!' Their host smiled humourlessly. Firkin found himself thinking of dead fish.

'Tonight'ssss Ssssssspecial isss essspesscially, ahem, appetisssssing, unt isss highly rekommended,' Vlad oozed, rubbing his hands together.

'Ooh, what is it?' asked Hogshead, salivating desperately.

The gaunt figure leant over and pointed at the menu with a long grey index fingernail.

'Is there a lot? Only me an' Firkin have been walking all day and we're tired an' I'm starvin'.'

'I haff enough for my . . . er, your needssss, Ssssir!'

'Is that what we could smell as we came in?'

'Almossst ssscertainly, Sssir.' The corner of his mouth twitched slightly.

'Ooooh, well I want some. What about you, Firkin?'

'Er, what . . . ? Yes, okay,' he said, looking up from the menu.

'Isss everythink alrright, Sssir?'

'Yes, yes, fine, er . . . I'm a bit tired that's all,' he lied.

'Two ssservings koming rrright up,' and with a brief flourish Vlad had disappeared silently into the kitchen, leaving the two boys alone again.

'What a strange accent he had. Seemed nice enough, though,' said Hogshead, his stomach rumbling expectantly.

'I'm not so sure. There's something not right about him, but I don't know what.'

'He was light on his feet for such an old man. I didn't hear him go out. Or come in.'

'Why do you say he's old?' asked Firkin.

'Well, being bald and only having two teeth . . . I just assumed . . .'

'Yes, I noticed that too, and what about the way he . . .'

'Heer iss your meal, gentillmen.' Vlad was back with two plates of steaming hot food. He placed them on the table, produced cutlery and two napkins from his top pocket, wished them both 'Bonn appiteeeth!' and was gone.

Hogshead grabbed his cutlery and joyously began tucking in. Firkin stared at the selection of chips, beans and neatly bread-crumbed spheres of what he fervently hoped was chicken, and sniffed suspiciously. It looked good. It smelled very good. His stomach gurgled desperately.

'Not hungry?' asked Hogshead around a mouthful of beans.

'I'm letting it cool a bit . . . by the way, what is it?'

'Don't know really,' replied Hogshead, 'something to do with what you get out of chicken mines . . . I think!'

Firkin was starving. His stomach rumbled again. There was something not quite right about this place and he didn't know what, but it probably wasn't the chicken nuggets.

His fork wavered in indecision.

He hoped it wasn't the chicken nuggets!

His stomach won. He tucked in ravenously.

The most striking feature of the kitchen in Vlad's Diner, is that it is not a kitchen. It may have been in the past, and it may be in the future, but right now, as Firkin and Hogshead hungrily stuff themselves next door, it is quite definitely not a kitchen. It's just a junk food factory.

A place for warming things up, slamming them on a plate and whacking them on to as many tables, in front of as many people, as physically possible.

A few minutes earlier Vlad had swooped in, scooped two helpings of chips and chicken out of the deep-fat fryer, perched unceremoniously on top of the range, waited by the glass-fronted thing till it went ping, threw two helpings of piping-hot beans onto each plate and scurried back into the restaurant.

He was now sitting watching the two boys, through two tiny holes in the back of one of the pictures. His tongue darted across his pale grey lips in anticipation of what was soon to come.

'Oooh, sssuch lovely boysss!' he whispered to himself, '. . . And sssuch healthy appetitesssssssss!'

He watched Firkin finish his last mouthful and sit back, then stood and scurried back out.

Firkin put his fork down, wiped his mouth, and sat back. He had to admit it, that was good. He was full.

'Iss everythink to your ssssatisssfaction?' hissed Vlad, startling Firkin once again.

'Lovely, that was!' enthused Hogshead. 'Can we have some pudding now?'

'I sssssee dat Ssssir hasss ein healthy appetite. Dat isss gut. Ein healthy appetite ssshowss a tasssty – er, healthy body,' he licked his lips. Firkin fingered his collar again uncomfortably.

'Er, I've only got a bit of room left.'

'Vell, may I tempt you mit ein ssslice of Ssssschwarzwald Kuchen or sssome lemon ssssorbet or La Mort au Chocolat?'

'No thanks,' said Firkin, 'I'm full up.'

'Oooh, yes please.'

'Vhich vould Ssssir like to be ssserved vith?' he asked Hogshead and giggled slightly to himself.

'The first one,' chose Hogshead at random, not having a clue what any of them were.

'Very gut Sssir, although Death By Chocolate isss ein popular choisssse! Sssss sss sss!' and again he was gone, quickly and silently whisking the plates away.

'Hogshead, I don't know why but I don't like this place. Old Vlad gives me the creeps. We'll never get to the castle if we don't get moving. I think we should get away as quick as . . .'

'Your desssert Ssssir,' said Vlad, thrusting a plate under Hogshead's nose and looking suspiciously at Firkin.

'Er, no thanks, we're just about to leave . . . ow!'

Firkin kicked Hogshead swiftly under the table and motioned to him to keep quiet.

'. . . room. Leave room. That's what he meant. Let his firsts go down before, er, before . . .'

'. . . I ate my pudding,' finished Hogshead proudly. Firkin grinned feebly.

'Dat isss fine. Take your time. I never like to rush a meal, er, cussstomer,' Vlad corrected himself quickly. 'Take all der time you vant. Ssssome koffee, perhaps?'

Firkin nodded a reply, more to give himself some breathing space. Hogshead busied himself with the difficult and onerous task of polishing off a huge slice of gateau. Vlad hurried off to fetch the coffee.

'Hogshead, forget about that, we've got to get out of here.'

'Look at all this chocolate . . . !'

'We've got to go. I don't like it here.'

'. . . and it's got black cherries in it.'

'Come on, forget about the cake.' Firkin was tugging at Hogshead's arm.

'Oooh, it's lovely . . .'

'Come on . . . come . . . oh!'

'Your koffeessss, sssir.' Vlad delivered the cups of steaming coffee, and again was gone.

Firkin sat down. He could'nt believe Hogshead could be so thick. Wanting to stay and finish his pudding! He was smiling contentedly now. Doesn't he understand? There's more to Vlad Langschwein than meets the eye.

Absentmindedly, Firkin reached for the coffee and drank it down.

Hogshead was grinning like an idiot and pointing wildly into the air. He started laughing. Hysterically.

Vlad smiled his dead-fish smile from behind the picture. His two sharp, thin teeth glistened as he licked his cold, grey lips.

Hogshead was going green. 'Where did that albatross come from?' Firkin felt light headed. 'Why have I got an elephant on my nose?' he thought. 'Who put my toes on Hogshead's ears?'

Everything started to spin round and . . . 'Hello carpet . . . I love you carpet . . . oh no don't run away, please.'

All too late. Firkin realised that there had been significantly more than coffee, milk and sugar in the coffee.

All the colours began to fade.

Everything went black and white.

Then just black.

Rosch Mh'tonnay stood on a small rise overlooking the eastern

81

border of Cranachan, and addressed the hundreds of men, in thick yellow coats, standing expectantly before him. Most of them held pickaxes, some wedges and some huge lumphammers. All wore yellow hard-hats. Behind him stood a row of huge empty metal containers, painted the same yellow. This was the team that would carry out the biggest civil engineering project of OG 1025.

'Okay men,' he shouted as the sun twitched blearily skyward. 'You all know why we're here and what we've got to do. The line you see in front of you is our target. We haven't got long so I want to see lots of sweat and toil from you all. Good luck!' As he pulled a battered whistle out of his pocket, his men raised their tools and stared at the line snaking away, left and right as it ran parallel to the cliff edge. They had all heard Rosch Mh'tonnay make similar motivation-enhancing speeches before. He felt it was his duty to address his men before embarking on any major civil engineering project. Especially important ones, like this, the biggest this year. He breathed deep, put the whistle to his mouth and blew. The first impact of hundreds of expertly wielded pickaxes exploded in the morning stillness. Rosch Mh'tonnay swelled with pride, he was incredibly proud of his men. Particularly today. He was in charge of three hundred and fourteen men on a contract of national importance. He thought back to the moment, just over a week ago, when the tall, thin, black-clad man had burst into his works office. At first he had looked up in fright as he recognised, almost instantly, the Chief of Internal Affairs.

He pulled his heavy boots off the table and sat up quickly as Fisk strode over the bare floorboards, grabbed a chair and sat down. The back-clad figure stared disdainfully at the mess of parchments, catalogues and brown-stained mugs of cold tea on the civil engineer's desk.

'Ooh, ahh. Hello, Sir,' burbled Rosch, 'er, come about the progress report on the Steppe scheme? Well it's here, I was just finishing it off and I was going to deliver it myself, er, personally, er . . .'

'That is Gudgeon's pet project. Its progress is of no interest to me. However, the men are. I want them!'

'Sir? I had no idea. I thought they were vicious rumours. Do you have anyone particular in mind? I'm sure that they'd be honoured by your, er, interest.'

'What? No, I want them all!'

'At the same time?' The civil engineer's eyebrows squirmed up his heavy forehead.

'Of course. They are a team aren't they?'

'Well, I know a few of them are always seen together but I don't think . . .'

Fisk glared, distastefully, at the numerous calendars that lined the wall behind the overweight civil engineer. Glossy parchment images depicted voluptuous women with little covering but the various architectural implements they modelled. He was particularly fascinated by the girl with the theodolite.

'What are you burbling on about? Do you want this job or not?'

'Job? I thought, er, oh. Job. Yes.'

Rosch's eyes widened as Fisk unrolled a map of the eastern border and handed him a letter of authorisation, bearing the signature and seal of King Grimzyn himself. They widened further as he listened to the detailed description of the project, supplied by the Chief of Internal Affairs.

'. . . and it needs to be finished within two months. Can you do it?' he concluded.

'Phew! It's a big job that. Couldn't do it without more men.'

'I repeat. Can you do it?'

'I'd 'ave to take the men off the Steppe scheme.'

'And could you do it then?'

'I should think so. Yeah, leave it to me.'

'Excellent.' Fisk rubbed his gauntlets noisily together.

'Oh, Mh'tonnay,' he added, threateningly, 'I don't need to tell you that our little discussion has contained information of a very, ahem, delicate nature. If this leaks out, I shall personally see to it that you are found at the bottom of a deep, dark excavation. In tragic circumstances. Do I make myself clear?'

'Crystal, Sir. Crystal.' He swallowed nervously.

'I shall expect work to begin immediately.'

They stood and in a moment Fisk had gone. Rosch Mh'tonnay looked sheepishly at his unshaken, outstretched hand, sat down heavily and wiped his brow.

*

In the distance someone was playing merry hell with the biggest pair of concert timpani you could ever possibly imagine. His huge arms, glistening with exertion, pounded rhythmically in a brain-crushing paradiddle. Alarmingly he seemed to be getting nearer.

Outside, a skyful of overweight thunderclouds scrummed and tackled a pair of medium-sized glaciers in a ground-shaking, bone-crushing game of no-rules rugby. And they were getting nearer. Pangea, Gondwanaland and several small continents were playing leapfrog. They were getting nearer too.

Or at least, that's how it seemed to Firkin as he lay with his eyes tightly closed, hoping it was a bad, bad dream and praying it would all go away.

Half a dozen small earthquakes joined the seismic throng as he opened one eye. Several thousand rabid wildebeest jostled for position as they stampeded through the fug in his head. What have I done to deserve this? he thought, as a wave of zebra followed. He lay on his side and whimpered, hoping the rabid ungulates would settle down. Why do I feel like something the hyenas dragged in? Sparks of memory glistened in the dark mud of his brain. There was something about chicken nuggets, coffee and a gingerbread cottage. Oh, yes . . . and Vlad Langschwein.

'Gut mornink, gentillmen. Did you sssleep vell?' said the bald head inches away from Firkin's face. Breath whistled between the two tiny sharp teeth as it smiled coldly and asked, 'Breakfassst?'

'Usssggrnttlbleurgh!' It was the best Firkin could do.

'I vill kom back later.'

'Uurgh.'

The head turned and bobbed away.

Firkin heard the sound of a key turning in a metal door. It was difficult to miss. To him it sounded like it had been played through 600 kilowatts of Marshall Amplifier; turned up to eleven!

Dimly it dawned on him that perhaps this devastating headache probably had something to do with the gingerbread cottage and Vlad Langschwein, and the future probably didn't look too rosy.

One herculean effort and several herds of wildly stampeding ungulates later, Firkin sat up and woozily looked around.

Hogshead was on another bed across the room, still asleep. The room was quite bare apart from the two beds but it didn't feel too unpleasant. Except, of course, for the iron bars in the windows and the big iron door. There was a cupboard against one wall, in which Firkin could see their bags.

Suddenly a small but very important question appeared above his very low mental horizon. It was very simple but it struck Firkin like several bolts of lighting. It was this: 'Why are we here?' Not the complicated and philosophical 'Why are we here?' but the 'Why-are-we-being-held-in-a-small-room-in-a-small-cottage-in-a-forest-by-a-bald-man-with-only-two-teeth-and-a-strange-accent?' sort of 'Why are we here?'

Firkin had an awful feeling that he was beginning to suspect why. But he didn't want to believe it. Or even really think about it.

Shortly an inhuman groan announced Hogshead's struggle with the rigours and demands of consciousness. His face told Firkin that he hadn't been the only one to receive certain chemical additives. Hogshead had a headache.

Firkin had began to recover; now he only felt mostly dead.

'Who's playing those timpani?' groaned Hogshead.

'Your head,' whispered Firkin.

'Wha . . . oooh, don't shout so loud!'

'I'm whispering.'

'Yeah – you and whose megaphone! I feel horrible.'

'I knew. We were drugged last night and now we're being held prisoner.'

'What – oh, come on, this is one of your games isn't it, Firkin . . . isn't it? Go on, tell me it is! . . . Please? . . . pretty please.'

'It's true.'

'Oh. Bleaurgh . . .'

'Gut morgen, Gentillmen. Breakfassst now, ja?'

'No,' said Hogshead.

'Vhy not?'

'I don't want another dose of whatever-it-was and chips.'

'You vill not need dat now. I haf you here,' replied Vlad very matter-of-factly. 'Breakfast?'

'I'm not hungry. Go away.'

'Eat sssomethink. You vill tassste, er, feel better. You vill.

85

Lovely breakfassst. Yum, yum.' Vlad pushed the tray through the hatch in the door and was gone.

It sat there on the floor and glared at them. The breakfasts they had eaten in the past were mere snacks compared to this feast. You will have seen a full English-type breakfast fry-up: bacon, eggs, sausages, beans, black pudding, mushrooms, fried bread and so on. These breakfasts had all this. And more. Much, much more. Mountains of food, cooked to perfection, sitting there almost willing the boys to sink their cutlery in and devour them.

Somehow each breakfast seemed to be calling out, 'Eat me. Bite me. Devour me. You'll feel better when you've had a slice. I've been cooked especially for you and it has been my ambition for years to be eaten by you and only you, I'm just the way you like it. I will be almost as delighted as you when you eat me and then I will know that you will have been satisfied by me. Go on, have a bite.'

It was too much for them. They succumbed to temptation and, against their will, tucked in with glee. Each mouthful seemed tastier than the last and each bite seemed to cause little shrieks of delight from the breakfast (the sausages were especially good at this).

Rashers of bacon seemed to leap onto their forks and beans queued up in fork-sized groups sending up cheers as they were lifted mouthwards. Once the fry-up had gone it was the turn of the toast and marmalade to make their presence known. Amazingly, all the toast was hot.

Soon it had all gone and they sat back on the beds feeling very full. Firkin was surprised that he had put so much away, especially since he hadn't been hungry before.

On a particularly nondescript morning in OG 1025 the sun rose in the Talpa Mountains to the accompaniment of a whistle and the impact of three hundred and fourteen civil engineers. The occupants of Middin were jolted rudely awake and, their curiosity thoroughly pricked, they struggled blearily into the once-still morning air to see what the hell was going on.

The Prospector looked up at the brightly lit cliff and scratched his head. The cliff sported a fringe of tiny yellow men all vigorously hammering and pickaxing away.

The villagers watched in mild, almost academic, interest as the tiny Cranachans laboured above their heads. Soon, as there appeared to be little excitement, and neckache began to set in, the villagers drifted off, one by one, to start the day. One or two muttered something about the sanity of the Cranachanians. Others took the view that they were on their side of the border and so, as long as it didn't affect them, they could do what they liked. Besides, what could that lot digging away at the top of that cliff do to us? It's probably a site of historical importance or something.

The Prospector had his doubts about these theories, fuelled by an enormous mistrust of virtually anything Cranachanian.

He stared at the cliff top and tried to figure out what they were up to.

'There is a castle in the clouds . . .' sang Courgette happily as she skipped towards the well in the woods. Her long hair waved down over her shoulders in rich red cascades. It was the rich, red hue that squirrels would give their eye teeth to be.

It was a lovely morning and the grass was still covered with silver pearls of dew. Here and there, small pockets of mist lay in hollows in the ground.

Her father had once told her that they were lazy clouds that hadn't got up yet. She didn't believe him, of course, but she did like the sound of it. It made her giggle to think of clouds tucking themselves into hollows, some putting false teeth into jars next to them, some setting alarms for the next morning, then all settling down to sleep. Her agile mind flew off into a whirl of fantasy. Do clouds dream? Do they snore? What happens when it's frosty? She laughed and told herself she was silly.

She was right.

Courgette turned off the path, when she spotted the tree with the little carved symbol on the trunk, and carried on towards the well. Her bare feet were wet from the dewy grass and her toes began to tingle. She loved running and skipping through the woods. It made her feel so alive and free. She much preferred it to the inside of the castle, all dark and cold and empty. A crow croaked somewhere overhead. She stopped and listened. Another rasped a reply through the thin still air. She bent down, picked a large mushroom, and ran on towards the well swinging the bucket and chewing happily. She skipped over a fallen log, round the big tree and was soon at the well. The person responsible for building this well certainly had a feeling for classical garden architecture. It was everything a well should be. Short, round, made of natural ingredients and covered in green and yellow lichen. It even had a little pointy slate roof. She swung the bucket over the edge and dropped it, watching the handle spin faster and faster, and listening for the sound as it hit the water. It always seemed to take longer than she expected. There was a sharp slap, followed by a long echoey rumble as the sound bounced up the well shaft. She grabbed the handle and began winding. If it had been a long way down, it was further coming up. She pulled and wound the bucket up inch by inch until it appeared over the rim and she was able to swing it on to the wall.

Breathing heavily from the exertion, she took a drink and filled her own bucket. Wiping her brow on the back of her hand, she sat off back to the castle, stopping only once to fill her pockets with fresh mushrooms.

'Hogshead, I've been thinking,' said Firkin.

'Mmm? What?'

'Do you remember what you thought when you first saw this place?'

'Er, I thought it couldn't possibly be real. It must have come out of a fairy story.'

'Yes, it did. Can you remember the story?'

'Er, it was something about two children lost in a wood and left to starve by an evil stepmother, who find a gingerbread cottage and get caught by a witch . . . I think.'

'Yes, but there was more than that wasn't there? What happened to the children?'

'They sailed away on a duck!'

'No . . . why did the witch want them?'

'Oh, that. Why didn't you say? She wanted to eat . . .' He stopped. His face went pale. 'Oh . . . Firkin . . . Do you think? . . . No . . .' He shook his head. A look of pleading started to grow in his eyes.

'Well, can you explain the breakfast? Were you hungry before it arrived? I wasn't and I ate more than I normally would in a week!'

'Er . . . but . . .'

'. . . and look at the door . . .'

Hogshead had to agree it was a bit over the top for a guest room. Even in the most security-conscious hotels.

'Oh, no . . . what do we do, what do we do, we've got to get away, I don't want to be ea-ea-ea-'

'Don't say it. It won't happen. We are the heroes. It can't end this way and besides . . .' he paused.

'What?'

'. . . I don't know. I just thought I might have had an idea if I kept talking long enough.'

'Oh!'

Silence fell between them and each wandered off into their own thoughts.

Hogshead was close to panic. His eyes bulged. The prospect of being eaten was bad enough, but eaten by someone so creepy . . . And foreign. Ugh! He had to get out. But how?

He looked around the room. There were bars on the door and on the window. They hadn't seen the bars when they came. He felt so stupid and wretched. They should have noticed bars on a gingerbread cottage surely. A gingerbread prison. That was it! A gingerbread prison was made of . . . gingerbread! They could get out and Hogshead knew how!

'I've got it, I've got it, I've got it!' He started clawing at the walls furiously.

'Hey, calm down . . . what have you got?'

'The answer. We can escape,' he babbled, clawing wildly at the wall.

'How?'

'. . . Gin-gin-gin-'

'What?'

'. . . gin-gin-'

Firkin stared at the growing pile of gingerbread crumbs at his feet. 'Gingerbread is edible . . . we can eat our way out. Yeah!'

Firkin leapt at the walls and started tearing and biting.

He couldn't believe it, Hogshead was right. His hands sunk in as they pulled great chunks off the wall in a frenzy of ripping and tugging. Stubborn parts they bit through. Within minutes there was a deep hollow where they had been working and a large pile of crumbs behind them.

'Ha, ha, it was so obvious! We should have thought of it sooner,' said Hogshead ecstatically.

'Yeah. If we carry on like this we'll be out soon!'

'Hee, hee. Ow . . . There's a really hard bit here . . . '

'Yes, I've got a hard bit too.

They carried on ripping and tearing and gradually from underneath a layer of thick, yielding gingerbread was revealed a normal, solid stone cottage, and try as they might, chewing their way out of there would be impossible. Firkin cursed at not having been born with tungsten-carbide fillings.

Hogshead couldn't believe his eyes. His plan had seemed to be so close to working. He flung himself across the room onto the bed and began to sob in despair and exhaustion.

'We're trapped, w – w – we're trapped and w – w – we'll – we'll be ea – ea – ea – waaah!' he buried his face in the pillow and cried.

In another part of the cottage Vlad was writing a note on a small strip of parchment. It was exactly the right size to fit in the carrying tube, which in turn was exactly the right size to fit neatly on the leg of one of Vlad's carrier pigeons. He knew he should have reported the capture of the two boys sooner; immediately he had suspected them to be heading for Castell Rhyngill, so his orders said. But in this part of the forest the last few years had been so quiet that Vlad had begun to crave company. The job didn't keep him occupied as much as it might. What was the point of being a lookout for Snydewinder if there was nothing to look out for. It wouldn't matter to Snydewinder if the message was a few days late, thought Vlad. I've captured them. They are going nowhere.

He put the quill down and set off to see to his prisoners.

'Oh, hello. Back so soon?' Val Jambon patted his daughter's head affectionately as she placed the bucket by the sink. The stone slabs of the kitchen floor were decorated with a trail of tiny wet footprints, and the occasional splash where Courgette had struggled in with the bucket.

'Look what I've got!' she squeaked, knowing how much her father liked mushrooms.

'Mushrooms!' He cringed. More flamin' mushrooms, he thought. Every blinkin' day she brings me flamin' mushrooms.

She unloaded her pockets onto the large oak table and stood back proudly.

This, thought Val, has gone too far.

'Oh, thank you Courgette. Very nice. Er, does anything else grow in the woods?'

'Yes. Lots of things.'

'I thought so. Well, why do you always bring me mushrooms?'

'You like mushrooms,' she answered simply and grinned, like a spaniel on Valentine's Day.

'Let me show you something,' said Val as he turned and opened a cupboard. A wave of roundish white fungi tumbled onto the floor and lay in a heap around his ankles. Courgette's face fell.

'I do like mushrooms,' he said as he stepped out of the off-white heap. 'But not that many, not every day. Bring me something else tomorrow, eh?'

She nodded pathetically and stared at the heap of mushrooms on the floor.

I'd better not tell her about the fourteen drawers and six cupboards full of the damn things she's brought in, thought Val. It'd break her heart. One day she'll learn sense. I hope.

Val Jambon was a very open and loving man. He could easily be everybody's favourite uncle. His outlook on life was strangely childish and miraculously he'd never learned the art of holding a grudge. His motto was 'A friend in need is a friend to feed.' He had devoted almost his entire life to cooking in some form or other. He'd spent years learning the art of food preparation, dessert creation and menu planning, so that now there was not a great deal that he couldn't boil, stew, fry, roast, fricassee or steam to perfection. His favourites were sweet, sticky cakes and puddings. Fortunately, so were the King's.

Val handed Courgette a piece of apple pie, disappeared into the far end of the kitchen and rummaged in various cupboards while the coal-fired range kept pots boiling and ovens baking. Courgette chewed her pie absently and probably thought about pink rabbits. Or something.

At that moment, way above them, far away at the other end of the castle, a hand reached out for the bell cord and pulled. The red cord went tight as it transferred the vertical motion of the tug, through several pulleys and several hundred yards, into a horizontal jangling of a bell in the kitchen. Val looked up at the bell, then the clock, then across to Courgette.

'Breakfast for *le Grand Fromage*, I think.' He stood up, hastily assembled a tray, and set off on the long walk to the King's bedchamber.

Courgette's pink rabbits frolicked in the small green meadows of her mind.

The hairs on the back of Firkin's neck suddenly leapt erect as he sensed breathing behind him.

'Isss anythink amissss?'

Firkin turned sharply and stared into the pale watery eyes of Vlad Langschwein as he looked through the bars in the door.

'No. I think this is a perfectly normal reaction after being locked up for so long. Don't you?' he snapped.

'None off my other victi . . . er . . . guesstss hass exssperienssed ssuch trauma. But denn none haff tried to eat the wallsss. Are you feelink hungry perhapsss?'

'No. Don't give me any more food.'

'I ssshall haff to fix thessse wallsss when you haff gone.'

'Why have you got gingerbread walls?'

'To make der illusion more complete,' he gloated. 'Everyone hass a childhood memory off der taless their mother told dem off fairy casstless unt cottagesss in foresstss. Vould you haff invesssstigated ssso closssely if the vallsss were ssstone? Vould you haff entered my trap? A mousse trap needsss itss cheessse. Ja?'

Firkin felt almost defeated.

'Unt now it'sss time for lunch!'

'I don't understand this. Why are you feeding us?'

'You look a little on der thin ssside to me!'

'I've heard about your type. You drink, you don't eat! You're a vampire!' he yelled accusingly.

'Oh, pleassse, pleassse, how wulgar, don't usse dat vord. It'sss ssso insssulting and degrading. It makesss me sssound like dose mosssquitosss or leechesss. Pah!' he spat. 'Don't confussse me mit dose parasssitesss.'

'Why are you feeding us? You only need our blood!'

'Vell, I got a little tired off der liquid lunch, a bit fed up off der old routine. Now don't get me wrong,' he said surprisingly chattily. 'I like ein gut bite-out asss much asss anyone. It'sss hard to beat der challenge off sssedussing der innocent vomen mit der hypnosssisss; der exssitement off der clossing in on der bare neck glisstenink in der moonlight unt finally der exsstasssy off der bite . . . But after der firssst few hundred timesss der novelty vearsss off. I tried it from behind, unt mit der voman on top unt even in ein vagon, but after all it'sss jussst nibble, nibble, ssslurp!'

The two boys' eyes widened in horror and revulsion.

'I needed more,' continued Vlad. 'Sssso I converted disss old cottage unt lured sssmall children inssside. I sssoon developed a tasste for sssomethink a little more, ahem, sssolid.'

Hogshead started to shake, his mouth opening and closing as he mouthed silently, 'No, no, no, no.'

'I haff quite a recipe book now.'

Hogshead's eyes were wide with terror.

Vlad started to salivate and his small grey tongue darted across his lips.

'But you two are not ready yet!' he added. Firkin was not very relieved to hear this.

His eyes became colder as he became agitated.

'You vill eat more. It'sss time for lunch mit tea unt cakesss. Ssss, ssss, ssss.' He turned and was gone. Firkin felt sick. He had only half believed that Vlad could be a vampire. But now that he'd heard it . . . heard that it was true . . . that this creature was going to eat them . . . He shuddered.

Within seconds Vlad returned and shouted, 'Now you vill eat!' and pushing the tray through the opening, turned and left them alone again.

Firkin couldn't believe it. Despite the feeling of nausea and the fact that he had been stuffed only a few hours before, he looked at the tray groaning under a pile of fattening, calorie-laden cakes and couldn't resist eating. Hogshead looked up and also immediately felt hungry. Within minutes the food was gone, the plates were clean and the two boys' bellies were full.

Having now eaten and explored Hogshead's idea, there was little for the boys to do.

They lay on the beds and stared at the ceiling. Hogshead was depressed. Firkin was fidgety. There was a way out of here. There had to be. He needed something to do. His mind worked better when he could fiddle with something. He drifted to the cupboard, rummaged in his bag for a few seconds and took out a small rectangular cardboard box.

He forced himself to be cheerful. Well, attempt to be cheerful at least.

'Fancy a game, Hogshead?'

'What!' he shouted. 'How can you even think of playing games at a time like this?'

'Calm down. What else can we do? . . . And besides . . .'

'What?'

'. . . it helps me think!'

Firkin opened the end of the box, took out the cards and started to shuffle them. He gave the pack to Hogshead who, reluctantly at first, dealt them.

After a few games they calmed down a little, and soon all that could be heard was the gentle flicking of the cards, as they were dealt, and the occasional outburst of 'I won' or 'Beat you.'

The sounds carried through the bars in the door, out through the rest of the cottage until, like a tempting aroma rising from one of his dishes, it reached Vlad. Curiosity rose within him. He'd heard that sound before, a long time ago. As he approached the door he recognised it.

'Cardsss,' he whispered. 'Dey're playing cardsss!'

Vlad loved cards. It had been longer than he cared to remember since he had played anything but Patience, and now here were two opponents, ready to be tackled. A captive audience, so to speak. He congratulated himself on not having sent his note to Snydewinder. Cards were far more important.

'Right,' he decided, 'Snydewinder can wait. Let'sss haff a game mit dose two! Ssss, ssss, ssss!'

Vlad looked in at the two boys playing and felt a burst of

excitement run up his spine. Cards. A game of cards. He unlocked the door and entered the room. Firkin turned and completely failed to hide his contempt.

'What do you want?' he shouted. 'Get out!'

'You, you're playing cardsss,' he said, rubbing his cold, blue hands together.

'Well spotted!' came the sarcastic reply.

'May I join you?'

'What? You've got a nerve!'

'May I join you?' repeated Vlad courteously.

He turned and looked at Hogshead who was sitting with his mouth open. The vampire's eyes, if anything, looked colder and paler then ever. Hogshead's expression suddenly began to lose all signs of sentience; his shoulders sagged, he seemed to be losing his grip on the outside world.

'I really would apprecsssiate it if you could sssee your vay clear to allowing me to join in your game off cardsss,' he whispered staring hypnotically into Hogshead's eyes.

'Yes . . . please . . . do . . . join . . . us . . .' he said in a monotone, with a completely vacant expression.

'Ssssank you ssso much.'

Vlad sat down, picked up the cards and began to deal. Hogshead stared around in confusion, shook his head and looked surprised to see Vlad.

Firkin was furious, but could do nothing to stop this invasion of their game.

The vampire smiled a cold grey smile and slowly shuffled the tiny pack of cards.

Back in OG 1025, weeks passed in the little village, in the little valley, with little change. The residents of Middin were somewhat more irritable than usual, due entirely to the constant thumping and crashing of the Cranachan Civil Engineers that filled every daylight hour. At first, most of the residents had payed at least a passing interest in the goings-on on the cliff top. There really was little else to do at this time of year. Just wait for the seasons to turn before the lemmings came again. But gradually, as most of the villagers could see little difference from day to day, curiosity faded

95

to irritation and shortly afterwards to frustration and anger at the constant, merciless racket.

Several theories had been put forward to account for what was going on and all had been rejected as impossible. The most popular had been that they were mining something, but the Prospector knew, better than all of the villagers put together, that there was nothing of value worth mining up there. Nothing mineral, anyway.

It was another early evening in Middin and, like many of the previous evenings of late, the Prospector sat outside his hut, drink in hand, staring at the yellow-fringed and now slightly lower, cliff top.

'Suppose I'd better make sure my knives are sharp for this coming season,' he said to himself, and took another sip of Twisted Lemming. 'I'll get Wyllf to give me a hand, if he's not too busy in that garden of his. Don't know why he bothers. Moss, moss, moss. And backache. That's all he gets.' He took another long, leisurely sip and started upwards again.

'Damn nuisance these workmen, wish they'd clear off. If they hang around up there much longer, makin' all that racket, the lemmings won't come.'

Suddenly he gripped his glass tightly.

Several images flashed through his mind in quick succession. The parchment ultimatum from Cranachan. The night with Vice-Captain Barak. His thoughts went back further. The mysterious black figure with the sextant. And now the work on the cliff . . .

He felt that somehow they were all connected, he'd thought that before. It was the type of nagging thought that lodges itself somewhere in the back of your head and will not go away. Like an inaccessible itch somewhere between your shoulder blades. It was a thorn in his mental flesh, scratching, irritating. But now he knew why.

He closed his eyes and looked again at the mental picture that swam before his mind's eye. He concentrated hard. The grip on his glass failed, it slipped and smashed on the rock by his side. He didn't notice. In his mind his hands smoothed out the huge map on the desk in front of him and he peered closer. The familiar mountain contours leapt out at him, the forests away south on the lowlands, the rivers, the streams. And there, almost ignored, almost

96

impossible to see, a black dotted line following exactly a dark brown contour line, marking the top of a cliff.

The final line had been drawn, the picture was complete.

He cursed violently at his stupidity as he stood up and then ran inside. Why hadn't he thought of it sooner?

Was it already too late?

He had to move.

And fast.

Vlad felt a thrill run through his body as he dealt the pack of cards to the three of them sitting on the floor. His cold grey fingertips slid joyously over the smooth shiny surface of the cards. For the moment the boys' impending mealdom was postponed. Their status had been raised to worthwhile opponents. Of course, it could very easily be returned, at a moment's notice, to 'lunch'. They would just have to play their cards right.

Vlad finished dealing and looked up at the boys. He smiled like a month-dead hake, turned over his cards and stared in disbelief at the hand in front of him. Hogshead fidgeted nervously as he sorted out his own hand. Vlad rubbed his eyes and looked again at the neat fan in his hands.

During his extensive travels he had seen a great many variations on the themes of spades, diamonds, clubs and, his favourite, hearts, but the pack he was now staring at defied all logic in a flagrant breach of all normal pack styles. There were no aces, no kings, queens or jacks. The hand in front of him was made up entirely of picture cards illustrating all kinds of strange creatures.

'Vhat kind off pack off cardsss isss thisss?' he shouted in frustration. 'I vant to play cardsss.'

'These are cards.'

'Not real cardsss. I recognissse nothink.'

'You mean you've never played with cards like this before?' asked Firkin.

'Yah. Issn't dat vhat I jussst sssaid!'

Hogshead turned and started to explain to Vlad the intricacies of the game as best he could. Firkin only half listened, struggling to catch onto an idea hovering on the tips of his synaptic junctions.

After a few minutes they were ready to play. The game went

slowly as Vlad tried to use all that Hogshead had told him. Inevitably, he lost. This didn't go down at all well, but he dealt again, determined to win.

'It may be childisssh,' he consoled himself, 'but at leassst it'sss cardsss.'

Firkin's thoughts were not on the game so he lost the next one and the third game was accompanied by the sound of Vlad grumbling agitatedly under his breath. The boys caught snippets of '. . . not proper cardsss . . .' and 'sssstupid game . . . sssstupid . . .'

Hogshead squeaked with delight as he reached out quickly, snatched a card from the heap in front of him and declared that he had won. Vlad cursed a little louder.

Suddenly Firkin's idea clicked into place. He knew exactly what to do. He reached out, gathered the cards and began to deal again. He felt a surge of adrenalin through his body as he tried to control his voice.

'Another game?' he said quietly, with only the slightest quiver.

The cards were dealt before Vlad even realised that he'd had the chance to refuse. Vlad picked up his hand and continued to mutter under his breath. The game commenced. Vlad, now familiar with the characters of the pack, played well. Or so he thought. All he needed was Murrion the Shepherd and he'd win. One card. Despite his annoyance at the game's juvenile nature he was quite excited at the prospect of victory. Oh, yes, he thought, I'll show these two.

Hogshead put down his card. Vlad almost spat as he saw Mote the Wood-Nymph, followed by Quip the Jester from Firkin. One card, one card and he'd win. He threw away Pun the Jester, useless without Quip now that he'd thrown away Gleek and Jibe earlier. Hogshead reached out and snatched up Pun. Slowly and deliberately, in a way calculated to cause the most irritation. Hogshead lay his cards on the floor in a neat fan.

'I've won!' he purred smugly.

Vlad exploded. He threw his cards onto the floor and stood up. 'Zzatt isss ein ssstupid game! Not proper cardsss. RRRRUB-Bissshh. Farrrr too childisssh.' His face was red and his fists were clenched. He cursed to himself. Twelve years waiting for a game of cards and he'd lost. To two children. Four times! Oh, the shame!

'Now if it had been sssomethink more, er, adult, then you vould haff sssstood not a chansssse! Huh.'

It was time for Firkin to make his move.

'Oh, yeah,' he taunted, 'says who?'

'Ssssayss me!' shouted their captor.

'By more adult you wouldn't mean something like poker, would you?'

Vlad stopped cursing and stared at Firkin. His curiosity had awoken.

'Vhat did you sssay?' The corner of his mouth twitched.

'Poh . . . ker!' whispered Firkin, sensing a rapid change in Vlad's mood.

'You sssurely can't play sssuch a game?' Vlad's pale eyes looked hungry. He stared intently at Firkin.

'I'm the best poker player in the whole of the Talpa Mountains. Try me!' Firkin had laid his bait. Outside he appeared calm but inside he was shaking with surging adrenalin and his pulse raced.

Hogshead couldn't believe his ears. Firkin's definition of poker was a long piece of metal used for rattling coals in a fire. He'd never played in his life, and now he was challenging a very, very angry vampire to a game. It's all over, he thought, Firkin's brain's turned to mush – he can't think straight. The pressure's too much.

'Vhell, vhat are ve waiting for! Deal!' Vlad rubbed his cold hands in anticipation.

'I can't.' Give him one more run on the line, then reel him in, thought Firkin. Nearly there. Calm. Calm.

'Vhy?'

'Well, when I set out I knew my only company would be Hogshead here.' Don't babble, he told himself. 'A fine companion, but sadly lacking in poker skills.' Calm. Slowly. 'I thought it unwise to bring a pack of real cards with me.'

Hogshead wiped his brow. Firkin had no intention of playing after all.

'Zat isss no problem. I haff a pack sssomewhere.' Got him!

Hogshead's jaw dropped open as he watched Vlad turn and leap out of the room. Firkin moved a fraction of a second later.

'Firkin, what are you doing? You've never played poke . . . ow.'

He was pushing Hogshead out of the door. 'Come on . . . grab your bag . . . go, go!' He half-pushed, half-kicked Hogshead out of the room, then turned, grabbed the cards and ran after him.

A few doors away, drawers were being ripped open and cupboards emptied in a frenzy of wild searching.

'Vhere are you, little cardsss?'

The two boys ran furiously in the opposite direction and burst through a pair of double doors into the main restaurant area. Their flight was masked by the noise being made by Vlad, as he pulled yet more drawers out and upturned dozens of cardboard boxes on the floor.

The boys cannoned on, Firkin catching a chair with his bag and sending it spinning across the polished icing floor. Hogshead reached the front door first, grabbed the handle, turned it and whumped into the layer of marzipan veneer with the combined momentum of both Firkin and himself. It was locked. The two boys collapsed, winded.

Deep in the cottage, the frenzied search continued and a loud crash signified the emptying of another cardboard box.

Firkin shook his head, trying to clear it. He turned away from the door and lurched across the restaurant. He picked up the chair, turned and ran red-faced toward the huge sugar window and in one massive effort hurled the chair.

Suddenly things seemed to start to happen in slow motion. Fifteen million fragments of sugar glass exploded in every direction as the chair shattered the window. Firkin overbalanced on the shiny icing floor and careered into the wall underneath the window. The chair landed in the clearing outside, somersaulted twice and ended in three pieces arranged neatly around a tree stump . . . and dimly Hogshead became aware that it had suddenly gone very quiet.

'Boysss, I haff found zhem!'

Firkin stood first and somehow managed to drag Hogshead upright and shove him, still winded, through the window. In a second, he was with him in the afternoon sun, half-pulling, half-running and half-falling across the clearing and away into the trees.

'Found dem!' shouted Vlad, victoriously. 'Ready to play now, boysss?'

Branches slashed at their faces but they ignored them and pushed on through, their pulses racing. Deeper and deeper they ran, putting the greatest distance between them and the cottage as possible before Vlad discovered . . .

From way behind them came a blood-curdling scream, as Vlad found the boys missing. They ran even harder, panicked at the sounds of crashing and banging as Vlad tore the room to pieces searching for them. They kept running. They ran until they both collapsed on a bank and lay panting. They hadn't a clue how long they had been running – time does funny things when you panic – but they both knew their bodies could carry them no further.

'Phew! But we- we've got to keep g- going,' panted Hogshead, looking back with wide eyes.

'Calm down. We . . . we'll be okay, for the moment.'

Hogshead looked at him.

'What?'

'He won't chase us, phew, in the daylight,' said Firkin. 'Well, at least that's what Franck told us,' he added to himself.

They both lay there struggling to get their breath back and gradually started to calm down.

After a few minutes, Firkin plucked a blade of grass from beside him and began to chew at it. He calmly turned and began to rummage in his bag. He pulled out the pack of cards, slipped Murrion the Shepherd out from his sleeve and gently pushed him into the box.

Hogshead looked on amazed.

'You cheated?'

'Only a bit.'

'I had a feeling I shouldn't have won.'

Firkin smiled with the grass between his teeth.

'I'm sorry, do you want to go back and explain?'

Hogshead's face turned pale as he heard the words. He turned to face Firkin, shaking his head in disbelief.

Firkin grinned at him.

'You ratbag! Don't joke about things like that.' Half joking and half in annoyance, he thumped Firkin as hard as he could on the arm, then lay back on the grassy bank and looked up at the sky for the first time in far too long.

'You know,' he said after a few minutes, 'there's one thing I still don't understand.'

'Mmm?'

'How on earth did you figure out he was a vampire?'

'Ah, elementary, my dear Hogshead,' Firkin said, prodding him with the end of the grass. 'There wasn't a trace of garlic anywhere on the menu.'

Fort Knumm

In the deepest, darkest part of Fort Knumm's cold heart, a slab of air lurked. It was warm, clammy and it pulsed. Low, almost subterranean, bass frequencies throbbed through it with a regular heavy rhythm. If it had a solid physical presence it would have biceps like thighs; a penchant for leather and studs; hobbies including advanced club wielding, part-time skull crushing and occasional major limb realignment; and an expression of such malicious wickedness as to make grown ogres scream and run to Mummy. Of course, it hadn't always been like this. It had started out the same way as all the other bits of air. Quite content to swirl around people's feet or play with their hair, or occasionally remove a chimney pot for sheer devilment. But when the fans had stopped in Ye Silver Spitoone . . . it began to change.

Air is such a flighty thing that its character is not so much determined by breeding as by its environment. Things rub off. It's hard not to pick up some of a person's characteristics if you've been right down deep inside their alveoli. So when the fans packed up in Ye Silver Spitoone – the haunt of the meanest band of social dropouts to stalk Fort Knumm – where bandits, cut-throats and assassins drank, ate and gambled next to mercenaries, murderers and wild men . . . what chance did an innocent few litres of air stand?

It grew up quickly when the fans stopped. The lack of air conditioning allowed the air to become conditioned. It learned to take care of itself. It learned to smoke and was now soaked in alcohol and other chemical additives. It had changed. Its mother wouldn't be proud of it anymore. It was no longer the sweet little breeze that riffled through banks of autumn leaves. It had learned to be wicked, almost malevolent. If you looked very carefully into some of the darker recesses, especially in the moments before an argument or fight broke out, you might even have seen a wide cheshire cat grin. It wasn't just air any longer . . . It was Atmosphere.

Propped against a tall tree in a huge forest, an old man sat reading. The late afternoon sun glinted off the bolts of lightning, sequin moons, stars and tacky, enamelled signs of the zodiac which decorated his long black cloak and pointy hat. A battered green rucksack lay crumpled next to him.

This was Vhintz, one of the last of a dying breed – the Travelling Sorcerer. He, like the half dozen or so still remaining, would move from town to town, casting spells, mixing potions and performing feats of general conjuring designed to make life a little easier.

He'd had a hard morning of magical scissor sharpening and paracosmic shoe reheeling, and was now doing his homework. Four years ago, in about OG 1034, his father had enrolled him on a correspondence course for low-level magic users. Some of the courses he'd found useful, like 'Sleight of Hand for Beginners', 'Elementary Hocus Pocus', and 'Advanced Codology'. These told him all he needed to know about looking suitably mystical while mending dripping taps or curing warts.

Over the years he'd found that you could pass off all sorts of practical solutions as magical. You just had to look and sound right.

In a recently published paper, the Thaumaturgical Board of Philosophers and Psychologists had presented some newly acquired data about the perceived worth of Travelling Sorcerers in the market place. Belief in the Sorcerers' worth, the board concluded, is made up from a mixture of factors split as follows: 15 percent based on the effect actually achieved; 38 per cent on the body language used by the Sorcerer; and 54 per cent on the tone of voice. Amazingly they found that this added up to 107 per cent, thus illustrating beyond a shadow of a doubt that some people are just born to be conned.

Vhintz may not have understood all things magic, but all things gullible were as clear to him as spleens to X-rays. He had based his entire career on this fact.

Today he was reading his homework on 'Advanced Incantations'. He'd always found real magic very difficult. Well, impossible, actually. He felt sure that he could cast a spell, if only he could understand the ASCII Characters*. Today was the day. He had it. He was sure. He felt good today.

He reached over and pulled out another book from his bag. It was large, leather-bound and suprisingly heavy. Strange runes and ASCII's decorated the cover. It looked very old. And very magical.

It was.

His grandfather had given it to him when he was too young to know about such things, saying, 'Guard this, keep it safe. I see dark times ahead. Vhintz, stop gurgling. Wars, starvation. All here in this kingdom. No. I don't want your rattle. This book, if used wisely, will save the kingdom!' He paused, listening: 'Whoops! Must dash!' He had run out of Vnintz's nursery, cloak tails waving, and disappeared rapidly down the corridor, followed a few seconds later by thirty or forty pairs of very angry-sounding, heavily booted feet. It was the last that was ever seen of his grandfather. Vhintz never discovered where he got the book from. Or from whom.

But all that had been years ago. Right now, in this small clearing in this huge forest, a personal first was about to be made. Vhintz was sure that today, after years of preparation, was the day that he would cast his first real spell.

He looked around him. All clear. He opened the large leather book and peered at the yellowed pages. He took a history-making breath. Slowly, with his finger under every word, he began to read. His eyes scanned the page slowly, he concentrated hard. He tried to live every word, rolling the shapes around his mouth, trying them on, wearing them. Something was happening. Beads of sweat, testament to the effort of concentration, blossomed on his high forehead. Gradually, strange things began to happen. The words moved slowly in random directions. He could recognise the individual letters, even the odd word, but the whole thing was nonsense. It was like trying to read a page of a newspaper that had been pasted to the bottom of a swimming pool.

* All scripts, logos, symbols and hieroglyphs invented and used by the Advanced Spell Casting and Influential Incantations Board are subject to copyright and are known collectively as ASCII Characters in magic circles.

Tutting with frustration, he closed the book. He'd do it one day.
It was just a matter of time, he hoped. Exhausted from the burst of
mental effort he closed his eyes to think about what he was doing
wrong. Soon the warm sun, the gently chirping birds and the
soothing buzz of nearby bees worked their own special spell.
Quietly, Vhintz slipped away into a calm and shallow sleep.

The two boys walked wearily through the forest. The cries of
temper and frustration from Vlad had faded hours ago. Fortunately, Franck had been right about daylight and vampires.
    'Stop!' said Firkin. 'Look!'
    'What?'
    'Over there.' Firkin pointed.
    'What? I can't see anything. Except for that tatty old signpost.'
    'Yes. That's it. A signpost.'
    'Oooh.'
    They walked towards it. Firkin reached out and pulled a branch
away. Dusting off what seemed to be years of grime, he read:

                    FORT KNUMM   12 miles

Fort Knumm. What pictures that conjured up! Solid fortifications
rising huge from moated banks. Curtain walls crowned with
ramparts, trodden by garrisons of crack troops. Banners flying.
Trumpeteers ready to herald the approach of friends; and columns
of archers ready to welcome great foes. Terminally.
    Sounds impressive. It would be if that were the case.
    True, there is a fort. A tiny moth-eaten motte and bailey stands
forlornly neglected in the middle of the town. It was built at the
time when forts were *de rigueur* and every town worth its
condiment had to have one. It was the first fort in the area and
attracted people from miles around. Always quick to make a few
shillings, the craftiest townspeople turned their hands to, well,
handicrafts. All types of produce were on sale – all handmade.
Wicker baskets, cat baskets, coloured wax candles covered in
strange shapes, small soaps with herbs in, honey and jam in tiny
pots, small vessels containing bath oil. Tons of the stuff, all made
in Fort Knumm. In a rare flash of effective civic planning, the

Mayor set up a collective association for all the crafts persons of Fort Knumm enabling the distribution of their wares throughout the town and maintaining a fair price for the goods produced. A delivery network was put into operation and shops were soon offering goods for sale, all displaying stickers proclaiming the fact that they were made by the 'Fort Knumm Hand Masons'.

The tourist trade boomed. Prosperity followed.

Expansion of the town was strictly regulated and architecture was subject to tight controls so as not to destroy the 'Olde Worlde feel' as the Mayor had so picturesquely called the less than sanitary collection of seething dwellings surrounding the fort.

This state of affairs continued for a good few years and quite a few people got quite fat on their profits. They became inward-looking and not a little complacent. Not to mention lazy. Too late, they realised that other towns had their own forts and Fort Knumm wasn't special any more. The number of tourists dropped savagely. The townspeople tried bravely to ignore their dwindling income and hoped the outside world would still come to visit. It didn't. Money became scarce. Tourists became scarcer and now the town was a sorry collection of desperate salesmen, criminals, assassins, murderers, insurance agents, etc. . . . .

Of course Firkin and Hogshead knew none of this. Compared to Middin, Fort Knumm was a town of riches, a city of splendour, a glittering metropolis.

In the early evening and after several hours of hard walking, the two boys passed through the town's gatehouse. The archway held up two huge, rotting wooden gates, miraculously still supported by four hinges, consisting now mostly of rust.

Through the gate the main street stretched off up the hill. Each side was lined with shops huddled tightly together. The fronts of the buildings leaned out at strange angles where the timber frames had buckled over the years, and the top storeys crowded out the light. It was almost as if the architect had tried to capture the moment when a pair of huge rolling waves start to topple against each other, and turned them into a row of timber-framed houses.

They walked slowly up the street looking into the shop windows.

'You look like a discerning sort of gentleman, if I may say so, sir! But I sense something missing from your life. What you need is this! Impress the ladies with your immaculate grooming.' The salesman thrust a small wooden box at Hogshead and proceeded to demonstrate the 'Ye Olde Travelling Companion'.

Hogshead stood, amazed, as he was shown the nail clippers, the nail file, a small tooth pick, a device for removing stones from your boots, three different sorts of knife, a pair of scissors . . .

'. . . all contained in an easy-to-carry wooden pouch. Yours for only . . .'

'Come on,' said Firkin grabbing Hogshead by the arm.

'He's got one,' he said over his shoulder to the salesman.

They moved on a few feet.

'Into every life a little darkness comes!' hailed the nearest shop. 'Banish those dark times with . . . this!' A hand, followed by a small shabby man, shot from the doorway carrying a tastelessly carved wax candle. It stood about twelve inches high and must have weighed several pounds.

'Light your home with this exquisite example of wax craftsmanship. The specially designed wick gives a slow rate of consumption to ensure a long life and an ambience to . . .'

'No thanks!'

'Heat and light from the same device . . .'

'No, it's too heavy. We are travelling.'

'Light your way forward with ease. See the path ahead!' He waved the candle frantically.

'No,' said Firkin firmly, ushering Hogshead forward.

'You'll regret it! You'll see!' he quietly unsheathed a four-inch blade and waved it significantly.

Firkin ignored this unconvincing threat and moved on.

'This is an amazing place,' said Hogshead looking around. 'It's a, a thingummy of shopkeepers.'

'A nation . . .'

'Eh?'

'. . . of shopkeepers.'

'What . . . No that's not right. It's . . .'

'Do you have difficulty finding the right words? Ever stumble over definitions?' came a voice from their left. 'Well, gentlemen, today is your lucky day. I can offer you, here and now, a complete pocket-sized, latest-edition dictionary. And I'll throw in your very own Thesaurus, fully house-trained of course! Ha, ha! Impress the maidens with your knowledge of word play. Whisper grammatically correct love poems! What do you say, gents? You look like men who know a good deal when they see one . . . Hey, whaddyoubothsay?'

'I've read it. Not a very good plot.' said Firkin dismissively.

'You won't get a better deal, let me tell you!'

'Did you say meal . . . I'm starving.'

'There's got to be a place up here,' said Firkin encouragingly, 'somewhere.'

They passed a small skinny man sitting on the floor surrounded by drawings of faces.

'Evening sir.'

'Evening,' replied Hogshead politely. 'Nice day,' he added conversationally.

'Looks like rain . . .' came another voice '. . . don't want to get wet now do we? How impressed would the maidens be if you turned up wet? I've got just the thing in here . . .' he trailed off as he ran into his shop.

'Let me sketch your picture, sir. Only take a minute, sir. A perfect souvenir. I can even frame it for you, sir. Let me sketch . . . ow!'

'Oh shut up, Boz. These are my customers!' said the umbrella-man kicking the poor artist. 'As I was saying. Ahem. The light portable way to stay dry. Easily assembled, readily avail . . .'

'. . . but you've got such sketchable features . . .'

'. . . able in many colours to suit your outfit. Fashion umbrellas. You won't get a better . . .'

'. . . in charcoal, ink, or coloured pencils? Take your pick, sir . . .'

'Stop!' shouted Firkin. 'I've had enough. I don't want an umbrella, thank you, and if I bought a sketch it would get scrunched up in my bag.'

'I can supply a carrying tube if you wish, sir.'

'No. I don't want one. Now, please could you tell us where we could get something to eat.'

They appeared to think about this.

'Well, I don't see why we should tell him. I mean he hasn't bought anything, has he? Supply and demand, you know. I know where he can eat and he don't!'

'Yeah, that's right. We know where the pub is and he don't!' Boz grinned.

'I don't think we should tell him.'

'That's right. We won't tell him. It's a secret that it's over there and first on the left. Ow . . . !'

'What the Dickens did you have to tell him that for?'

'It just came out. I didn't mean it.'

Back in OG 1025 the Prospector paced nervously up and down in the ante-chamber of the Conference Room of Castell Rhyngill. He could hear his heart pounding, filling the room. Adrenalin surged around his body from a cocktail of nerves and fear. He knew the reputation the King Khardeen of Rhyngill had for avoiding all unnecessary expenditure and the often ruthless way he achieved this. Rumour had it that his favourite saying was something along the lines of 'More pain, more gain.' Especially when setting new tithe levels.

The door creaked open and a hand beckoned the Prospector inside. He smoothed back his hair, attempted to straighten his shabby jacket and nervously followed.

He walked past the geometric displays of weapons festooning the walls, and stood before the centuries-old oak table. The decades-old King of Rhyngill, sat dozing behind it.

'Ahem! Your Highness. Sire!'

The King jolted awake and looked about startled.

'Sire,' resumed the clerk, 'May I present Franck Middin, the Prospector.'

Franck bowed before the ageing king and waited nervously. The King looked at a small bowl before him and took a suspicious mouthful of what looked like porridge.

'Well?' he said irritably in response to the clerk's nervous cough. The King peered over a pair of half-moon glasses and wiped his mouth with a grubby-looking handkerchief.

'Your Highness,' began Franck nervously. 'I beg audience for a hearing on a matter of urgent Kingdomnal importance.'

'Eh . . . What d'you say?' The King raised his ear trumpet. 'C'mon out with it. Haven't got all day!'

'Sire, I come on a matter of urgent Kingdomnal importance,' repeated Franck patiently.

'Impotence! Who said?'

'Importance, Sire. Very important.'

'Damn right it is. Can't have rumours of Kings bein' impotent. Not true anyway. Haven't you seen me son then?' The King rummaged about in his cloak pocket. 'Thought we'd been round the whole kingdom. Ah, here. Look.' The King showed off a small painting of his son framed in a small heart-shaped frame.

'There, isn't he lovely!'

Franck was never sure what to say at times like these.

'Er, yes, Sire. He's got your nose.'

'My nose? What about my nose?'

'Nothing, Sire. I meant he looks a little like you, Sire.'

'Mmmm.' The King scowled as he put the picture away again. 'What've you come about anyway?'

'Sire, I'll come straight to the point.'

'Damn good idea!'

'I believe that what has rapidly become our greatest export, a product desired by all walks of life, a substance which I myself have had a large and immensely important role in establishing, an interkingdomnal symbol of stature and . . .'

'Get to the point!' snapped the King, playing idly with his handle-bar moustache.

Franck coughed and rewound his thoughts.

'Sire, our lemming skin is in danger.'

'Eh . . . What?' For the first time the King was genuinely interested. 'What danger . . . What?'

'Sire, I have reason to believe that Cranachan is attempting to steal this and all future seasons of lemmings from under our noses.'

The King leant across the oak table and stared at the Prospector. A small finger gesture urged Franck on.

'Almost a year ago I was given this.' He handed the clerk a roll of parchment. 'It is a declaration of ownership of the region of the Talpa Mountains where the lemmings breed and grow and a concurrent claim, therefore, to their skins.'

111

The King looked up, his face pale as the information sank in.

'Hate legalese. Is this true?'

'Yes, Sire. But in reality they have no claim on the skins once they enter Rhyngill air-space, as they do so of their own free will, and we have no import/export agreement with them.'

'That's alright then. Isn't it?'

'Well, your Highness, it would be if events hadn't taken a turn for the worse. This year, and it will be the first time this has happened in history, when the lemmings come they will land on Cranachan soil.'

'On their side of the border?'

Franck nodded slowly.

'Impossible . . . they can't move the border without my permission . . . *I* can't move the border without my permission! And I'm the King!'

'They haven't touched the border, Sire.'

'Don't play games with me. What's going on? What's different now? What's moved?'

'The mountain.'

The King stopped in his tracks. His blustering furore had lost all its bluster. He stared over his glasses, tapped his ear trumpet on the oak table, placed it back against his ear and said quietly. 'Mountain?'

'Mountain,' confirmed Franck.

'That's what I thought I heard you say.' He fiddled with his moustache.

His Imperial Highness, the King Khardeen of Rhyngill picked up his spoon and slowly stirred the now inedibly tepid bowl of porridge. Inside his head aged neural pathways, clogged with years of mental dereliction, were rapidly cleared by the machete of righteous indignation. His face changed, became somehow younger, somehow more alive.

'Damn it all,' he said, 'That's just not on!' Dropping the spoon with a muffled splat, he raised himself to his full height, stared at the clerk and shouted, 'Fetch the War Lords of Rhyngill . . . NOW!'

After a cursory bow in the general direction of the King, the clerk ran, his head reeling with the command. 'The War Lords!' *They haven't all been together for, oooh, well, since before I was*

112

clerk, and that was after I was, or was it before I was, no after, definitely after, must 'ave been otherwise I wouldn't 'ave gone to . . . blimey! That is a long time. Whilst the War Lords were gathered from the far recesses of Castell Rhyngill, Franck told the King the whole story. He produced maps, drawings, sales figures, projected sales figures, breakdown profit and loss predictions, seasonally adjusted Talpine unemployment figures; he illustrated the Cranachan Civil Engineers' efforts on the cliff top; reams and reams of parchment were pulled out of his case and proved conclusively the danger their lemming skin was in. If they didn't act quickly and decisively, OG 1025 would be the last year that any lemming skin came from Rhyngill.

As Vhintz, the Travelling Sorcerer, dozed in the afternoon sun his mind threw off its shoes and ran gaily through the fresh fields of his collected memory. It pushed open a door and peered inside artificially darkened room. It looked down on the backs of row upon row of wizardly heads. A figure stood on a small dais at the front of the room and shuffled a wad of papers. Vhintz's memory gestured to a mage on the end of a row, shoved him along the bench and sat down to listen to the lecture. A magic lantern produced an image on the wall behind the lecturer, the topic of the talk. It said quite simply:

Some Facts About Magic

The lecturer coughed for attention, the lights dimmed a little more and he began . . .

'To be truly magic; to possess the ability to cast spells without the aid of a spellbook: to conjure or juggle reality and twist the rules of cause and effect around one's proverbial little finger is not genetic. One doesn't have to be the seventh son of a one-eyed sea-dog's mistress-in-law to stand more, or less, of a chance at effective thaumaturgy.'

A murmur of mirth rippled through the audience.

'To cast a spell effectively, you have to "understand". All it takes, fundamentally, is the ability to create and shape words to

113

focus the correct type of magic onto a particular subject, however unwilling.

'Everybody knows that if you get a coathanger, bend it to the right shape and shove it in the top of a small transistor radio, music comes out. It's the same with magic.

'But *words* are the coathangers of magic.

'Magic is all around us, it's everywhere, running parallel to us in time and space and all it takes to unlock the ethereal vault is the correct arrangement of words.

'Of course, you've got to know what you're doing. The key to this burgeoning ethereal dam of ancient power is a skill more fundamental than the essence of sentences, more directed than diction or grammar, more correct than assonance. Much more ancient and deeper than any mere work of ordinary literature. To use magic properly you have to be an adept in the ancient craft of "spelling".'

A hand raised itself in question. The lecturer was ready before it was asked.

'No, no! Not the sort where the arrangement and sequence of mere letters is important. This is far superior, ultimately more holistic. To be adept at true "spelling", a deep and intimate knowledge of pace, paragraph alignment, adverb convolution and third-party infiltration parameters is essential.

'Otherwise you may as well take one book, chew it into very small fragments in a very small space and wait for chance to arrange the fragments properly.'

Vhintz's memory, feeling curiously uncomfortable, stood and crept out.

'Are you sure he said "First on the left"?' whispered Hogshead nervously.

'Yes. Didn't you hear him?'

'That's what I thought he said but this doesn't feel exactly right. It's a bit on the dark side.' Hogshead looked about him nervously and moved closer to Firkin. A small pack of rats watched in surly disinterest as the two boys crept down the narrow back street. The pavement, if you could sully such a grand appellation with the strip of uneven ground whose unfortunate duty it was to occupy the

114

space between the two rows of shabby buildings, glistened faintly in the dim quarter-light of the street. It seemed very strange to Hogshead that it did glisten, since it hadn't rained for weeks and he would be surprised if any rain would get in here anyway.

'Did he say how far down the first on the left?'

'No, it had better be soon otherwise I'm turning round and . . . Look out!'

Above the street a window opened and a figure appeared holding a large bucket. Too late, Hogshead looked up. Still talking to someone inside the room, the figure absently upended the bucket in the careless way one carries out an irritatingly familiar domestic chore. Too late, Hogshead moved. Firkin turned away and cringed visibly as a cascade of savoury, and not so savoury, domestic refuse honoured Hogshead with its unwelcome and horribly wet presence. The window closed, the incident below passing unseen. Hogshead stood and glistened pavementally. A long potato-peeling snaked off his forehead, followed by several pieces of carrot. He shook his head in disgust and dislodged a few more potato-peelings.

'Ooh, darlin', you wanna watch where you walkin' – 'specially round 'ere.' A tall woman emerged from the dark shadows of an unseen ginnel into the lighter shadow of the back street and looked pityingly at the dripping Hogshead. 'They're animals round 'ere, love. Animals I tell yer.'

Almost as if to prove the point a large rat slithered quietly across the street and swiftly disappeared, narrowly avoiding the sharp toe of the woman's boot.

'You ain't from round 'ere are yer?' she asked as Hogshead attempted to clean himself up a little.

'No,' answered Firkin, 'How can you tell?'

'Well for starters you'd 'ave been watchin' out a bit better, and besides I ain't seen you two 'andsome darlin's before on my patch, an' I know everyone on my patch. It's my job, see?' She looked at the dripping Hogshead and smirked.

'Come on, we'd best see about cleanin' you up, love.' Without even waiting for an answer she disappeared into the shadows.

Hogshead looked blankly at Firkin who shrugged his shoulders in reply.

'Come on, darlin's. Don't know 'bout you, but I ain't got all night.'

The two boys stepped into the shadows and followed the woman as she led them down narrow alleys, through gaps in fences, round dark and dingy blocks until she stopped suddenly and disappeared through a peculiarly pink doorway. Reluctantly, but with nothing else in mind they stepped inside. The floor felt strangely bouncy and Firkin looked down at the shaggy pink material on the floor. A long slender finger appeared from a side door and beckoned them inside.

The sound of hot running water and the smell of fresh oils and herb balms greeted them with a strange but welcoming aroma. The woman turned off the taps and approached Hogshead.

'Alright, love. Let's start 'ere shall we?' She reached out and began to expertly undo the buttons on Hogshead's jacket.

'Bit smelly, aren't you, love? Not to worry, we'll soon 'ave you smellin' like a rose. You can go nex' door wi' Bharbra,' she said to Firkin as another tall, and remarkably scantily-clad, woman entered and smiled at him.

The grime from the last few days, the dim red lights and the worried look on Hogshead's face all disguised the fact that he was almost definitely too young for this type of personal attention. The aroma of the oils and his sheer exhaustion made him almost blissfully unaware of the fact that in a moment he had been completely and expertly stripped. Maisy smiled sweetly at him as she removed his final garments and helped him into the hot bubbling bath.

'I'll leave you in there while I go an' clean these up. All part of the service, darlin'!'

She shook the heap of clothes, checking for loose change, as she left the room and the swiftly relaxing Hogshead.

The War Lords of Rhyngill is, without doubt, a grand title, full of power, courage and glory. It calls to the forefront of one's mind a band of men ready to join battle at the drop of a hat, bristling with aggression, armed to the teeth; standing to represent the military genius of the kingdom; the strategic pinnacle of Rhyngill; all enemies' worst nightmares incarnate. Only in the worst times

116

were the War Lords gathered. It was generally believed that, as each of the four inherently held more aggression than your average battalion-at-arms, bringing them into close proximity with each other would cause an unstable and extremely dangerous environment which, if handled correctly, could bring about a swift and definite end to any war. Rather like several kilos of highly enraged plutonium. It was mainly for this reason that conference rooms were so large.

And so it was without fanfare, or announcement, or even a whispred welcome, that in OG 1025 the War Lords entered the conference room. It was strewn with parchment charts, a thin-looking man with bottle-green glasses pointing to a chart of market forecasts, and their King enraptured. And looking surprisingly young.

Franck turned to greet the War Lords. His jaw dropped limply open before he could control himself.

It was immediately, and painfully, apparent to Franck that decades of peace had done terrible things to them.

Three old men rattled into the conference room and creaked toward their thrones. A fourth entered in a rickety bath chair.

'What's all this about, eh?' asked Lappet frostily. 'I was having a nice game of backgammon with old Rachnid here. Keeping the strategies up to scratch, don't y'know!'

Rachnid nodded and, balancing precariously on his stick, somehow managed to ease himself into his throne.

Bateleur, a spritely octogenarian with black sparkling eyes, an alarmingly sharp-looking hooked nose and a mane of dense black hair, looked around enthusiastically.

'Who's for a good old thrashing then?' he squawked. 'Could do with a good scrap!'

'Should've gone before you came,' cackled Brumas from his bath chair.

'Shut up, you old bat,' shouted Bateleur, poking Brumas with his long and pointed stick.

'Only four more to bear off. Would've won, you know. Void now of course,' continued Lappet in a world of his own.

'Who you calling old?' shouted Brumas hoarsely, his jowls slapping the side of his face. 'I'm in my prime, fit as a flea, ready for

117

anything.' He slapped his barrel chest in a gesture of manliness, and promptly collapsed in a fit of coughing.

'Gentlemen, please,' shouted the King Khardeen. 'If you could put aside our differences for a moment, I do appreciate that you haven't all been together for a long time and that there is a lot of catching up to do, but if I could just have your attention. This is serious!'

'Reminded me of a game few years back. Four to bear off. Two dice throws. Did it! Yes, did it don't y'know!'

'Lappet, pay attention.'

The King, having put his foot down with a firm hand and gained the ageing War Lords' attention, proceeded to explain in minute detail the situation in which they found themselves. He referred to Franck's graphs, maps and detailed forecasts. He spoke for minutes, embellishing the truth with rabble-rousing phrases more and more as he went on while Franck just watched, nodding occasionally. '. . . and so Gentlemen,' he concluded, 'What are we going to do about it?'

A gentle snoring floated over from the bath chair.

'It's obvious, I'd say!' shouted Bateleur, waving his stick.

Brumas, jolted awake by the sudden shouting, sat up suddenly and looked around in confusion.

'What's so obvious?' asked Lappet.

'Act of aggression stealin' our thingummies. Need a good kicking I'd say. Sire,' shouted Bateleur, in his high croaking voice, 'I move we take action. Of a military nature, of course. Haven't had a good scrap for ages.'

'Ever tried senna pods?' asked Brumas unhelpfully.

Rachnid suddenly found his voice, 'You mean w-w-w-war!'

'No, backgammon,' crackled Bateleur sarcastically, 'What do you think?'

'Two a day, you'll be fine,' continued Brumas, in a world of his own.

'Don't you think that that's a little bit violent?' whined Rachnid.

'You call yourself a War Lord!' squawked Bateleur, slamming his fist into the table. Rachnid turned very pale.

'What about you, Lappet? What do you think?' asked the King twirling his handle-bar moustache happily.

118

'Must admit. Challenge of strategic planning in enemy territory appealing. Concur with military action decision.'

'Right, that's settled then. I declare this motion of war carried,' declared the King, peering over his half-moon spectacles. 'Let preparations begin.'

Franck, speechless by the speed of the decision, looked around bewildered. He hadn't expected it to come to this. Well, not that fast, anyway.

''Avin a nice time in there, are we?' asked Maisy with an edge to her voice that hadn't been there before.

'Yes, thank you,' answered Hogshead politely from under a mound of pink bubbles in the bath.

'All scrubbed nice an' clean?'

'I think so.'

'Well, 'ere's yer clothes. 'Urry up an get out!'

'Are they dry? Only it's not healthy to put on wet clothes. Especially at night because . . .'

Hogshead drifted away as he saw the expression of irritation on Maisy's face.

'I'll, er, 'urry up an' get out then. Er, could you pass me a towel, I'd like to get dry first, please.'

Maisy passed the towel and waited, fidgeting impatiently.

'Could you look away, please?' asked Hogshead, 'I'm going to get out now.'

'Don't worry 'bout me, darling. I've seen it all before.'

Hogshead blushed, realised that she was right, and shyly got out.

'Why are you angry?'

''Cause yer wastin' my time. If you ain't got any money I don't want you 'ere.'

'You invited us in. I didn't realise we had to pay.'

'You ain't really 'ad anythin' worth payin' for yet, darlin'. That would've come later.' With that she pouted just a little. The effect was lost on Hogshead.

'We'll have some money soon and treasure. That's why we're here,' he said cheerfully, towelling his hair furiously.

'Oh no,' cried Maisy in despair, 'Not another one come 'ere to make 'is fortune. Don't yer know that Fort Knumm's days of

119

makin' people's fortunes 'as gone. Take my advice, darlin', get out while yer can.'

'No, you don't understand. We're on a mission.'

She threw her hands in the air.

'Oh, it gets worse. Bleedin' missionaries. I knew you weren't from round 'ere.'

Hogshead pulled his trousers up.

'No, it's a secret mission.'

'Look, love. I ain't interested. I just want you out of 'ere so's I can get someone else in. Someone with a bit o' money. I've got a job to do.'

She ushered the still damp Hogshead out into the clammy late evening and shut the door.

'Wait, wait. Firkin!' He pounded on the door as he realised his best friend, in fact his *only* friend at the moment, was still in there.

'Open up. Firkin!'

Suddenly the door burst open and the damp, and feebly struggling body of Firkin was hurled out of the door by a remarkably butch-looking young lady.

'Wait, wait!' cried Hogshead through the closing door.

The door stopped, opened slightly and a deep voice snapped in irritation. 'What d'you want?'

'Well, I want to know where we can sleep.'

'Got any money?'

'Not much.'

'Not my problem then is it?'

The door slammed firmly and finally shut.

Firkin groaned and sat up. 'What was all that about?'

'I'm not really sure. I think Franck mentioned places like that. I can't remember what they're called.'

Firkin looked blank.

'Oh, you know. We went in with dirty clothes and came out clean.'

'Something to do with grass?'

'Yeah. It's on the tip of my tongue.' Hogshead thought hard.

Firkin's brow furrowed in concentration.

'Got it,' he cried, after what seemed like an age.

'Come on, tell me.'
'A Lawn Dirette!'

In the history of Castell Rhyngill, the few short weeks after the War Lord's meeting in OG 1025 had to be the most hectic. An excitement raced through the corridors and halls like a dispossessed demon on a narcotics binge. No one was immune to its fever. Even the resident pack of black rats in the kitchen twitched a little more nervously than usual.

It was the excitement of preparation. Checking this, making sure of that, doing the other, telling someone else to do the this, that or the other that you yourself hadn't the time for. It was a delegator's paradise. It was very like the excitement that exists just before a summer holiday, only different. Different in two fundamental ways. This was serious and some people might not come back.

And through it all a small boy wandered, soaking up the atmosphere but not understanding a thing of what was going on. Prince Klayth watched as columns of foot soldiers marched in the courtyard outside the tithebarns. He walked through the stables and watched as the cavalry prepared their tackle. He drifted in and out of groups of people in furious preparation. And all the time he heard the same word. War.

Rhyngill was in the final stages of the preparation before going to war against the neighbouring kingdom of Cranachan. The War Lords had strategised and planned for the event. Brumas had requested and received a specially constructed battle bath-chair. Everything was ready.

Suddenly Prince Klayth noticed a change. He awoke one morning and instantly sensed a difference. He climbed out of bed and tip-toed across the room. Quietly he opened the door and crept out. He looked first at a pair of huge black boots, then the long flowing cape of office and finally the huge bearded face of his father, the King Khardeen, forcing a smile as he peered down at him through his half-moon glasses.

'Hello Daddy,' whispered the tiny Prince, 'What're you doing here? Where's Mummy?'

'In a safe place, son. Safe place.' The King bent down, picked up the young Prince and walked over to a nearby chair.

'Why?' asked Klayth.

'Because I'm going away and I want you to be a big boy for me.'

Klayth looked up and stared at the bearded face of his father's face. He looked very old, but somehow very strong, like a gnarled tree.

He'd been on the throne a long time and, up until five years ago, had been worried that he would never have a son and heir. This wasn't through lack of trying, as most of the women of court knew only too well, it was just one of those co-ordination things.

But just over four years ago Klayth had arrived and the King's worries were over. Now he had an heir he could get back to the things that kings were supposed to get up to. He could give his son something to emulate. He could get out of the castle and continue the reign of tight, "but oh so fair", terror and extortion that he knew and loved. Years of enforced absence from the warring and pillaging circuits were ended after one night's passion. How he actually managed it at his age was a talking point for weeks afterwards. 'Son, I want you to be King like me for a little while. You'll be alright, Maffew and Burnurd will look after you.'

Klayth stared tearfully at hs father. He wasn't sure why but he felt as if he wasn't going to see him again.

'That's settled then,' said the King quietly as he put the Prince down and walked out of the room. Klayth didn't answer. How could he answer, or even express any kind of opinion when he hadn't the faintest idea of what was going on?

He drifted aimlessly back into his room and stared absently out of the window. A few minutes later he watched as the King, the four War Lords and an armoured bath chair led the first column of troops out of the front gate, over the drawbridge and away into history.

Klayth turned away from the window and felt very, very small.

The Travelling Sorcerer was still dozing in the warm rays of the late afternoon sun. The moon on his cloak sparkled in time with the rise and fall of his chest. Next to him lay the ancient leather-bound book, crumpled unceremoniously where it had fallen from his lap. Vhintz's mouth hung open slightly and he almost snored. A blissful picture.

Fortunately for him he was completely unaware of the ugly creature watching him from the other side of the clearing. Had it

122

possessed lips it would have been licking them in anticipation as it observed its prey. Had it possessed hands they would have been rubbing each other expectantly. Had it a heart, it would have picked something its own size. Over there, in direct sight, was the makings of a very good meal indeed. A feast ripe for the taking. And it was hungry. The creature's eyes scanned the distance between itself and its prey. It surveyed the route, checked the cover, looked for signs of ambush. All clear. It was very, very hungry . . .

It started to move, slowly, towards the innocently sleeping old man. Carefully, stealthily, it undulated its way across the clearing. Keeping low, out of sight. Nearer and nearer it came, its jaws quivering in excitement. Digestive juices welled up in its stomach as it eyed the meal, helpless, before it. It closed in. The old man slumbered on, defenceless, oblivious. Saliva surged hot in its mouth. It dragged its inhuman body nearer, raising its head. Nearer. Saliva-stained jaws glistened briefly in the sunlight. A final flash of beauty before the carnage. Its head lashed mercilessly down, then from side to side as its jaws sliced deep. A frenzy of ripping and tearing. Gorging. It scattered dismembered fragments everywhere in its desperate attempt to satisfy its aching hunger . . .

As the sun's reddening rays illuminated the scene of carnage and destruction below, the creature, its burning hunger sated, heaved its bloated body away to digest the heavy feast.

A chill wind blew forlornly across the old man's body, stirring the tails of his cloak. Its eyelids flickering unconsciously, hideous convulsions racked the body as its nerve endings fired in the dying seconds of an afternoon nap. Vhintz yawned expansively and scratched his shoulder. Smacking his lips and stretching, he reached out, closed the old leather book and returned it, carefully, to his rucksack. He stood, stiffly, stretched once more, massaged his back, then headed off towards the next town leaving a slightly warm patch of tree trunk, a man-shaped patch of flattened grass and a tiny pile of freshly chewed, age-yellowed parchment.

A gentle gust of wind picked up the shreds and hid them under a pile of last year's leaf litter.

Not far away, a bookworm gently snored as it digested an afternoon feast.

*

Far down the wrong end of a dark, wet, cobbled alley several dozen of the meanest criminals in the whole of Fort Knumm were having a wicked night out.

This was nothing unusual.

They always had nights out.

There was always some excuse.

They were incredibly inventive in their reasoning. If there was no new escapee joining their merry throng to be inaugurated, then there was always the *anniversary* of a new escapee joining the throng, or maybe a new murder to celebrate, or perhaps even an over-generous thief buying rounds for his friends from the proceeds of his latest raid. In Ye Silver Spitoone a friend was easy to find. Anyone without a knife at your throat, kidneys, etc.

In Fort Knumm the criminals knew how to party. They were always down 'The Spit', as it was affectionately known. They loved the Atmosphere. And it loved them.

The call to party was obligatory. No excuse for absence. None. Not even murder. Even your own!

Tonight the usual crowd were in. Ikhnaton the Assassin was at the Skull Table* with Aznar the Bouncer. A crowd of lowly muggers and thieves looked on.

'Set 'im up!' yelled Ikhnaton above the throbbing din.

Aznar bent down, inserting a coin into the side of the table and began arranging what appeared on the table top.

Skroht'm the Barman wrestled with several homicidal lunatics as they argued about the price of the last round.

The rest of the clientele either amused themselves watching the bar brawl or fleeced each other in thousands of different ways at little tables jammed into the rest of the dim dark hostelry. It was a good Atmosphere. Especially for being bad.

'It's my break!' shrieked Ikhnaton, standing nose to nose with Aznar and knifing three sneak thieves for effect. A pale black grin appeared in the air. The Atmosphere was hotting up.

'Bu' I setimup.'

* Skull is a game played on a flat slate with six pockets, two hatchets and no rules. Well, there are rules but these are 100% variable and depend on two things:– (a) who can shout the loudest, and (b) how much he's had to drink.

'Are you ARGUING?' replied Ikhnaton, nonchalantly fingering a thirteen-inch gutting knife.

'. . . er . . .'

'It's my break,' repeated Ikhnaton in a whisper that somehow everyone heard.

Before him, on the flat slate table, were five almost spherical objects arranged in a passable triangle.

He stood up to his full height, narrowly avoiding the low oak-beams, clenched his teeth and brought down his hatchet on the nearest sphere. A bone-splitting crack was heard as the sphere shattered.

The muggers and thieves shouted their approval as the pale grey ooze mingled with the already congealing blood on the table and dribbled away down the pockets.

'ONE! Ah ha ha!' yelled Ikhnaton and arranged the hatchet for a second strike.

This time, two recently deceased skulls shattered under the onslaught and the thieves went wild. Audience participation was an essential part of the night life in The Spit. If you weren't seen to be enjoying other people's playing, then soon those other people would be seen to be enjoying playing with you. Not necessarily in one piece.

Over the other side of the bar, Skroht'm had finally convinced the lunatics of the price of the round by adding their heads together. Ikhnaton raised his hatchet for another strike and stopped. He stared towards the door and blinked in disbelief. Two new faces stood in the doorway and blinked. The rounder one coughed. It suddenly went very quiet.

The Atmosphere held its breath.

It hadn't taken long for Firkin and Hogshead to decide that sitting in the gutter of the filthy alleyway that passed just outside 'Daisy and Maisy's Plesure Parlor' was not a good idea. It was bad enough not knowing precisely where you were in a strange town, and Fort Knumm was certainly strange. But sitting outside one of the seedier of Fort Knumm's many evening entertainment venues, as the evening rapidly approached night, was not only highly undesirable but foolhardy in the extreme. As the evening drew on, the size of the clientele frequenting the pink pleasure palace grew, as did the level of their intoxication. Huge thugs leered precariously over the two tiny figures and breathed heavy, alcohol-laced, breath at them. In the end the decision to move was taken, not from any positive sense of direction but more that 'anywhere else is better than here'.

At first, they adopted the Brownian navigation technique, a methodology beloved of aimless tourists searching for sights of historic interest in a foreign town. That is, rattle about randomly until something, anything, looks familiar. Sadly, as they were searching for a destination of which they knew neither the name nor appearance, this method was completely and utterly useless. A slightly more thoughtful approach was needed. Since they were heading for a hostelry, expressly designed for the sole purpose of purveying wines, spirits and vast amounts of beer to thirsty and/or alcoholic punters, would not it be advisable to ascertain the direction and intensity of airborne alcoholic vapours and proceed in a direction opposite to its decay gradient thus facilitating the timely discovery and ultimate arrival at its source? They followed their noses.

This was not as simple a task as would initially be expected. Fort Knumm had so many different, conflicting and, worse, *nauseating* smells that following any one in particular proved extremely difficult. They roamed aimlessly in the dark back alleys close to the outer wall. They walked in ever-quickening steps past groups of huge leering thugs, smoking things that gave off a dark blueish smoke that hung in the air in a very relaxed way. Several times, especially near to the wall, they had to retrace their footsteps as they turned a corner to find their way forward blocked by a dead end. All the time rats scurried past on unknown missions and around them, the cockroach-infested buildings hummed with life. The vertebrates were outnumbered, hundreds to one, by the other residents with significantly less backbone.

Eventually, Firkin and Hogshead turned into another, equally repellant, backstreet and walked warily on. Ahead of them, on the right, a building was making a lot more noise than expected. Raucous laughter, mingled with the occasional sound of breaking glass and screaming, filtered out into the street. A low subterranean pulse throbbed rhythmically.

Above the two boys heads hung a faded sign. It was in desperate need of repainting but if you stood and squinted hard enough in the gloom it was still possible, just, to make out the words 'Ye Silver Spitoone'.

It has been said that the name was due to an unfortunate series of events involving a dyslexic, and partially deaf, sign writer, an intoxicated amateur historian and a misplaced, but none the less genuine, sense of loyalty to the King on the part of the then landlord. The landlord, wanting to honour the King in the naming of his newly refurbished hostelry, decided to use a legend he had once heard about royalty being royalty because they had something silver in their mouths when they were born. The identity of this silver thing eluded him so he consulted an amateur historian friend, and regular drunk, who assured him that he knew. The landlord then commissioned a sign and renamed the place.

The presence of the King was requested at the unveiling and renaming ceremony. On the day, sadly, things did not go according to plan. The landlord, after a passable speech, proudly unveiled his new sign. The King's face dropped, the crowd went wild, mainly with laughter, and the landlord was last seen struggling between two Black Guards. The King ordered the sign to be left there as a reminder that the King's birthright is a noble thing. 'And by the way, it's a *spoon*!' he had declared, stomping imperiously away.

What became of the landlord nobody ever knew. Mostly people suspected that whatever it was, it was almost certainly not likely to be in his health's best interest. 'The landlord,' it was said on the streets, 'was well and truly in the spit, without a paddle.'

That had all been years ago, and probably wasn't entirely true, but the locals liked it. Firkin and Hogshead stood outside and listened to the bawdy singing. They looked at each other, took a deep breath and walked into Ye Silver Spitoone.

Abruptly the drunken cacophony stopped. A thick carpet of silence fell. The two boys stood in the doorway. Hogshead coughed. The Atmosphere smirked a malevolent smirk.

Over to the left a group of men were holding hatchets up above a large slate table. Other people, creaking in rust decorated armour, sat in small secluded corners, drinking the odd gallon or

127

two of some brown liquid. Several people had hands in other people's pockets. Firkin walked slowly towards the bar. A group of dazed-looking men wearing fur coats moved out of his way.

He scaled a bar stool and sat staring up at the huge, sweaty bulk of Skroht'm. The current and well-respected, well-feared, well-rounded Landlord.

'Landlord,' said Firkin in a manner that he hoped sounded brave, 'We . . .'

He looked around as the sound of frantic running feet signalled Hogshead's arrival at the bar.

'We would like some food . . . Please . . . If it's not too much trouble?'

'Oh, you would, would you?'

Firkin felt beads of sweat apppear on his forehead.

The huge bulk of the Landlord moved ponderously towards him. He wiped his hands on a towel. An innocent gesture, but to Firkin it spelled menace, with a capital 'M'. Followed by a capital 'ENACE'. He wore an apron and a vest and both looked like he'd been doing so for months. He stood in front of Firkin and filled the space behind the bar. "We'd like some food"? Wouldn't we just? Ha, ha, ha!' he bellowed. You could have heard a pin drop.

'Yes, please.'

'Who's "we"?' said the Landlord peering over the bar. 'Not the 'royal we', one hopes. Haw, haw, haw!'

The audience of assassins, muggers and wild men moved forward in their seats, sensing some fun.

'Er. No. Him and me actually,' replied Firkin, gesturing to the crimson-faced Hogshead.

'Any more of you is there? Whole wagonload outside? Or is this it, actually?'

A malevolent grin winked briefly in a distant corner.

'This is it. Just us two.' Firkin swallowed uncomfortably.

'Aw, what a shame! We all likes visitors in here, don't we, Gnorm?' He nudged one of the mountainous men on his left, who nodded wildly and laughed out loud.

'Arr,' said Gnorm.

'Please could you tell us what's on the menu?' Firkin asked.

'Oooh. Mark at that! "Menu" he says. All posh like.'

The landlord was enjoying himself. He felt like he was on the stage and the audience were beginning to enjoy it. He leaned theatrically over to Firkin and said, 'We don't call it an, ahem, "Menu" in here. 'Fraid it's called "A List". You says "Landlord, what's on the list?" Okay?' Several of the younger sneak thieves began rocking back and forth in obvious amusement.

Firkin felt very uncomfortable and was convinced this whole episode was slipping out of his hands. He swallowed again. Took a deep breath and . . .

'Landlordwhatsonthelist?' blurted Hogshead with his eyes tightly shut. The whole pub fell about in laughter as Firkin shut his mouth in embarrassment.

'Oh yes, lads. I'm so glad you asked!' laughed the Landlord as he handed Firkin a well-thumbed and almost transparently greasy piece of parchment. His face brightened. 'There you go. Hope you didn't mind our little game. It's just that we don't get many new faces in here very often. So we likes to make the most of it when we does. I'n't that right, Gnorm?'

'Arr,' said Gnorm.

Two enormous hands reached out of the sky and lifted Hogshead on to a stool placed next to Firkin.

'You just choose what you want an' let me know,' said the Landlord, placing two frothing drinks in front of the boys.

It suddenly occurred to them that it had been almost a full day and they had drunk nothing (except a little bath water but that doesn't count). They both snatched for the drinks, guzzling them down in a few seconds. The contents of the glasses tasted a bit funny to them but it was wet. And very welcome.

'Cor. Got a bit of a thirst on, eh lads?' said Skroht'm, passing another to each of them. These disappeared almost as quickly and were replaced by a third each.

The game of Skull continued in the far corner and the Atmosphere returned to normal. Normal in the Spit was a heady mixture of about 45 per cent cigarette smoke, 20 per cent pipe tobacco, 19 per cent alcohol fumes, 13 per cent exotic, and probably illegal, narcotics and about 3 per cent oxygen. Thus proving that if you want to create an atmosphere, oxygen is probably optional.

The boys, their thirst far from slaked, took another drink each.

Time and tide, it is well known, wait for no man. Things change, new inventions are invented, old discoveries lost in the mists of time are rediscovered, ancient cities uncared for fall into disrepair and ruin, muscles and skills atrophy from underuse and annual subscriptions to magazines end. So it had come to pass, in OG 1025, that Bateleur discovered his subscription to *Strategist's Monthly* had not been renewed.

This was one tiny symptom of the effect that years of self-inflicted peace, while the King produced a son, had reaped on the military splendour of Rhyngill's War Lords. A few others included the normal cocktail of arthritis, cataracts, greying hair and senility. Although in the case of Rachnid this was difficult to prove, he'd always been mad.

Not only had the might of the War Lords crumbled from chronic underuse but the outside world had not stopped advancing. New techniques for gaining a tactical advantage had been dreamt up, improved manufacturing processes had enabled larger, sharper and bigger weapons to be produced, and training programmes designed to enhance military skills and courage had been brought into widespread use.

Unfortunately, one of the facilities an ageing mind does not seem to lose is the capability to initiate and sustain a sense of righteous indignation. In fact, if anything, with increasing years this grows exponentially. And indignation can be a powerful force.

This held true for the War Lords of Rhyngill. Having champed at the bit and, metaphorically, pawed the ground in frustration at the lack of any type of even remotely warlike activities for the past twenty-two years, they were more than ready to leap into battle at the dropping of a hat. However, in this case it was more the dropping of trousers.

For the first time in twenty-two years the War Lords had some real power and, like all decently addictive vices, this shot straight to their heads. They bullied and cajoled everyone in sight, sent memos of a highly petulant nature to those out of sight, and, after a very cold start and a few short-lived squeals of protest, they galvanised the rusting war machine into action.

Riding high on indignation the War Lords cried 'Havoc', and loosed the troops of Rhyngill. It was only after two and a half minutes, as they watched Rhyngill's finest being rounded up again, that Bateleur realised that it may have been a mistake, after all, not to have renewed his subscription to *Strategist's Monthly*.

Ah well, he thought to himself as he was frog-marched into Cranachan, at least we had a good reason for losing. I mean, how were we to know that we'd be outnumbered, outmanoeuvred, outweaponed and outright losers.

It was an extraordinary victory, the Cranachan tactics were impeccable. It all went precisely as planned.

As the massed forces of Rhyngill, in full battle dress and in attack formation, passed through a particularly narrow valley, a single Cranachan foot soldier had leapt nimbly out from behind a small juniper bush. Using the universal language of mime, as laid down in the Gin Ether convention guidelines on battle etiquette, (a heady and difficult-to-swallow cocktail of concepts and treatment rights that invariably gave the reader a splitting headache) the single soldier halted the entire advancing army. He pointed up at the cliff edges and then, like an air hostess illustrating the location of emergency exits, he directed the collective Rhyngillan attention along the length of the valley. As their gaze tracked the whole valley walls, more and more Cranachan soldiers appeared. Each carried bigger and sharper weapons than any of the soldiers from Rhyngill. As a show of strength and sheer weight of numbers it was designed to impress. It did. The military equivalent of stage fright swept the ranks of the Rhyngillan army. They whimpered, shook and finally gave up.

The Right Horrible Khah Nij watched with immense satisfaction. An easy victory over those spineless creatures, he thought, how they can even dare to call themselves vertebrates is beyond me. Just like a holiday that was – weeks of preparation and planning, running around like headless chickens for days before, and then Poof! Gone in a flash. All you've got is the memories. The paintings won't have come out on that one, it was too quick, and that back lighting plays havoc with the artist's eyes.

He watched the round up for a few minutes, pocketed his copy of last August's *Strategist's Monthly* and set off back to Cranachan.

'So what brings two small strangers like you into our cosy little hostelry?' asked Skroht'm leaning over the bar towards Firkin and Hogshead.

'We're looking for ashasshassinss,' blurted Hogshead. The five or six pints of strong ale that the two boys had sunk in rapid succession to slake their thirst were beginning to, er, free their tongues, shall we say.

Hogshead's phrase had managed to blurt itself at one of those incredibly inopportune moments when everyone in the room who is speaking takes a breath. In the next three nanoseconds the following things happened:

1   every single piece of throwing, slicing or maiming cutlery in the room was unsheathed and readied for throwing, slicing or maiming,
2   all exits were sealed and covered,
3   Hogshead was removed from his stool and pinned to the floor by two of the longest and sharpest-looking swords he would ever see,
4   Firkin wished Hogshead had kept his mouth shut,
5   Hogshead wet himself. And agreed with Firkin.
6   The Atmosphere held its breath.

'Shtob!' Firkin shouted.

All eyes turned to look at him. An occasional blade glinted in the gloom.

'I, er, fink I'd better, hic, make this a lille clearerer.'

Hogshead's eyes were pools of inebriate panic. Everyone looked at Firkin. Nobody said a word.

'Ahem, well.' He took a large swig of a drink and stood up on to the bar. He swayed gently from side to side and looked out of one and a half eyes. He took a deep breath and grinned at the watching crowd. It was now or never.

'We're ron a mizzion,' shouted Firkin.

'Oh, no . . . missionaries,' came a voice from the back.

132

'No, no, no. Itsh . . .' He looked around conspiratorially and put his finger to his lips. 'Shh . . . Itsh a, hic, a sheecret mizzion,' replied Firkin.

'Spies!' cried one of the more nervous sneak thieves. It was the last thing he ever said.

'Tell us why you're here or we might have to make up a game to find out,' whispered the deep clammy voice of Skroht'm inches away from Firkin's ear.

Firkin jumped. Took a large drink and tried to steady his nerves. The crowd was getting restless.

'Pleeshe, pleeshe,' shouted Firkin, 'we need, hic, we need . . .'

'A bucket!' came a voice from the crowd. Deafening, raucous laughter filled the Spit.

'. . . your help,' finished Firkin feebly. Hogshead couldn't see a great deal from his position on the floor but somehow he had the distinct feeling that it wasn't going well. He also felt rather funny. Almost as if he couldn't control himself properly. The ground was moving, he was *sure* the ground was moving. He closed his eyes – it seemed like a good idea. They shot open again; the ground *was* moving! Oh no, he thought, not again! Way above him, and seeming to be further every minute, Firkin was launching into what he fervently hoped would be a rabble-rousing speech to get the band of desperate assassins he needed for his mission.

'Gennlemenn, we are enterinng dark timesh . . .'

'The lights in 'ere 'aven't ever worked properly, eh Landlord?' shouted a member of the crowd.

'Our kingdomm 's in a baahd, hic, way . . .'

'So're you, mate. Said 'e needed a bucket, didn' I?' Laughter roared once again.

Firkin struggled on: 'The ratesh of tax are crripplnng, crripplnn, hic, crrrrrppl, verry high. We've got noh food, my shishter ish shtarvinng an'ill.'

'Aw, Gnorm, get the violins out!'

Firkin took another swig and pressed on. 'Neely all our food goesh to one playsh. The Cassle and the King. The Cassle musht be full of treashures and food! It musht be!'

The crowd started to talk amongst itself.

'Thatsh why I'm 'ere. Gennlemnnn, we need a groop ovv, hic,

133

trained ashash . . . ashash . . . asshhh . . . men to come with ush
and rid our kingdom onshe adn f'rall from the evil an' wicked
King!'

The crowd had lost what little interest it may have had.
Treasure, yes, they were interested in that, oh yes, riches beyond
their wildest dreams, the unimpeachable power and respect that
money brings, yes please, but having to kill kings for it? Oh, no.
Right out. Too much hassle by far.

The background noise and hubbub began to increase as other
conversations started.

Firkin was either oblivious to the fact that no one was listening
or just too drunk to notice.

'. . . rewards will be shplendid,' he continued, unheard and
ignored, 'Wee'll share out all the treashuresh to everyone. But
there will be, hic, many dangersh. Cassle guards have greaht big
sshpiky scchwordsses and huge ashk . . . askes . . .
ahhkkxxxx . . .'

Firkin's rabble-rousing speech was drowned in the background
noise of a pub full of disinterested people.

'. . . no, lissen,' he struggled bravely on. 'Evryeewon who
comsh with ush will be, hic, rich! Rhuch bee yon yhure whildesht
dreeeee . . .' He raised his flagon, slipped in a pool of beer on the
bar and disappeared in mid-sentence. Nobody except Hogshead
and Skroht'm noticed. The landlord stared at the prone figure of
Hogshead, pinned like a butterfly to the floor at the end of two
very sharp swords, shook his head pitifully and signalled to the
sword holders. They each received a flagon of fine ale for their
devotion to duty and promptly forgot all about the quivering
figure on the floor. In a matter of minutes life had slithered back to
the depths of depravity that pass as normal in Ye Silver Spitoone.

Fisk strolled casually towards the main Cranachan communication centre. The fingers in his gauntletted hand tapped on the sides
of the cages that lined the room through which he now walked. A
dull avian murmur, and the rattling of beaks in steel feeding-
troughs, rose in intensity as the black-clad figure agitated the
pigeons in their cages. He hated the smell of these stupid birds. He
hated the fact that the whole internal communication system of

Cranachan depended on the ability of a pigeon to find its way back here from a place, who knows how far away and who knows where? For a thrusting executive in the Cranachan council it was frustratingly slow and irritatingly unidirectional. Fisk hated it. It was so old-fashioned; in OG 1025 there should be something better. Who knows how long it would take? The pigeon might stop for a rest, or it might get mugged by an itinerant bird of prey, or even seduced by some buxom and broody pigeonette. What guarantee was there that the damn fool bird wouldn't just up and fly away carrying a piece of information of huge importance just for the hell of it? Just because it could!

What annoyed and frustrated him more than that though was the fact that during unusual and exciting times, like expeditions or wars, pigeons only worked in one direction. Take a pigeon with you, then send it back with a message. People sent him messages. People told him what to do. What good was a system of communication when you couldn't shout at people? How can you lead if you can't give orders? That relies on trust and this was one of the many worthy attributes that Fisk held no truck with.

He stopped and pulled faces at the occupant of a nearby cage. He tapped on the front and chuckled to himself as the pigeon backed away.

'Auwwwk!' he shrieked, in an attempt to frighten the poor creature. 'Auwwwk. AUWWWK!'

'Sir,' a communications scribe stood in the open door to the communication centre. Fisk looked up and smoothed back his hair slowly.

'What?'

'Sir, a message is just coming in.'

'At last!' He ran past the scribe and burst into the landing room. A pale grey pigeon fluttered gently in through the open window on to the large stone ledge, its claws scratching on the rough surface. 'Grab it!' shouted Fisk.

An assistant scribe leapt for the bird, struggled slightly to contain its flapping, then presented it feet first to Fisk. He tore impatiently at the tube on the leg and, after much squawking from the bird and Fisk, removed it and walked over to the table. He cursed profusely as he looked at the scratches and scuffs on his gauntlets and wondered again at the stupidity of a system that uses birds not shy about using their claws. Fisk opened the tiny tube, pulled out a roll of parchment and read:

Mission accomplished Stop Prisoners taken Stop
Two and a half minutes Stop That's forty shillings
you owe me Fisk! Stop K.Nij

Fisk cursed and headed off to report to King Grimzyn.

Damn! He knew the Rhyngillans were stupid, but to fall for the plan in last August's *Strategist's Monthly*, well, Fisk couldn't believe it. He had been prepared to stake twenty shillings on it. But for a victory in under three minutes Fisk had been prepared to double it. An easy claim as he didn't believe in the August strategy working. He cursed again. He shook his head. The spineless Rhyngillans had just lost him forty shillings!

Cursing once more he added, to his already very long list, the whole of Rhyngill as something else to despise.

The manic timpanist had returned with a vengeance and was now merrily rolling and paradiddling through the befuddled and terribly tender neurons in Firkin's brain. Hogshead didn't feel too good either.

They were lying in the gutter of the grotty backstreet that glistened outside Ye Silver Spitoone. Everywhere else in the world, either now or at least some time today, the sun would rise. It had climbed, like an orange giant's bald head, over the Eastern Tepid Seas to look down on the last few sturdy Raft-women left standing after a strenuous nocturnal insurgence (military, of course); its rays sparkled and danced, blue and silver, on the glacial wastes of the Angtarktik; all across the half of the world it could reach, the sun was up and sunning. Everywhere, that is, except Fort Knumm. There, in the damp dark heart of the Fort, it could almost have still been the middle of the night. But for someone not a million miles away, it was still far too bright.

'OOHHHHGHNOHHHH!' groaned Firkin as he opened one red-rimmed eye experimentally. 'NOT AGAIN!' Someone had carpeted his tongue in the night. The timpanist thrummed onward.

'OHHHGODO-GODO-GODO-GOD!' A dim but hugely embarrassing recollection of last night began to form. It sauntered jauntily up to Firkin's memory and, with the neuronal equivalent of the point of an umbrella, poked him sharply in the synapses. It stepped back to watch the effect.

Firkin's face went a very strange colour, sort of red and green at the same time, as embarrassment and nausea fought for supremacy. His face muscles thrashed about in sympathy as disbelief struggled with evidence in a half-nelson. Firkin lost. He looked up at Hogshead, opened his mouth and said, 'Wha . . . ?'

His face hadn't changed minutes later, after Hogshead explained about being forcefully ejected from the Spit and spending the night in the alleyway. The Landlord was a little dischuffed to find that the pair of them had barely enough money to pay for the drinks in their glasses, let alone the food and several previous drinks they'd consumed. They had been lucky they didn't have any broken legs but the Landlord benevolently let them off because, in his own words, he 'hadn't 'ad such a good laff f'ra long time, eh, Gnorm?'

'Arr,' Gnorm had agreed.

Firkin looked bad. He felt worse. He wanted the ground to swallow him up.

'Grndswallermeeup,' he said, looking down between his knees. Hogshead reached for a bucket.

High up in one of the tallest towers of Castell Rhyngill a man was busy. His thin, bony hands worked quickly and efficiently cleaning out the dozens of cages in the room. It was a dirty job. He wore old overalls, large boots, a cloth cap and a black leather eyepatch. With a final flourish he swept the last of the cages and threw the pigeon back in, locking the door quickly. 'Awwwk!' he shouted, relieved now that was over. It was a chore but it had to be done. Nobody else could do it. Nobody else in the castle knew about the thirty or so pigeons he kept up here. It was his secret.

He looked up at the sound of flapping wings and tiny claws landing on the stone window-sill. He snatched nervously at the pigeon and, keeping it at arm's length, pulled it inside. Hunching on the floor he held the bird upside-down as he untied the piece of paper from its leg. He unclipped the nearest cage and threw the bird in, dislodging a few feathers.

He unravelled the thin strip of paper and read:

Due to forthcoming Royal Feast, next supply wagon
will call early on the 19th Stop Make sure it
is filled Stop
OR ELSE Stop

He calculated quickly.

'Today!' He spat at the pigeon.

He detested them back there in Cranachan, always changing the plans on him at such ridiculously short notice. He hated this assignment. Hated the kingdom. He ground his teeth together. He longed to get out of Rhyngill.

'Bah!' he barked. Several of the pigeons flapped and a few feathers drifted gently to the floor.

Snydewinder changed his clothes, and slunk out of the room, triple-locking the door as he left.

'Who-so-ever puts their foot in this tiny sandal is the true born . . .'

'Frankly, Sharlett, I don't give a damn!'

'. . . do you like peaches?'

The voices were back.

'. . . nibble, nibble, slurp . . .'

'. . . bloody 'ard work fendin' off damsels an' maidens every day.'

They were getting louder.

Random disconnected phrases rattling inside his head again.

'Oh, Pierre, take me all ze way to Maybeland!'

It was becoming unbearable.

It was one of the worst nightmares he'd had.

'. . . 'ow many fingers am I holding up?'

He awoke with a start. More dreams, more voices. He shook feverishly. Why me? Why now? Voices from all the books he'd

138

ever read – well, eaten – shouted at him in the night. His stomach ached. He felt exhausted.

'Something I ate, must it have been!' groaned the tiny bookworm, feeling very sorry for himself.

He was right.

Ever since his illicit feast, while the Travelling Sorcerer slept, he'd been having these dreams. They were getting worse. They were getting louder and more frequent.

What the innocent bookworm didn't know when he'd tucked, so ravenously, into the old leather-bound book at Appendix IIIb was that:

(a) it was a Sorcerer's book,
(b) it was a magic book,
(c) it was a very old book,
(d) it was a *very* magic book, and
(e) he'd regret it!

He also didn't know what was now happening.

Magic books have to be printed by special printers. They don't just decant the ink onto the paper surface; they inkant the words into the paper's substance, bonding the thaumatin dyes with the very essence of the parchment thus making a network of definite, and permanent, wave guides to maximise amplification of specific magick signals. The spacing of the words is critical.

A simple punctuation error, during a printing run of 'Ye Ancients' Almanack of Magicke', caused a feedback loop in one of the relocation spells. It was discovered too late to rectify and resulted in the instantaneous disappearance of two printing presses, three typewriters and all of the paperclips in the office. The have never been found.

Right now, deep inside the bookworm, things were happening. Things that, in the natural order of things, shouldn't ever be happening. The lignin making up most of the parchment was being rapidly, and irreversibly, dissolved, freeing the inkanted words from the pages. These words, free from the constraints of a two-dimensional page and now toys in the playrooms of chaos, were coalescing, grouping in a new and altogether more meaningful pattern. A pattern so fiendishly complex at all levels, that scale is an irrelevance. A pattern that transcends the mere macroscopic. A pattern that bridges the space–tome continuum. If it were possible to see it, it would look something like a series of small upturned breakfast bowls mounted on a coathanger.

What the bookworm didn't fully realise, yet, was that the stomach-ache and the visions were only the beginning. The time was rapidly approaching when there would be enough free words to achieve a critical mass event.

An event that would open a new chapter in history.

An event that would shake the very foundations of reality.

An event that would be, for all involved, a very novel experience.

King Klayth was in his public chambers wearing his early-morning lounging robes. Honouring the greatest tradition of his missing father these were, almost inevitably, black. Breakfast dishes lay on a tray beside him and he sipped delicately at a cup of steaming tea.

'Sire, I crave your Regal company this fine morning. May I enter and speak?' Snydewinder greeted the King in the time-honoured fashion and, without waiting for a reply, walked straight in.

'No, you may not!'

'Sire?'

'I am still breakfasting.'

'But you are in your public chambers, Sire. Therefore, anyone may crave an audience. I would not even have considered entering had you been within your private quarters. It would have been beyond the . . .'

'Yes, yes. What do you want?' said Klayth irritably.

'Sire,' said Snydewinder with forced cheerfulness. 'It is a splendid morning. I have taken the liberty of saddling the horses. May I suggest, your Highness, that a morning of hunting and horsemanship away from the castle would be the perfect opportunity to allow the tithe, er, allow the timely rehearsal of your riding skills.' He rubbed his gauntlets nervously together and swallowed hard. 'A morning's hack in the forest, Sire, and the cart would, er, the *start* would be perfect for your day.' He ended on a forced grin.

The King sipped his tea silently.

'The horses are ready and champing at the bit, so to speak, Sire. It will be too late soon, the best part of the day will have gone.' Snydewinder glanced nervously out of the window.

His lounging robes creaking gently, the King took another mouthful.

'It is fitting that a high skill level in all the noble pastimes is maintained by a person of your Regal stature, Sire.'

'I don't feel like it. Go away.'

A look of horror flashed briefly across the Lord Chancellor's face. He snapped it back under control.

'But, your Sireship, it's important, a matter of life and death . . . er, a matter of life and death could be avoided if, if, I, er, you constantly keep your riding skills in trim.'

A whingeing note of desperation clung to the edge of Snydewinder's voice.

'It's too early in the day.'

'But, Your Altitude, I . . . er . . . the horses will be disappointed if . . .'

Snydewinder began to fiddle with the buttons on his jacket. Klayth could see that he was unsettled. A sneaking curiosity got the better of him.

'We wouldn't want to upset our fine beasts, would we?' Snydewinder looked up and relaxed visibly. The high hunch in his shoulders settled a few inches.

'No, Sire. Not at all. May I take it, then, that you will be accompanying us this morning?'

'Yes. Make it so and do inform Burnurd and Maffew.'

Klayth sipped at the steaming cup of Urlgray tea.

'It has been done, Sire.'

'Very good.'

'We shall assemble at the front drawbridge and await you at your earliest convenience . . .' He turned and rushed away. 'Sire,' he added over his shoulder as an afterthought.

The King sipped again and, not for the first time, wondered suspiciously about Snydewinder. He felt sure he was up to something. After a few moments, he put down the tea cup, rose, and went to get dressed for the hunt.

141

Between the outer castle defences and the inner curtain wall a group of four horses stood patiently in full hunting tackle. The two huge castle guards fed them sugar lumps and patted their velvety noses. Snydewinder fidgeted with the straps, kicked stones and muttered irritably to himself. If the wristwatch had been invented, he would have been glancing nervously at his – every few moments – cursing as vital seconds slipped inexorably out of reach. He suddenly dashed away from the group and looked out through the castle gate, then hurried back, animatedly fiddling with some of the buttons on his jacket. Something was definitely on his mind.

'Ah! Your Highness! So good to see you on this fine morning.' Snydewinder's voice sounded thin and strained as the King walked towards the group.

Ignoring him, Klayth walked over and patted one of the horses affectionately.

'Morning, Burnurd. Morning, Maffew,' he called.

'M — m — morning, Sire.'

'Mornin', your 'ighness.'

'Shall we go now? *Please*, Sire? *Now*, Sire?' Snydewinder glanced quickly through the gate again.

The King mounted his horse and settled into the saddle. It felt good. He liked riding.

Burnurd and Maffew climbed ponderously onto their muscular destriers and Snydewinder, like an overwound marmoset, twitched and leapt onto his steed.

Soon the four horsemen were walking their horses out of the castle and across the drawbridge. To Snydewinder, it seemed to take forever to cross over the green, lily-laden moat several feet below. He was constantly glancing over his left shoulder. He seemed to be looking for something. Or someone.

Once across the drawbridge, Snydewinder let out a huge blast on the hunting-horn and spurred his mount into action. The others followed him into the trees and accelerated away from the castle.

A few moments later two horses pulled an empty wagon out from behind a large clump of trees and headed slowly towards the castle gate.

*

Several miles away from Castell Rhyngill – and a few hours later – two figures slouched in the shade of the trees. The smaller, rounder one was still panting from the effort of half-dragging, half-steering the taller, thinner one out of the gutter of the filthy backstreet that slouched outside Ye Silver Spitoone.

'I'm hungry,' said Hogshead, conversationally.

'Humph!'

'Are you hungry?'

'Humph!'

'I bet you are!'

'Yes, and I feel awful! I've failed. I'm sorry, Hogshead, I shouldn't have got you into this mess. I was stupid, you're my best friend, I shouldn't have let you come.' Firkin blubbed.

'You didn't, I followed you.'

'I should have told you to go back.' A tear, matched by another in his left eye, began to trickle silently down his grubby cheek. 'I wouldn't have listened. We're a team.'

'Well, I've failed you, and I've failed Dawn.' Firkin sniffed wetly. 'Look at us. Look at where we are.'

'Where are we?'

'*I* don't know! And I don't know what to *do*! We've got no money. No food! No maps! I don't know where we are. We've got no assassins. I've still got a headache and if I knew the way, I'd be off home right now!' Firkin's voice quivered with emotion. 'But I can't go back. I don't know what to say to Dawn. I've failed you and I've failed her. I've failed!' He rolled over and sobbed pitifully into the grass, one elbow squishing in something brown and unpleasant.

Hogshead fidgeted uncomfortably. Yes, he's right, he thought, but look how far we've come and how much we've done.

His thoughts were disturbed by a far-off sound. He listened. Quietly and far off he could hear, through the rustle of leaves, a horn being blown. He heard it again, louder this time. Getting nearer. Fast. The ground rumbled slightly.

He shook hs friend's shoulder, but Firkin had already noticed the noise and was looking around confusedly. His eyes still shone.

Accompanying the horn was the low drumming of four heavy horses. Getting louder. Firkin sat up, sniffed and wiped his eyes.

143

Hogshead crouched behind the log he'd been sitting on. They could hear the four horses but caught no sight of them through the dense screen of trees. The hooves got louder. The horn got louder. Firkin crouched apprehensively. The ground shook as if it was about to explode.

Suddenly, out from the trees burst forth four of the biggest horses the boys had ever seen. Firkin crouched transfixed, as they galloped towards him. Their nostrils flared and they panted hard. Sixteen hooves battered the ground in mile-eating strides. All the riders wore black. The first rider tugged hard on the reins and leant forward over the giant neck as the huge beast hurled itself over the log. The rider yelled in exhilaration. Before they had touched the ground the second horse and rider were airborne, arcing slowly over the boys. Defying gravity in a heart-stopping leap. The third and fourth were soon over, their bellies seeming to take forever to pass over the two boys' heads, sending lumps of soil raining down from the horses' hooves.

Firkin watched with growing annoyance as they galloped away, shrieking wildly, through the wood with capes flapping. He was certain that the first one had been wearing a small crown. He stared after them brooding as he brushed soil from his back.

'What the . . . ? Who was . . . ? We could have been trampled!' struggled Hogshead, his face growing redder.

Firkin said nothing, his brow deeply furrowed, scowling as he thought. Hard.

Quietly he turned to Hogshead and said, 'A hunting pack. Yes, and the King; but not in that order!'

'Wha . . . ?'

'The answers to your questions.'

'Oh . . . so that was . . . THE KING!'

'I'm pretty sure it was.'

'How do you know?'

'Well, it stands to reason – big horses, well fed; big guards, well fed, wearing black armour: and, er, a crown. Sort of a bit regal. And he could have trampled us! He didn't even see us! Could have mown us down, kept going and . . .'

Firkin drifted off. He felt very small and very angry. The enormity of his task struck him and with it were fired the furnaces

144

of righteous indignation. How dare he try and run me down in the forest? How dare he ignore us so completely like some insects? How dare he treat Dawn and everyone else in Middin like animals? Well he's gone too far, he isn't going to get away with it any more.

Firkin knew they needed help desperately. Their task would be impossible without it. But a small spark of determination shone out in the gloom. He must keep looking. For everyone's sake, he had to carry on. He owed that to Hogshead. Fort Knumm had been useless but there had to be somewhere else. Keep looking, it's just a matter of time. Firkin stood up, picked up his bag and started off determinedly after the four horsemen.

He felt a tug on his sleeve. It was Hogshead.

'Not now, please. Not yet. We can follow soon. But, but I'm *starving*!' he howled.

Firkin wanted to set off immediately but he suddenly realised that he'd been pushing Hogshead too much. There was an obvious trail to follow, sixteen sets of hoofprints and numerous broken branches snaking away through the forest.

'OK,' answered Firkin. 'If I go over there, and you go over there, then I'll see you back here in ten minutes with all the nuts and berries you can find. Don't get lost. And, er, good hunting.'

'Oh, yeah. Very funny.' replied Hogshead with a hint of sarcasm. Relieved at Firkin's change of heart and still a bit shocked by the riders they smiled at each other and turned to the vital task of scavenging.

The two percherons strained in their heavy harnesses as they pulled the fully-laden wagon out over the castle drawbridge. The iron-rimmed wheels creaked across the uneven wooden surface. The two men, sitting in the front of the wagon, didn't worry about the noise. They knew there was nobody in the castle to hear them. A tug on the reins gave the horses the order to turn left. Not that they needed telling. They'd done the journey hundreds of times and could easily find their own way home, over the border, then up and over the Talpa Mountains.

The wagon jolted as it left the end of the drawbridge unevenly, dislodging two small carrots from one of the sacks. His mission successfully accomplished, the driver straightened up the horses, and the wagon trundled off steadily down the track, away from Castell Rhyngill.

They looked in trees, in bushes, under trees, behind bushes. Nothing. They covered an impressively wide area in a very short time, but Firkin came back to the clearing empty handed.

'What a waste of time,' he complained.

Shortly afterwards Hogshead picked his way through the undergrowth with his hands clutched tightly together. He had something and he didn't want it to escape.

'Just you wait till you see what I've got.' He moved over to the tree stump which stood in front of them. 'It's all I could find, but it'll be something. Get your knife out.'

Hogshead opened his hands and put his catch on the tree stump. Firkin stared open-mouthed.

'It's all I could find,' repeated Hogshead apologetically.

'We were looking for food! Not things to put in matchboxes as pets!'

'I know it's not much, but . . .'

Firkin stared again at Hogshead's offering. It was small and pale green and looked up at them defiantly through two large, round, unblinking compound eyes. Two feelers stuck out of the top of its head and ended in balls. Its tiny jaws worked and flexed in agitation. It didn't look very tasty. Firkin turned away in disgust.

'. . . it's better than nothing,' ended Hogshead limply.

'Not much. You can have it . . . I'm not hungry.'

'You can have half if you want,' said Hogshead waving his knife for effect.

'No thanks.' Firkin walked away toward a slightly denser patch of trees. 'I'm going to have a leak,' he said.

Plucking up his courage, Hogshead leaned over the small greenworm and grinned a cold grin. 'Hello lunch,' he said, licking his lips as he raised the knife high.

He sized the worm up against the blade.

'Are you sure you don't want any?' he called again.

'No,' said Firkin disappearing behind the trees. 'Hurry up!'

Hogshead told himself that it would taste fine. It was mostly

146

protein, nice healthy protein, with a bit of roughage. Franck had told him about tribes of pygmies that lived on worms all the time. Lots of them. Alive. Suddenly he wished he hadn't thought of roughage.

'I am very hungry,' he said to himself. 'It's either him or me.' He gritted his teeth raised the knife and closed his eyes. As he brought the knife down . . .

'No, no, halt,' shrieked a tiny piping voice.

Hogshead stopped and looked around. All he could see around him was a few trees and his newly acquired lunch. He was sure he'd heard a voice. Must've been the wind, he thought.

He raised the knife again . . .

'No, no, halt. Hear me, did you not?'

Hogshead opened his eyes. The tiny worm had drawn himself up to his full height of three-quarters of an inch and was staring defiantly into Hogshead's eyes.

'Lunch will I not be!' squeaked the worm.

Hogshead's mouth hung open idiotically.

'To eat me you do not want.'

'. . .' said Hogshead.

'A not nice taste I am. Yuck.' The worm made a spitting gesture. Impressive with a mouth full of mandibles to control.

'. . .' repeated Hogshead and twitched the knife.

'No, no. Three wishes you can have!'

'Wha . . .'

'Three wishes . . . for you . . . the knife put down.'

'What do you mean, three wishes? How?' he dropped the knife.

'Mmmh! Not normal, since my last meal, have I been feeling. Dreams of weirdness, strange characters out into my consciousness are leaping. Disturbing it is! Mmmh!' He put his head on to one side and continued staring into Hogshead's eyes.

'Yeah, but what's this about the wishes?'

'A tactic of delay, the use of your knife to prevent. These characters here can I bring.'

'What characters? Where from?'

'Books . . . a *bookworm* I am, you see! From the Chapter Dimensions I can bring them, upon your reality to impinge!'

'Cooh . . . big words!'

'With books not all I do is eat!' the bookworm somehow frowned and looked hurt.

'You can conjure up people from books?'

'Anyone . . . the space–tome continuum something to do with is.'

'Anyone? . . . How?'

'Your eyes close, and me, who you want, you tell . . .'

'If this is a joke you'll still be lunch!' threatened Hogshead, trying to remind himself that he was boss.

If the worm had possessed fingers they would have been well and truly crossed.

Castell Rhyngill

Three decibels below the threshold of human hearing a tiny sound began. If you had been standing in the small clearing, in the large forest, about half a mile from Fort Knumm, where some very strange events were about to occur, you would have been able to hear it, sounding like a glass cicada on a hot Mediterranean evening. A brittle sharp-edged sound. It chirruped louder. Another chirruping started at the same frequency. And another. And another. Something like a badly tuned transistor radio would be tickling the inside of your ear.

Hogshead could hear it. Firkin thought he could hear something. The chirruping rose in intensity but still remained in perfect unison. Hogshead looked around for the source. It seemed to be coming from nowhere. Any everywhere. Gradually, a harmony note began to become distinguishable. It too rose in intensity. A perfect minor third. The sound grew louder by degrees.

Firkin could hear it. He walked back, from behind the trees, to where Hogshead was standing.

A fifth rose in the sound to give a harmonic minor chord. It was beautiful. And irritating at the same time, like a choir of mosquitoes.

Hogshead saw a tiny speck of silver dart past him at the edge of his vision. Then another. The fifth grew stronger. It now sounded like hundreds of brandy glasses having fingers rubbed round their rims. It was hypnotic. Several silver specks flew in from the left and began to spin round the others, forming a tiny milky way. The hairs on the back of Firkin's neck began to vibrate in sympathy.

The two boys stared in wonder. The bookworm had his eyes tightly closed. Small static discharges flashed between his antennae. The sound grew louder still as more silver specks flew into the clearing. Gathering. Coalescing.

A seventh rose above the root of the chord. A tension could be felt. The sound became uncomfortable. The inside of the boys' heads began to itch. It grew louder still. More and more uncomfortable. The air became thicker with the silver specks swirling in the clearing. It was getting hard to see. The seventh grew louder. And louder. And then . . .

Silence. Perfect, complete silence. The chord had resolved into nothing and the million silver specks coalesced instantly into . . . a round, porky gentleman, wearing a greasy apron, a very off-white chef's hat, and a tray of the most delicious-looking shortcrust pastry pies. Hogshead stood and stared in utter disbelief. He rubbed his eyes, blinked, stared at the bookworm, and looked again. The Pieman was strolling around the clearing, as large as life, as if he owned it all.

'Larvely pies, larvely pies. Get y'r pies 'ere, nice fresh pies. You, sir, y' look a little on the 'ungry side, if y' don't mind me saying so. A good 'olesome pie inside y' would be the best thing, you mark my words.'

Firkin and Hogshead stared dumbfounded.

'I see it but I don't . . .' started Firkin.

'Pie . . . pie . . . pie. . .' whimpered Hogshead as he stared at the man before them.

'Freshly baked 's morning these were, only th'best ingredients used, tradishnal recipes. . .'

'. . . believe my eyes!' finished Firkin.

'. . . porky pies, steak'n'kidney pies, game pies. . .'

Hogshead began to dribble as he moved in a trance towards the Pieman. He was transfixed by the expanse of golden-brown pie crust steaming gently. He couldn't believe his eyes.

Neither could the bookworm.

It had worked. It was easy. He hadn't had to say any magic words. He just thought about the Pieman, then it happened. He had felt his tiny conciousness split into millions of even tinier fragments and shoot off in every direction. Searching. Infinitesmal silver sparkles racing into another dimension. Seeking. Magic bullets bearing the Pieman's name, shooting into the void, searching for the minuscule fragments of character residing in every book. Plunging through libraries, raiding bookshops, careering along shelves, snatching the fragments from the books and bringing them all together to focus on a central point. Then, like copper sulphate crystallising instantly from a supersaturated solution, each individual fragment pulled itself towards the next in a burst of nonentropic implosive energy until suddenly, standing in the middle of the forest, as if he'd been there all the time, was the Pieman. He'd been collected from all the nursery-rhyme books all over the world to now stand solidly real in front of an amazed Firkin and Hogshead. And an almost equally amazed Bookworm.

Hoofsteps echoed across the green sward in front of the castle, breaking the stillness, as the four horsemen returned from their hunt. King Klayth, breathing heavily, reined in his mount and stopped before the drawbridge. His horse panted heavily from the exertion and stamped restlessly on the soft ground. The two castle guards thundered by on their destriers, clattered over the drawbridge and disappeared into the castle. Syndewinder followed closely behind and yelled, 'Good ride, Sire! Most enjoyable!'

Klayth didn't have a chance to answer before the Lord Chancellor had crossed over the drawbridge and turned out of sight.

How strange, he thought. I'm sure he was smiling. Amazing what a good hack can do!

He made to move off, into the castle, but stopped. Something had caught his eye. There, on the ground, a few yards away, lying muddily in a fresh horseshoe print was a small carrot.

He hadn't seen that on the way out.

There again, he told himself, I wasn't exactly looking. It's not that obvious really.

He looked again at the soft ground and, even though he couldn't be absolutely certain, it did look as though a heavy wagon had rolled out of the castle gates and away down the track towards the mountains. He shook his head thoughtfully, shrugged his shoulders, made a mental note to ask Snydewinder about it, and rode over the drawbridge back into the castle.

'Let me see if I understand this right!' said Firkin slowly to a wildly overexcited Hogshead. 'You are trying to tell me that this is all that bookworm's fault?'

'Ch'tin.'

'What?'

'It's his name.'

'Ch'tin?'

'Well, that's what it sounded like. He made a funny noise through his mandibles that sounded like . . . er, well, Ch'tin.'

'Alright – so this is all Ch'tin's fault?'

'Yes,' agreed Hogshead, nodding as if there was no week-on-Tuesday, let alone tomorrow.

'And you're trying to tell me that the pies we have just eaten were produced by a Pieman who, up until three minutes ago, was a collection of words in books scattered all over the world?'

'Yes,' said Hogshead.

'And that the weird sound and the funny silver things were all the bits of his character coming together to make him real. . .'

'Yes,' said Hogshead.

'. . . and right now he's real as you and me. . .'

'Yes.'

'. . . and you wanted the Pieman . . .'

'Yes.'

'. . . and we've got two more wishes. . .'

'Yes.'

'. . . and we can get anyone. . .'

'Yes.'

'. . . anyone at all. . .?'

'Yes.'

'Do you really expect me to believe this!?'

'Yes.'

'I thought you'd say that.'

Ch'tin nodded almost as wildly as Hogshead.

Firkin sat and looked very thoughtfully at the bookworm. It stared back at him smugly.

'Er, 'scuse me, lads,' said the Pieman, 'but if that's all you'll be wantin', I've got to be gettin' off to the Fayre now, so I'll see y' 'round, okay.'

'No, no, you must come with us,' pleaded Hogshead. 'Please,' he added.

'Bu' I've gorrall these pies to sell.'

152

Firkin stood up, slipped Ch'tin carefully into his pocket and strolled up to the Pieman. Slipping one arm round his greasy shoulder he began to explain about the fact that they were heading towards Castell Rhyngill, and how nice 'Pies by royal appointment to His Majesty the King' would sound and besides, there'd be all these other people in the Castle, you know, er, knights, scribes, maidens, ooh yeah, lots of maidens I should think, you'd have no problem with your looks, yeah, lots and lots of maidens, probably sell all you could make, every day, and a little bit extra, eh, know what I mean? Soon they fell silent, each in his own thoughts.

The Pieman dreamed of new recipes, Royal recipes, when he wasn't thinking of maidens, that is.

Hogshead dreamed of hot steaming pies.

And Firkin thought of all the heroes in all the books he'd read. And for the first time in his life, in that clearing in the huge forest, he really thought, seriously thought, about magic . . .

Courgette sat on the huge oak kitchen-table with her feet dangling over the edge. She kicked them backwards and forwards absently. She stopped, picked up a spoon and began pressing it on to her legs leaving little red ovals that faded slowly. Val Jambon was busy at the other end of the kitchen putting the finishing touches to a post-hunt snack for the king. Courgette had watched him for the last fifteen minutes as he had chopped, sliced and diced several different edibles. Several pots simmered gently on the huge black stove. He was busy. She was bored.

Bored, bored, bored. I want someone to play with, she thought to herself, or even a pet. 'I'm going to fetch some water,' she declared out loud, jumped off the table, picked up the bucket and skipped out of the room.

'Oh, jolly good,' called Val over his shoulder absently.

The door that Courgette went through didn't lead directly outside, of course. That would be too easy for any marauding troopers to invade through. It led to a small ante-chamber, which featured thirty or forty arrowslits, pointing inwards, through another door and into a dark passageway. This was only just wide enough for Courgette as she skipped away, down under the curtain wall, then under the moat, then on uphill slightly, to finally emerge from a very natural-looking cave entrance in a hill near the castle.

This passageway had been invaluable in the castle's past, as it allowed supplies to be brought in during times of siege. Of course it too had its defences. As well as the arrowslits at various points along its length, there existed the facility to flood the tunnel with moat water. This had only been used once, but to devastating effect in the siege of OG 936 when King Stigg of . . . ah, but that's another story.

Courgette blinked once or twice in the bright morning sun and listened to the very late starters of the morning chorus chirping furiously to establish their territories. Several larks still trilled for supremacy in the morning air and Courgette listened attentively. Wrens tic-ticked to each other from the low bushes and far off a cuckoo could be heard. She loved the birds' songs. Dreamily looking upwards into the branches, she headed off towards the well, humming gently to herself.

All around the world, simultaneously, from all the copies of one particular fairy tale, fragments of one character were silently, and quite suddenly, removed. If you'd been standing in a particularly quiet library, listening very hard and looking at the right book, you may possibly have noticed an almost infinitely small silver streak enter the book and a microsecond later a slightly larger silver streak leave in the same direction. You may even have heard a very thin whooshing sound as this happened. If the book had been lying open, one of the pages may, possibly, have flicked slightly as if it had been blown by the tiniest gust of wind.

All these fragments, snatched from the surface of the pages where they had lain for years, were pulled by the magic silver bullets moving towards the same destination, coverging on one point.

That point was about two miles away from a huge rambling castle in a clearing in deep woodland. In the clearing stood Firkin, Hogshead, the Pieman and a tiny bookworm. They had put a good few miles behind them this morning, a testament to the nutritional content of the pies and Firkin's determination to see this mission through.

The foursome stood watching the tiny silver galaxy as it gathered before them. The mosquito choir was in fine song again and, as another group of silver flecks shot in from the left, the seventh began to rise within the chord. The Pieman scratched his head, static electricity arced to earth on the bookworm's antennae, it felt like a thunderstorm was about to break. Louder, higher. They held their breath. The air was swirling silver. Firkin prayed for the chord to resolve, the hairs in his nostrils quivered, he desperately wanted to sneeze. The sound grew louder. And louder. And . . .

Suddenly silence fell in the clearing, almost as if it had been plunged into an anechoic chamber, and Firkin sneezed. As he opened his eyes he realised they had company. One very large man stood facing them in brilliant medieval dress armour. He stood with his legs slightly apart and his armour shining, reflecting the afternoon sun. His visor was down. A two-handed sword was sheathed, almost casually, across his broad back. At his left hip hung a shorter, and highly decorated, fighting sword and his left arm held a small round shield, decorated with a crown in bronze, with two ribbons, on a beige background.

The two boys fidgeted, excited that it had worked again. Ch'tin looked smug. If he'd had fingernails he would have been polishing them on his chest.

Firkin walked apprehensively towards the figure and raised his voice in what he hoped would be a suitable manner: 'Hail, your Majesty.' He bowed a long, deep bow.

The enarmoured figure stood motionless as if it had been cast there.

Firkin looked around. Hogshead and the Pieman grinned sheepishly and waved their hands encouragingly, mouthing, 'Go on, go on!'

'Erm. Hail, your Majesty. Er, humbly do we crave thine allegiance to the just and noble cause which we have taken upon our humble selves. Sir.'

Firkin struggled with his feeble attempt at High English.

'We pray,' he continued to the gleaming metal monolith, 'thine arm wilt see fit to guard and protect, with the aid of thine faithful sword, by your side. . .'

The figure uncrossed his arms and slowly raised its visor. Two piercing blue eyes stared out from the shadowy interior.

'. . . the ability to enable our troth to be pledged in . . . oooh.'
Firkin looked into the two eyes. 'Hail,' he added limply.

'What's all this "thee" and 'thine' business, eh? I ain't 'eard owt quite so daft fr'ages.'

Firkin stood and stared. Hogshead fidgeted nervously.

'Would you like t' try one of my larvely pies, Sire?' said the Pieman, seizing an opportunity for a sale and stepping forward to break the silence.

'Ast tha got a pork pie, wi' pees? It's got for t'ave pees wi'it.'

'Sadly no, sire. I'm a purveyor of pies. Pealess pies, unfortun'ly.'

'Oh, ne'er mind. I ain't so hungry anyroad. Now then,' said the knight sitting down on a tree stump, 'what wuz you rabbitin' about jus now, eh? Summat about noble causes, or summat?'

'Er, yes,' stuttered Firkin, moving towards the shining knight and scratching his head in a state of confusion. Franck never told me he had a funny accent, he thought. This was going to take some getting used to. The knight removed his helm and placed it on the ground. Long flowing jet-black hair cascaded around his shoulders. He was clean shaven, with a chin that could only be described as noble. He had a face that looked honest yet forceful. He fitted every young maiden's dream. Tall, dark, handsome: a knight in shining armour.

'Well you see, Sire, it's like this . . .' began Firkin as he describe their plight so far.

Prince Chandon listened attentively, occasionally asking questions in his broad accent. When Firkin had finished, the Prince stood up, drew his two-handed sword with an easy flourish and held it skywards. He looked fantastic in the clearing. The sun glinted off all his highlights giving him a fairy-tale quality.

'I, Prince Chandon, will join yer quest an' come along wi' ye. I'll stand beside ye an' protect ye from all kinds o'arm.'

'Ooh. Thank you,' said Firkin.

'You're so kind, Sire,' agreed Hogshead.

'Well, its t'least I can do,' he replied modestly. 'An' besides it's ages since I 'ad a good scrap! There's jus' one thing, though. I'm supposed for t'be a bit incognito like, so's no one really knows who I am. Sort of a secret mission like you, like. So you'd best all me PC from now on.'

His accent made it sound more like 'Percy'.

'That's fine, er, Percy, but why is it a secret?' asked Firkin, hoping he could understand the answer.

'Well, I don't want no one t' know I'm 'ere. No disrespect like, but . . . it's not t'type o'thing roy'lty should be gerrin' up to.'

Firkin looked up blankly. He thought he'd caught the gist of it.

'It's nowt t'do wi all deeds o'bravery an' stuff. No. That's smashin'!' The Prince looked over his shoulder and lowered his voice conspiratorially. 'Its all t'girls, like. They won't leave me alone, y'know. It gets bloody 'ard work fendin' off damsels an' maidens every day. I like the rescuin', that's great fun, like. But they're allus so bloody grateful after. I've got 'undreds of 'em after me. It gets a bit frightenin' sometimes!'

The Pieman stared enviously and muttered something under his breath about chances being fine things.

'So, if ye've still got a wish left,' said the Prince, changing the subject, 'who's it gon t'be, eh?'

Firkin told him. Curiously, his own accent sounded weird now. 'Aye, bloody good idea.'

Hogshead asked the bookworm for their third wish.

They stood in the clearing expectantly. Ch'tin drew himself up to his full height (three-quarters of an inch), closed his eyes and started thinking. Now he'd got the hang of it, and he had an audience, he succumbed to the temptation of moaning gently under his breath and twitching his antennae mysteriously. Just for effect. He swayed backwards and forwards as if possessed by strange spirits. He knew all eyes were on him.

'Expiallydoscious,' he squeaked (just for effect) and clapped his antennae together.

His consciousness exploded again as he became the focal point for the literary fragments. Almost instantly the brandy-glass hum began, gaining intensity quickly as the morphogenic field was assembled. The third rang out clearly above the root and was soon joined by the fifth. The tiny crowd stared into the growing cloud of silver motes, hoping to be the first to catch a glimpse of the rapidly coalescing figure.

Firkin's scalp began to itch as the seventh gained strength and the density of magic bullets approached critical. He held his breath, waiting for the resolution. A slight note of discord rang in the midst

157

of the now familiar chord. Abruptly, silence fell and another figure stood in the clearing.

'You . . .' it said. And immediately vanished leaving behind a glowing afterimage of a mass of whitish hair and a symphony of colour.

There was a thick awkward silence in the clearing.

Everyone stared at the bookworm accusingly as he furiously tried to shrug his non-existent shoulders.

'Look at me not!' he piped. 'My fault it is not. Understanding I am not!'

'Try again.'

Ch'tin closed his eyes and tried again. The glassy whine began and grew in intensity. The third rose from the root, increased in volume, then unexpectedly collapsed, earthing itself in a series of blue sparks that arced between Ch'tin's antennae, leaving a faint smell of ozone. The bookworm looked up, crestfallen.

'Sorry. Impossible now. Too much interference from somewhere there is. Somebody reading about him probably is.'

Firkin tutted, looked very fed up, and hugged his knees dejectedly.

Hogshead looked down at the tiny green bookworm and asked him to keep trying every ten minutes or so until he could get through.

The group of four sat down in the clearing with their backs against the tree trunks and listened to the Prince telling tales about saving damsels from dragons, evil witches, being burned at the stake, etc.

He told of other knights' brave deeds, and was just concluding the one about the knight who had rescued a maiden from being boiled alive in a huge tower, only to have his honour sullied when she'd then tricked him into making love with her.

'So, y'see,' he concluded, 'sellin' pies mayn't be as glamorous, but its loads safer, like.'

'Arr, suppose you're right,' agreed the Pieman, although secretly he would have liked to be in a position to risk the 'glamorous' life. Just once. Just a bit.

Suddenly the group became aware of a high-pitched whine.

158

Ch'tin had got through. The mosquito choir were back. Quickly the intensity ramped up as they all willed the figure into being. The chord grew stronger, the silver flecks flooded into the clearing from all directions and in a few moments it was like a silver blizzard. The pitch rose into discomfort, louder and sharper, and to an instant the final figure appeared in the clearing and stood motionless before them.

He was dressed in a cape the colour of E major decorated with all the signs of the zodiac, stars, moons, sigils and topped with a fur collar and cuffs the colour of C minor 7. The effect was at once gaudy and slightly discordant. He wore a tall hat that matched his saxaffron robes, perched at a jaunty angle on a head of long unkempt hair, that was, more or less, white.

He had a long nest of a beard and carried a wand horizontally in the crook of his armpit.

An icy stare fixed on to Firkin.

'Your name would be Firkin.'

'Yes, er . . .' he replied, startled.

'My name,' said the old man, 'is Merlot. Do you like peaches?'

'Worked it did. See, see. Mmmh?' whistled the bookworm.

He was drowned out by the noisy commotion coming from one of the bushes nearby. Branches waved, and leaves rustled and shook about furiously as a bad-tempered something tried to right itself. Suddenly, as if launched from a cannon, a tawny owl exploded from the bush in a flurry of feathers, leaves and baffled insects. It flew straight at Merlot at full speed, then, at the last moment, flared out its wings, flapped wildly, and settled melodically on his C minor 7-trimmed shoulder. It drew itself up to its full height, smoothed its tail feathers and folded its wings neatly. After a moment it had regained all its normal composure.

'Oh, what a lovely owl!' cried Hogshead.

The owl grew taller and closed its eyes almost completely.

'There is no owl,' it said in deliberate and measured tones.

'Oh, Arbutus, that's not nice, what?' said Merlot, reprovingly.

'Hmmph!' he said, haughtily. 'And I suppose disappearing like that in the middle of a chapter is "nice". Well?' Arbutus closed his eyes and did a very good impersonation of an owl sulking. He was.

'That was not my fault, as well you know.' He turned. 'This was

159

your doing. Hmmm?' Merlot stared long and hard at the tiny bookworm sitting sheepishly on the tree trunk.

'Very impressive. Bit off a little more than you could chew what?' He laughed at his little joke and a few crumbs fell out of his beard. 'You have a lot to learn about the etiquette of magic, my little green friend. You shall come with me for a little while.' The wizard held the tiny worm in his old lined hand and turned to Firkin.

'Well,' he continued, 'quite a band of merry men you have here young fellow-me-lad. Quite a band, what?'

'Er, thank you, yes. I'm so glad you could come,' he replied almost apologetically.

'No choice, what? Summoned I think they call it. Well, if you want to do all this King-killing business, I suppose we'd better be off. Strike while the thingummy's still erm . . .'

'Hot,' squawked Arbutus, pecking at a mouse's tail dangling from under the Wizard's hat.

'Yes,' finished Merlot. 'Come on you lot!' He turned, swirling his wand, and, without waiting for an answer, walked discordantly out of the clearing.

'First thing you need to know about summoning spells,' they heard Merlot say to the bookworm in his hand, as he marched away through the screen of trees, 'is you can't ignore them, what? Think of a telephone, oh you don't know about them, well think of a thing that's a very hard thing to ignore, then try thinking hard about ignoring it, see? It's hard, what! One time I was in the middle of a particularly huge . . .'

Merlot, apparently talking to the palm of his hand and with Arbutus perched proudly on his shoulder, had disappeared through the trees, his voice already fading.

Shrugging their shoulders, the others followed.

In an otherwise, almost, completely deserted kitchen, somewhere in the lower reaches of Castell Rhyngill, something moved. Or rather stalked. It knew it shouldn't be there. It knew there would be trouble if it was caught.

In a moment of carelessness, its foot fell on a splinter of a nutshell and cracked it noisily. It froze. The echoes bounced around the kitchen. Too loud and too long. It looked around slowly.

A pair of tiny black eyes peered out at it from behind a quivering set of whiskers and a cupboard. It couldn't see the mouse. If it had it would have ignored it. It was looking for human company; spies weren't normally mouse-shaped.

The rodent watched as the tall, thin intruder continued on its stealthy advance towards the grain store at the far end of the kitchen. In a few moments, the mouse watched it retrace its course carrying a hessian sack of bird seed.

A few hard grains dropped to the floor as the thief fumbled with the latch of the kitchen door, looked left and right into the corridor, and crept out. In a moment the mouse was alone again.

Ch'tin, his first day's lesson over for now, snoozed gently in Merlot's pocket. He had managed to make himself quite comfortable amongst the bits of string, straw, assorted fragments of cloth and scraps of paper that Merlot kept in there. The Wizard hated to throw anything away maintaining that 'just because I can't find a use for it now, doesn't mean it isn't useful, what!' His saxaffron robes were full of tiny bits of junk that normal people would have ditched without a second thought. How he actually managed to remain standing upright, carrying all that detritus with him, nobody was entirely certain.

There were a lot of aspects to Merlot's behaviour that people were not entirely certain about. Not least his extraordinary ability to know things that he really should not have even the slightest inkling of. There was a rumour that Merlot lived his life backwards and that he saw things by re-cognition. A rumour that he repeatedly remembered denying at some point in the future.

One of the things that the Wizard did know was how little the two boys knew about warfare. All their knowledge came from tales told by their parents or Franck way back in Middin. Merlot understood the reasons behind choosing Prince Chandon. He was a big knight with a big sword or two. He could serve the dual purpose of protector and assassin. Of course, the boys didn't realise that the reason that the Prince's armour was so bright, shiny and sparkled like new was the fact that it was. Brand spanking new. It was dress

161

armour. Thin, lightweight and designed to look good. It would almost certainly buckle and split if it was on the receiving end of any decent thrust or lunge.

Of course, this was of no concern to the Prince. Why should it be? The Prince's exploits on the battlefield were legendary. Hundreds put to death by his sword, whole battles won almost singlehandedly, kingdoms saved by his brave, heroic and unbelievably courageous acts. Everyone knew about them, from the lowest of peasants to the highest crowned heads. He had a very good press agent and a remarkably creative team of legend writers to make sure of that, er, fact.

He had no intention of actually going into battle. That was for other people. Slaves, serfs, illegal immigrants. They were the ones that joined battles, not royalty. Not Prince Chandon. Of course, he wasn't averse to swordsmanship and he was surprisingly good at 'scrapping', as he called it. But that was in the tournaments, when rules were rules and men stuck to them. No hacking when your opponent is down, no kicking, no punching, clean breaks when the whistle blows and, of course, the referee's decision is final. It came easy to PC to pledge allegiance to Firkin and Hogshead's cause. His idea of danger was twisting his ankle during a particularly strenuous tournament and his understanding of risk was attempting a difficult double chip off the last hoop in a croquet match, when a wager of fifty shillings had been called.

Firkin and Hogshead were good at 'swords'. Or so they thought. They were the best in Middin at fighting with sticks. They knew all the important words like 'thrust', 'parry', and 'ongard'. They hadn't even seen a real sword before. Let alone tried to pick one up. As for the Pieman, well he was a bit of a mystery, but he certainly didn't appear to have the necessary 'oomph' to be hugely adept with a sword.

No, thought Merlot, the direct approach of storming through the main entrance, overpowering the guards, killing the King and ruling the kingdom by brute force is not really a good idea for this bunch. Merlot chewed his beard as he thought hard. No, something a little more subtle, a mite more finesse, what?

Suddenly he turned and smiled at the tawny owl perched nonchalantly on his C minor 7-trimmed shoulder.

'Arbutus, my dear friend, this is what I would like you to do . . .'

It was no good. He couldn't concentrate. It was a good story he was reading, full of excitement, adventure and a bit of peril but he couldn't stop thinking about other things. He couldn't stop thinking about what over six hundred and forty-two years of food looked like. His imagination turned it over and over. He hadn't been able to get this thought out of his mind since the last meeting when he'd argued so strongly with Snydewinder. It was literally food for Klayth's thoughts. He imagined tithebarns jammed full of stuff. Row on row of vegetables packed in boxes stacked up to the ceiling; shelves and shelves of shallots and shellfish; piles of pies, peas and potatoes; mountains of meat! It must be an incredible sight. All that food. He closed the book and determinedly left the Library. He was going to see it for himself.

The tithebarns were sited outside the castle itself, in a huge courtyard surrounded by the main curtain wall. They were well protected from outside attack. They would have kept a fully populated castle fed for about a year in the event of a siege.

Thirty minutes later, Klayth stepped out of a small door at the far north of the castle into the courtyard. There were the tithebarns. He started to cross the courtyard. They were huge. Bigger even than he'd imagined them. They stood in two rows of six with their doors facing each other down a central space leading to the North Gate. Each barn looked big enough to hold at least two zeppelins and probably half a dozen hot-air balloons besides.

He was impressed.

He kept walking and after what seemed like a very long way, he drew near to the first of the barns. The doors at the front were mounted on rails and extended nearly the full height of the barn. They looked incredibly heavy. As he approached he spied a smaller man-sized door, set into the bigger door, and breathed a sign of relief.

He stood in front of the barn feeling small. His mind began to race again, thinking of all that lay behind this door. His hand reached out to the small knob and, turning it, he stepped into the vast, dark expanse. He'd been waiting for this. He stood with his eyes closed, waiting for them to adjust to the dark. Opening them

163

quickly he looked around at the incredible sight that surrounded him. His head reeled as he tried to take in the size of the place.

There were shelves and shelves in rows as far as he could see. Right up to the roof and away into the murky distance. It was almost like a study in perspective, parallel lines closing and fading, swallowed by the enormous cavern. The inside of the barn was huge. Massive. Enormous . . .

And completely empty.

So were the other eleven.

The cool grass rubbed against Courgette's legs as she strolled slowly through the forest, drifting gradually towards the well. She was playing a game with herself, imagining that she was a squirrel and tracing a path along the branches that would allow her to reach the well without touching the ground. She was doing fine. Along that bough, left at that rotten bit, down that thin branch, run and jump! Careful, careful, a long jump and a heavy landing. Now up that branch round by that owl, down across the . . . the . . . *owl*!

Her eyes ran back along the branch and there, sitting quite still, was a beautiful, male, tawny owl. Courgette couldn't believe her eyes. An owl! She stared transfixed at the motionless bird, trying to memorise its every detail. Slowly, one orange eye opened and stared down at her from the branch. Its gaze lanced down from above and pierced deep into her heart. In that moment Courgette felt an emotion that, later, she would come to know as love. Her heart fluttered momentarily and she gasped as she caught her breath. She trembled with excitement but fought to stand still so as not to scare the bird away. Gradually, like a heavy velvet curtain, the owl's other eyelid opened. It was beautiful.

Despite its beauty, Courgette knew that it was dangerous. She had heard of other animals like that – black panthers that appeared so sleek, calm and touchable could have your hand off in a moment's flick of a huge paw; tiny frogs, painted like Easter eggs, which were covered in poison and could kill in a moment if touched. It seemed to her that the most beautiful and brightly coloured creatures were often the most deadly. If Courgette had been a rabbit, race memory and instinct would have her thumping the ground with both her hind feet in abject terror. She would probably have only had seconds to live before winged talons snatched her from the earth and tore her life away. Abruptly, and deathly silently, the owl swooped from the branch and stooped towards her, its talons held out before it, its eyes shining with menace. The owl's cruel, fixed gaze held Courgette spellbound. Afterwards she was convinced that she had been hypnotised by those eyes, growing bigger and bigger and . . . For a heart-stopping moment, that seemed never-ending, the whole world was feathered wings and deafening flapping. She closed her eyes, and waited for the final rip of flesh.

Silence. It didn't come. She held her breath and stood perfectly still. After what seemed an eternity, she risked opening an eye. She could see nothing. She peered slowly over her right shoulder. Nothing. She moved her head back to centre and cautiously looked over her left shoulder. She jumped suddenly, for there, in full splendour, larger than life, was the owl. And it was sitting on her shoulder.

It had been such a gentle landing that she had not felt a thing. The owl looked at her and nibbled her ear gently. Her fear vanished.

'Ooh! You're pretty . . . what's your name?'

Arbutus almost told her.

'I bet it's something nice,' she continued, 'like Oswald or Sage or . . .'

Arbutus cringed.

'Oh. There you are, you naughty owl,' yelled Firkin running, on cue, from behind a tree. 'Come here, Arbutus, at once!'

'Arbutus!' squeaked Courgette with delight. 'There, I knew it was something nice. That's much better than Oswald or . . .' She felt sure that Arbutus had just nodded. Can owls grin? she thought to herself.

'Oh, Arbutus, I love you!' she declared. 'I've got to take you to see my father. Come on. You're such a clever owl and so pretty. I think that you're wonderful and . . .'

And so she continued.

Arbutus, of course, loved every minute of it. Courgette was completely captivated. A real owl, and it was seated on her shoulder. She walked back towards the small cave entrance and went straight inside. She vaguely knew that there were two boys behind her and that one of them owned the owl but that didn't matter. Not now, not when she had a real owl to show off.

She was completely unaware, however, of the man with the apron and tray of pies, the knight in shining armour and the real guardian of Arbutus* who followed on a short distance behind. She continued to croon and whisper sweet nothings to the tawny owl on her shoulder, as she led the whole band of would-be assassins into the castle.

Back in OG 1025, three months had passed since the, now legendary, two-and-a-half-minute war against Rhyngill. The three thousand or so prisoners had settled in to their new, high-security accommodation as well as could be expected. The lemming-skin harvest had gone exactly as planned, although the contract with Rosch Mh'Tonnay was under dispute as it wasn't actually necessary to use the new excavations for the purpose for which they had been ordered, and, as this work had interfered so drastically with the Talpa Mountain Steppe Scheme, the Scribe of Trade and Industry was holding out on the full payment. Quite a substantial legal battle was about to break out over this but, apart from that one minor fracas, everything in the garden of Cranachan was rosy.

Fisk had been riding high on the success of his idea which he felt sure would lead to a promotion. In fact, apart from an injury caused by an uncharacteristically careless error with an irately struggling pigeon, which resulted in him now sporting a black-leather eyepatch, life, for the Chief of Internal Affairs, was good. However, this was about to suddenly and irrevocably change.

In the Conference Room of the Imperial Palace Fortress of Cranachan, a tepid debate was about to become a heated one.

'. . . and the prisoners are behaving well, Sire,' reported The Right Horrible Khah Nij to King Grimzyn. 'We established a strict disciplinary regime early on, to which the prisoners are *requested* to adhere.'

---

* Nobody actually owns Arbutus. He just stays with certain people he likes. Especially those with a ready supply of mice.

'Very good. A very tidy victory. Well done!' enthused the King.

'Not quite, Sire,' said Frundle, the Lord Chancellor, almost under his breath.

'And what, pray do tell, do you mean by that remark?' asked the King.

'Well, Sire, Gentlemen of the Court, how are we supposed to feed three thousand prisoners of war whilst they are our, ahem, guests?'

The other four men suddenly found the ends of their fingernails, or the crack in the plaster on the ceilings, or a mark in the surface of the table in front of them very interesting.

'Well?' demanded Frundle.

A vague mumbling floated through the room. Fisk fiddled with the strap on his eyepatch.

'Sorry? I didn't quite catch that. Any great ideas, Fisk?'

'Er, yes, ha! Easy.' The Chief of Internal Affairs was caught in the spotlight of Frundle's attention. 'The, er, extra revenue generated by the sales of lemming skin will more than cover . . .'

'You must be joking!' interrupted Gudgeon. 'Have you seen the sales figures?'

'Well not recently, I've been . . .' floundered Fisk, glaring out of one eye. 'Are they, er, bad?' He knew he shouldn't have asked.

'BAD! BAD! If they were much worse we'd be buying the damn things back!' screamed the red-faced Scribe of Trade and Industry.

'What are you talking about?' asked the King.

Gudgeon picked up a chart that bore considerably more resemblance to the glide path of an average house-brick than a highly successful, profit-making enterprise. OG 1025 had been, not to put too fine a point on it, a disaster.

Fisk swallowed hard.

'Why?' demanded King Grimzyn.

'Don't know,' replied Gudgeon. 'Just after work started on our very expensive mountain-moving project as suggested by our right honourable friend here,' he took a breath and stared pointedly at Fisk, 'the sales figures for lemming began to drop. World wide. There has been talk of rumours.'

'Pah! Rumours,' scorned Fisk.

'What sort of rumours?' the King asked Gudgeon, while glaring at Fisk.

'Rumours of reports linking the wearing of lemming-skin garments with a series of mysterious accidents involving tall buildings . . .'

'Preposterous!' Fisk again.

'. . . and the loss of many wallets and handbags which appear to have jumped, some say almost suicidally, out of pockets and off shoulders.'

'I must say,' agreed Frundle, 'I have heard something similar.'

'I've even heard that some people have had their skins taken to a medium . . .' continued Gudgeon.

'Medium what?' interrupted Khah Nij, getting bored.

'Medium, contacter of spirits . . .'

'You mean like a licensed victualler?' grinned the Head of Security and Wars.

'No. Like crystal balls and mumbo-jumbo! It would seem that they believe that there is still a tiny bit of, well, er . . .'

'What?' demanded the King.

'Well, Sire, there isn't really a word for it!'

'Try.' insisted the King.

'Lemmingnosity.'

'You mean they glow in the dark?' chuckled Khah Nij.

'No. I mean, well they mean, that the skins have still got a sort of a part of their spirit in there and every full moon they . . .'

'All come out to play?' mocked Khah Nij, savagely. 'My other leg has got a whole peal of bells on. You can try to pull that as well. If you feel lucky!'

Fisk was bewildered. He fingered his eyepatch nervously. 'Are you trying to tell me that people have stopped buying lemming-skin produce because of a pack of unfounded and far-fetched rumours?'

'It would appear so,' answered Gudgeon.

'And that people's confidence in lemming-skin is ruined?'

Both Frundle and Gudgeon nodded. Khah Nij was beginning to find the whole petty episode a little too much.

'So what?' he shouted. 'This whole pathetic scheme has been a waste of time. Admit it. Let's just wash our hands of the whole shoddy affair.'

'We can't,' said Frundle, almost with regret. 'We've come this far. What would you have us do? Let the prisoners go, and tell them we're sorry for the inconvenience? Would you, Khah Nij, relish this thought?'

The Head of Security and Wars had to admit to himself that the old fossil had a point.

'At the risk of sounding repetitive,' began King Grimzyn again, breaking a rapidly deepening silence, 'what are we going to do?'

Gudgeon shrugged his shoulders pathetically and turned to Frundle. Khah Nij drummed his fingers on the table and stared militarily at Fisk. Frundle stared into space.

'Any suggestions? Fisk?'

'Er, me, Sire?'

'Yes.'

Why me, thought Fisk, why me?

'It was your idiot idea!' added the King, his eyes flashing with anger.

A wave of panic broke on the shores of Fisk's mind. He suddenly felt very isolated. Faces that were familiar to him suddenly seemed strange. Everyone stared at him. He felt like a caged animal. A very small animal in a locked cage, with a huge lion outside, holding the key.

'Well . . . I . . . er . . .' he struggled.

'Very helpful,' growled the King.

Fisk looked around for inspiration. 'We could . . . raid their larders. I mean, they fed themselves when they were in Rhyngill, so there must be some stuff there to feed them on.' He grinned feebly against a torrent of silence. 'No . . . aha . . . silly idea . . . too much manpower I suppose . . . silly me!'

'Are we taxing your brain too much?' mocked Gudgeon, laughing.

'Wait a minute . . . that's it!' shouted Fisk.

'What is "It"? Precisely?' moaned the King, head in hands.

'Tax!'

Frundle's ears pricked up.

'Tax!' repeated Fisk. 'They pay it to their King as a tithe. It gets delivered and stored in the tithe barns. All together.'

'How do you know?' asked Frundle.

Fisk had his methods and he wasn't about to tell them. He tapped the side of his nose with a long, black gloved finger.

'But what's the use of having all the tithes over in Rhyngill?' asked Gudgeon.

'All we need,' continued Fisk, his one eye shining wildly, 'is one man, with the ability to work in a foreign kingdom, in a position of power in Castell Rhyngill, and we're laughing!'

The other four men looked at each other thoughtfully, then looked at Fisk and did, in fact, start laughing. The Chief of Internal Affairs had a feeling that he had said something that he would, in the fullness of time, begin to thoroughly regret.

If she says 'Ooh, what a pretty owl' one more time, I'll have her ear off! thought Arbutus, as he remained perched on Courgette's shoulder. I am not 'pretty', he continued to himself. Regal, majestic, handsome . . . oh, there are so many words! Why does she have to use 'pretty'? Courgette's constant wittering had soon got on Arbutus' nerves.

'So, he's your owl, then?' asked Courgette, her voice sounding hollow in the small tunnel that led back into Castell Rhyngill.

'Well, not exactly,' answered Firkin. 'We're looking after him for someone.'

'Not very well by the looks of it,' she replied, cheekily.

'He flew off. He's very naughty sometimes.'

Arbutus tutted to himself.

'Yes, I expect so. Oh, but he's soooo . . . lovely,' cooed Courgette.

Close . . . very close, thought Arbutus, she nearly lost her ear then!

'He's a friend of ours,' said Hogshead.

'Who?' asked Courgette.

Now she's stealing my lines! thought Arbutus, typical!

'The man who owns Arbutus.'

Owns! Pah. How little they know. Arbutus tapped a talon gently in irritation.

'Well, where is he?' asked Courgette.

'He was following us.'

'He should be here soon,' confirmed Firkin.

170

'So should my Father,' said Courgette looking at Arbutus. 'I can't wait to show him!'

She reached out, opened the large wooden door and entered the Castle kitchen from the passageway. Firkin and Hogshead followed her in.

The two boys stopped and stared. They had heard and used the word 'kitchen' so many times that they knew exactly what it meant.* The same word, somehow, didn't seem appropriate for the place they had now entered.

It was probably the largest room they had ever seen. Both their huts would fit in one of the smaller corners. Down one wall stretched a huge black cast-iron stove upon which several pots simmered gently. There were shelves of gleaming copper pans, tureens, ladles, roasting tins and many vessels whose function the boys could only guess at.

A tray of biscuits lay cooling on a shelf. Jars, pots and sacks were arranged around the walls and racks of poultry and game hung along the ceiling. It smelled fantastic. Unfamiliar aromas raced about in there like wild olfactory demons. It was like the atmospheic equivalent of minestrone soup. But there was something missing . . .

In a kitchen almost the size of the village you'd been brought up in, one of the things you would reasonably expect to see is people. This kitchen, except for the two boys, one girl, one owl, and a now terrified mouse, was completely empty.

There are forces at large in the world that philosophers, poets and naturalists have observed since almost the dawn of time itself. They have given these forces names: Destiny, Fate, Hormones. They have classified them: chance and lady luck, *déjà vu* and conicidence, testosterone and pure lust. They have even seen, on rare occasions, the webs of effect that they weave upon their unsuspecting subjects. But, try as they might – and some have

* Kitchen(n): a tiny corner of a scrotty wood hut where you warm up turnip stew. Contains two pans, four plates and a small random selection of knives, forks and spoons. Often precedes other words, e.g., sink.

even had research grants from SERC* for their work – they have never really understood them. Some people experience them more strongly than others but we all feel them at some time or other, somewhere.

They are the forces that drive salmon miles up Scottish rivers to mate and die; or that impart the musical skill to write enduring symphonies to children barely out of nappies; or that turn wimps into romantic swashbuckling heroes and supply the courage to cross the piranha-infested moat, scale the castle walls, fight the castle guards and escape again having delivered the dark-blue box of chocolates to the waiting maiden.

These forces were affecting one of the three people entering the castle without permission. He'd felt them before. He felt sure it was something to do with the very nature of castles. Possibly to do with the way the stones were piled up in tall solid towers and thrust skyward in a soaring celebration of man's abilities. He was feeling very restless. Images flashed through his mind as he walked around the final bend in the tunnel under the moat and through the wooden door into the kitchen. Images of tall towers and spiral staircases. Visions of solid wooden doors splintering under the weight of metal-clad shoulder charges. Pictures of wimple-topped, scantily clad damsels-in-distress, bosoms heaving, wearing expressions of sheer gratitude tinged with – not a little unrequited and yearning – lust.

'Maidens!' thought Percy. 'Oh no . . . not again!'

* The Sorcerers' Eccentric Research Club. A body set up initially to provide a social club, and hence a function room, for the many and varied gatherings that festoon the Sorcerers' social calendar. Gatherings that, invariably, became so drunken and rowdy, so quickly, that, after arguing volubly with the landlord, causing a few fires and stress-testing to destruction the forgiving nature of anyone within a half-mile radius of their renditions of traditional Sorcering songs, a new venue is needed. The Sorcerers' Eccentric Research Club was a small wooden hut situated three miles away from any major conurbations, soundproofed, and supplied with enough different beers, wines and spirits to bring a small army to its knees. Sadly, though, being a research group, they had to at least appear to be researching something, apart from the bottom of a glass, of course. The Sorcerers' Eccentric Research Club did, therefore, with sufficient bribery, give grants. Rarely, vehemently begrudged and pitifully small but, nonetheless, the research fraternity was patronised by SERC grants.

172

This girl needs to read a dictionary! thought Arbutus, as she used "nice" to describe him for the nth time. Where n is large and extremely positive.

Courgette was sitting on the large oak kitchen-table swinging her legs in the space below. Firkin and Hogshead fidgeted in the empty kitchen waiting for the other three to join them. Arbutus turned his head almost completely round and, once again, considered the best way of removing Courgette's ear with the minimum of fuss. He liked to be prepared.

'Oh, Father, where are you when I need you?' asked Courgette rhetorically and sighed for effect.

'Where's everyone else?' asked Hogshead.

Courgette looked up.

'Everyone else?'

'Yes. You know, all the other kitchen staff,' explained Firkin. He knew all about this. Franck had told him.

'What other kitchen staff?'

'You know,' answered Hogshead, 'the dishwashers, the pastry chefs, the butchers, the . . .'

'What are you talking about?' asked Courgette, her face a complete blank.

Arbutus raised his eyes to heaven and tutted audibly.

'You have been in the kitchen before, haven't you?' asked Firkin.

'Oh, yes. My Father is the Chef,' she replied. 'To the King!' she added proudly.

'. . . and what about the other people?'

'Oh, yes . . . everyone.' She tickled Arbutus under where she imagined his chin to be.

'Er . . .' ventured Hogshead, feeling as though he had missed something, 'doesn't he get rather busy feeding all those people?'

'Oh, no. I help him.'

'Oh good, and who else?' Firkin was getting somewhere now.

'Just me,' Courgette said proudly.

'The two of you prepare all the food for the entire population of this Castle?' asked Firkin in awe.

'Yes,' she answered simply.

Suddenly, the huge wooden door into the castle creaked open.

173

A tall wizard wearing saxaffron robes floated in, with only the merest hint of a key change. He was followed by and even taller knight in very shining armour, and a short, fat, mildly greasy pieman.

'Ah, Arbutus! Found a new friend, what?' cried Merlot expansively and held out his hand.

A look of relief sprang to the owl's face and he flapped immediately towards the C minor 7-coloured shoulder he knew and loved.

'You would be Courgette, eh? Do you like peaches?' He smiled at the baffled young girl.

Arbutus pecked at a mouse's tail dangling from under Merlot's hat.

'I 'spect y'd like a pie better, wouldn't yer?' she was asked.

'Ah. This, my young lady,' interrupted Merlot, 'is our good companion, and purveyor of fine pies and pastries, on our long journey.' He extended his arm around the shoulders of the rotund gentleman. 'Mr Pieman!' announced Merlot.

'Charmed,' oozed the Pieman, touching his forehead.

Courgette sat bewildered and was lost as to where to look. So many strangers. All at once!

'And to my right, we have our protector, our brave and valiant knight. A man with a knowledge of history and etiquette, the long arm of the lore you could say, Prin . . . ahem, er, Percy.'

Courgette was enthralled. A knight. A real knight. In her kitchen! She had never seen a knight before. He stood massively in the kitchen, his head almost scraping the beams, gleaming brightly in spite of the thin layer of condensation covering him.

'Y'wot! Eh? D'yer say summat?' Percy looked about in confusion.

'Yes!' said Merlot haughtily. 'I have just been introducing you to this charming young lady, what?'

Percy focused his piercing blue eyes with difficulty and stared.

'No,' he said and shook his head. 'No. It's not 'er. She's not t'one. Not distressed enough.'

Everyone stared at the huge armour-clad man.

'Why am I stood 'ere in t'kitchen? She must be up that way!' He pointed to the other door that led to the rest of the castle and moved a step forward.

174

Firkin was horrified.

'Percy! Wait! Where are you going.'

The knight took a step forward.

'What are you doing? You can't go. What about the King? What about us?'

Firkin walked backwards in front of the giant metal-clad man and waved his hands wildly, trying to get through to him.

'Damsels,' was all he got by way of an answer.

Firkin began to get worried. He ran ahead and lay down in the path of the knight. As if in a trance, Percy stepped calmly over him.

'You can't go now!' yelled Firkin as he leapt at the knight from behind and grabbed his huge leg. The knight took two giant steps before his huge metal-clad hand gently removed the struggling boy from around his ankle and lowered his visor. All anyone could do was watch as Prince Chandon moved slowly, almost dreamily forward, then broke into a run. It was almost like watching an uncontrollable, knight-shaped steam train accelerating out of a station at full throttle. And just as unstoppable.

A few mintues later, as the last of the oak splinters settled, all they could hear was the sound of galvanized bootsteps clanging down an empty corridor.

That, and the occasional yell of 'It's alreet, luv. I'm comin'!'

The gentle avian murmur, from the thirty-odd draughty cages, high in the highest tower of Castell Rhyngill, rose slightly in volume as their occupants heard the key in the triple-locked door. As the final lock was released, and the door opened, another sound mingled with the cooing from the expectant pigeons. It was a curse. A human curse.

It was uttered quietly, but that did nothing to disguise the loathing, vehemence and frustration which it expressed.

Snydewinder was angry. This was nothing new. It seemed that even if everything was going right for him, and there was nothing to worry about, he'd invent something. The Lord Chancellor, it seemed, was in a constant state of vexed irritation.

Right now was no exception.

It was bad enough having to hastily arrange a hunting trip for the King and those idiot guards.

It was irritating at the best of times to have to climb the hundreds of steps up this blasted tower to feed these damnable pigeons! It was worse than ever today with this stupid sack that spilled more grain than it held.

But to have to do all this so that King Grimzyn of Cranachan could have a Royal feast . . . !

He swore again. Harder this time and kicked the cages for effect.

The pigeons moved uneasily and began to coo louder.

He tipped grain into each of their bowls and scowled angrily. 'Awwk!' he shrieked. 'AUWWWK!' Then he picked up a quill and a strip of parchment and wrote:

Mission accomplished Stop Royal Feast on the
way. Stop. H.Y.C.O.I! Stop. S.

He rolled it up, popped it into a tube and tied it to a pigeon's leg, keeping its claws at a respectful distance. He knew how sharp they could be, and winced as he thought about his eye.

Moments later, as he watched the bird fly toward the far Kingdom of Cranachan, he smiled a cold, evil smile. He felt marginally better now that he'd sent that. All the hassle he'd gone through this morning in arranging that hunting trip, all these damned pigeons, this damned Kingdom. It was a tiny, pathetic insult really, like putting two fingers up at someone through a wall, but it made him feel better, superior.

He cackled to himself as he thought again of the note. H.Y.C.O.I!

'Only I know what that means and they're all way too thick to work it out,' he whispered wickedly under his breath.

He leaned out of the window facing Cranachan, and the Talpa Mountains, and yelled at the top of his voice, 'Hope you choke on it! Ha, ha, ha!'

In one of the lower parts of the rambling castle, a tournament was taking place. The two largest occupants of Castell Rhyngill were locked in combat in the bare guard room. Burnurd looked at his opponent's position and struggled with his plan of action. He was

176

sure that there was a way that, with the minimum of effort, he could turn this situation around completely. Several schemes and plans hatched and floated, briefly, in the amniotic treacle of his consciousness, before dissolving slowly back into the neuronal sludge.

Suddenly, Burnurd stared hard at Maffew and began to grin in mock menace. The co-enzymes of doubt and confusion had worked furiously in his head. And failed. Despite their greatest efforts and seemingly against all the odds, he had hatched a plan. It would work. In a blinding flash of clear thought, it had come to him. He knew how to win. Almost immediately, a series of short clicks followed in quick succession, as Burnurd hopped his small black disc all over the draughts board. 'I won!' he shouted in victory and relief.

'What?'

'I won.'

'How?'

''Cos you lost. That's how.'

A cloud of sadness floated across Maffew's face as he realised that there were, in fact, no white pieces left on the board.

'Oh,' he said sadly, his deep voice echoing in the empty guard room. Then brighter, he asked, 'Best outta free?' Burnurd nodded and they began eagerly replacing the pieces on the board, stopped, had a brief discussion and finally agreed to place all the draughts on the black squares.

'Loser starts,' reminded Burnurd with a grin.

'Well, it'll be you next time,' taunted Maffew as he picked up his first draught and wondered where to move it to.

'Listen!' said Burnurd, staring into space, 'I can 'ear somethin'.' He scratched his head.

'Stop tryin' to put me off. I'm finkin'.'

'Can you 'ear somethin'?'

'I can't 'ear nuffin'.'

'I can,' insisted Burnurd.

Maffew cupped his huge hand to the side of his head, and listened. Burnurd explored the inside of his ear with a massive little-fingernail.

'What am I supposed to be listenin' for?' asked Maffew. 'I can't 'ear . . .' The castle guard's face lit up as he heard it.

'See. Told ya,' said Burnurd, smugly, as Maffew struggled to identify the new noise.

It had been very quiet at first. A distant pitter-patter, as loud as a mouse's tears. But it had grown louder, heavier, more ringing until now it had reached an intensity where it was very hard to ignore. A regular metallic pounding echoing on stone. Unmistakably, a very large man, wearing metal boots, was sprinting wildly down the empty stone corridor, just the other side of the guardroom wall.

Burnurd and Maffew's heads moved in unison, from right to left, as they followed the sound of the footsteps thundering by. Maffew still had his hand cupped to his ear. The heavily booted man passed by only feet away, and, almost as quickly as he had come, faded to silence.

'Wonder what that was?'

'Dunno.'

'Me neiver.' Burnurd shrugged his massive shoulders and said 'Your move.'

'Oh, yeh.'

Slowly, and with immense concentration, Maffew finally placed his white draught deliberately on the board.

Faintly they both heard a man yelling what sounded like: 'Don' panic, darlin', I'm on me way!'

In the castle kitchen a heated debate was under way. The youngsters stood in a small group and Firkin was grilling Courgette.

'Six!'

'Yes. Six!' repeated Courgette forcefully.

'But how come?' Firkin shouted. 'I mean, this castle is so big there should be thousands.' He threw his arms wide.

'Look, don't ask me why there's only six people living in this castle, there are. So there!'

She folded her arms and turned away. Hogshead walked around the table and continued talking to her, but a little more calmly.

Firkin tutted audibly and stamped away towards Merlot who was standing looking at the remains of the door.

'That girl is stupid!' complained Firkin.

178

Arbutus nodded wisely.

'Eh, what?' replied Merlot, absently staring at a small pile of grain on the floor.

'Stupid. How can she believe there's only six people living in this castle?'

Arbutus nodded again.

'Because there are,' replied the Wizard, poking the grains with his pointy shoe. The little bell on the end tinkled gently.

'But . . .'

'No "buts". It's true.'

Arbutus shuffled uncomfortably and stared hard at the ceiling. Firkin stood where he was and fidgeted nervously.

After a few moments, the Wizard looked up from the floor and concentrated his attention on Firkin.

'Now then, young man, all is not well, what?'

'No, I'm worried,' he answered after a few moments.

'Aha.'

'I don't know what to do now.'

'Uhu,' said Merlot, chewing his beard.

Firkin shrugged, then continued: 'I've come so far. I've put Hogshead through so much, and now we're here, in the castle . . . well . . .' For a few moments he sat there quietly, then he looked up. There was anger and betrayal in his eyes.

'It's Percy! I'm really annoyed with him. He's really let us down. He promised he'd help and he's gone and run off. It's not fair! We needed him. He's useless!'

'Now, now, don't be so quick to judge, young man.' Merlot's voice sounded warm and comforting, like a favourite sofa.

'I don't know what to do,' he said. 'We've come so close but I don't know where the King is.'

'Oh-hoh! Is that your problem?' exclaimed Merlot. 'Well, young man, why did you not say so?' He smiled wisely. 'Where,' he continued, 'do kings live?'

Firkin looked hard at the Wizard.

'Castles,' he replied sarcastically.

'And where are we now?'

'Yes, I know!' said Firkin impatiently and even stamped his foot. 'But I don't know where to look. We've never been here before. I don't know where to . . . go . . .' he drifted off as he followed the direction of Merlot's gaze. He looked across at Hogshead and Courgette.

He'd been staring at her almost all the time. She would have to be the most perfect guide! Firkin's spirits began to rise.

Damsels-in-distress, as their name would imply, exist not in the safe, suburban echelons of castle society. Oh, no. Not for them plush, ground-floor apartments, fitted with patio doors, offering year-round views of manicured castle gardens. Not for them the high-society dinners and balls, populated by bewigged and powdered gentry. Not for them freedom.

For the correct degree of distress to be achieved, these damsels must be exposed to calculated measures of hardship, discomfort and spinning-wheels. No damsel could be properly considered 'in-distress' without a small, rickety spinning-wheel at her feet.

But, for distress of the highest calibre to be fully realised, location is the key. It is a well known fact that the 'distress coefficient' of various criminally wicked tortures, is synergistically enhanced by the co-incident location at which the torture is inflicted. For instance, being manacled to a wall, in a bar, on a Hawaiian beach, with full waitress service, isn't really everyone's idea of absolute hell. Now, put that wall into a grimy, flea-infested pit of a cell, or a festering mass of fetid entrails and you'd be getting somewhere. It is for this reason that damsels-to-be-distressed are always found incarcerated at the top of tall, draughty towers, or thrust deep into the black rat-infested bowels of the earth with only cockroaches, or the occasional halitotic dragon, for company.

It was with all this firmly in mind that Percy was storming up the spiral staircase in the highest tower of Castell Rhyngill, his sword held out in front of him.

At the top of this tower, he felt sure, was the most distressed damsel ever to be . . . distressed! It was high, it was draughty, it was a perfect location. His feet clattered on the triangular stone steps and he breathed heavily with exertion. Higher and higher he wound, checking each door as he went. A trail of splintered and shattered doors illustrated his progress graphically.

Two floors, and four doors away, the thin bony figure of Snydewinder stared intently out of the window at the pigeon he had just released.

'Hope you choke on it!' he whispered to himself as he imagined his airborne insult winging its way over to Cranachan and the expression of the King when he . . .

Suddenly, he stopped, his daydream shattered by the pounding of reality. His shoulders tensed. He listened.

The sound of splintering oak echoed percussively up the tower. Snydewinder froze.

The Prince grumbled to himself as he looked around another empty room. He ran on up the spiral staircase.

Snydewinder was horrified. He could hear footsteps. 'Footsteps in my tower,' he thought.

Another oak door gave way noisily as Percy continued searching.

'What is going on?' thought Snydewinder. 'Footsteps! My tower. How dare they, I'll sort them out. We'll see about this . . .'

The penultimate door yielded noisily under Percy's weight.

One door away. Indignation took a back seat to blind panic and fled into the corner. Snydewinder was close behind.

So was a pair of size-fifteen metal boots powering the Prince noisily up the final few flights of stairs.

Without warning, the staircase ended and a door blocked the way. The top!

The Prince stood and panted on the stairs. In there, he thought. In there!

He looked up and down at the three locks and the huge iron hinges. In a moment, with the eyes of an expert doorbreaker, he had calculated inherent stress patterns, points of weakness and the exact spot – and force required to be applied to said spot – to effect swift and total obliteration.

Inside, Snydewinder was desperately looking for somewhere to hide. He was trapped and he knew it.

'Don't you worry. I'll be there in a moment,' shouted the Prince.

Snydewinder froze and in his state took it as a threat. He spied a tiny gap between a few of the bird cages and the wall. Blind panic convinced him it was big enough to hide inside. He dived for cover. The pigeons edged away from the flailing Lord Chancellor and wondered, in their mild avian, way what he appeared to be hiding from.

Abruptly, they found out.

There was a countdown of five booted footfalls before the world ended in an explosion of oak splinters, hinges, locks and the odd baffled woodworm.

The Prince stood framed in the door and looked menacingly about. The occasional feather drifted down in the settling dust.

Nothing else moved. Even the pigeons were quiet.

Snydewinder's eye was shut tighter than ever before in his life. Even his eyepatch had crease marks. He lay half exposed behind the cages and waited for the iron grip of a gauntlet, or worse, cold steel on flesh. Terror gripped him. Panic held him. His heart stopped. Frozen in electric tension . . .

'Oh, bloody 'ell. A pigeon loft!'

The Prince squinted briefly around for any signs of a spinning-wheel, saw none, smashed a gauntlet against the remains of the door frame in frustration and ran down the stairs to search some more.

Snydewinder twitched feebly behind the cages.

'Well?' asked Firkin grumpily, his voice echoing hollowly in the bare stone corridor.

'Well what?' snapped Courgette.

'Which way? You're the guide!'

The small band of intruders stood at the junction of five identical corridors. Their shadows flickered uncertainly as the torches on the walls guttered in unseen draughts.

'I don't know,' protested Courgette. 'I've never been here before.'

'So you're lost!' snarled Firkin, more out of frustration than anger.

'I wish I'd brought a ball of string,' whined Hogshead.

'I'm not lost,' said Courgette defiantly. 'Not lost at all! . . . It's just that . . .' Her voice trailed off. '. . . just that I . . . er . . . don't quite know where we are . . . That's all!'

'Oh, great!' Firkin folded his arms and considered the luxury of sulking. Courgette looked shyly at her feet.

'How many fingers am I holding up?' asked Merlot suddenly in the cold, brooding silence . . .

'What's that got to do with . . .' began Firkin.

'How many fingers am I holding up?' he repeated patiently.

'What's it got to do . . .'

'Stop arguing, young Firkin! How many?' The wizard stared hard into the young man's eyes.

'Well, three. But . . .'

'Thank you.' Merlot straightened up and counted off the corridors clockwise, one by one. He ended pointing down the third corridor.

'That way,' he proclaimed. 'Come on!'

Snydewinder shook the remains of a large, and once triple-locked, oak door out of his hair. He shook the last few feathers off his black leather robes. And then . . . he shook.

Fear, anger and a brooding sense of trepidation caused his unhealthily thin body to twitch uncontrollably. Questions screamed for answers, like a mob demanding justice at a witch hunt.

Who, or what, was that?

Why had it come?

What was it after?

Would it come back and finish the job?

There were more, hundreds more, but he couldn't cope with them all.

The hand of pure reason slammed the gavel of calm noisily on the block, yelled for order, and gradually quietened the screaming mob in his head.

In the resulting restless peace he was able to hear himself think. All his thoughts led down a narrow trail to a very similar conclusion. If the true reason behind his presence in Castell Rhyngill for the last thirteen years was discovered, then . . . well. It didn't bear thinking about!'

An image of a lion's mouth, salivating in anticipation, flashed through his racing mind. A shiver of cold panic lanced up and down his spine. Whoever, or whatever, had smashed down his door and entered his tower had to be stopped. Somehow.

Now was the time for action.

'Your move.'

'Is it?'

'Yes.'

'Why?'

''Cause I've just moved.'

'Oh, alright then,' said Maffew, happy with that reason, and slowly moved a piece one square forward.

'Hey, you're white. Put that back,' shouted Burnurd, indignantly pointing at the offending black draught.

'You sure?'

'Yes.'

'But I thought . . .'

What Maffew thought, Burnurd never discovered and Maffew rapidly forgot. Their discussion was ended abruptly with the arrival of the Lord Chancellor. He whirlwinded into the Guard Room, almost removing the door from its hinges and, panting hard, stared wildly at the two guards.

'Stand up. Quick. *Invasion!*' Beads of sweat glistened on Snydewinder's high forehead. 'Come on. Move. Now!' he shouted.

Burnurd and Maffew stood up slowly and glared at the irate Lord Chancellor hopping from one foot to the other, in intense agitation.

'Now?' asked Maffew, alert as ever. 'But we're still playing.'

'Yes, now!' Snydewinder picked up the guards' draughts board and flung it into the far corner of the room. Black and white pieces scattered everywhere.

'Game over!' He smiled a humourless smile. 'I want some action,' continued Snydewinder, trying to appear calm. He failed. His eye roamed the inside of its socket restlessly and showed white all around the pupil. 'Spies! Broken in. Hundreds of them. Catch them. Kill them! Exterminate them!' His voice ended at a pitch higher than was healthy.

He ran behind Burnurd and began to shove him hard.

'Move, will you!'

He ran back around the front and tugged impatiently at Burnurd's sleeve. 'Move. Now or I'll kill you!'

That did it. He probably would. He had no respect for life. Maffew had once seen Snydewinder pull all the legs, except one, off a daddy-longlegs and watch it struggle hopelessly round in circles. He had been giggling maniacally.

Right now he was hopping up and down, flexing his thin bony hands and staring wildly about him. Panic was driving him. And it had a heavy right foot. He looked almost like a rabbit in the headlights of a speeding forty-ton truck. But this rabbit was different. This wasn't a rabbit that would cover its eyes and hope the truck whistled by with inches to spare. This wasn't a rabbit that would turn and run, its white tail flashing alarm. This was a rabbit that was going to stand its ground. This was a rabbit with a plan!

Snydewinder ran out of the room with Burnurd and Maffew following slowly.

'Search the Castle. Find them! Arrest them!' he yelled wildly, 'And report to me in my quarters!' He stood for a moment, trembling like a blancmange on amphetamines, then, in a flash, turned and sprinted away down the long corridor.

Beads of sweat still clinging to his forehead. Snydewinder whirl-winded round the door of his spartan quarters, slammed it behind him and collapsed against it, his chest heaving as he gasped for breath. Wisps of panic swirled gently around his ankles, like dry ice in a low-budget horror film. He closed his eyes and shook. A dreadful image came, unbidden, into his head. He was staring up, out of two tiny eyes, inches above the ground. A menacing visage glared regal malevolence at him. He thumped the ground with his back paws; there was no sound. The jaws of the lion's head sneered, then opened, black lips framing yellow teeth. A skyful of golden mane, closing. He stared upwards into the red-black mouth of death. The breath of a thousand long-dead mammals screamed out from the cavernous throat. He heard his voice join the cacophony. Screaming. The jaws sneered closer, closer. Too close. In a mind-wrenching moment, as he felt the heat of the stifling breath on his face, the lion's face melted. Its features flowed in liquid horror as it rearranged, as quick as mercury, into the sneering face from thirteen years ago . . .

Snydewinder screamed, opened his eyes, and stood quaking

wildly. The sneering face of King Grimzyn still shone as an unblinking afterimage, burned deep into the back of his retina. Tentacles of panic slithered under the door, snatching at his ankles. He launched himself towards his desk and fled onto a chair, pulling up his legs and gripping them tightly. He buried his head in his knees and rocked slowly back and forth.

For the first time in thirteen years, Snydewinder was scared.

He had almost forgotten what it was like. Thirteen years of memories peeled back as he remembered the last time he had known anything like this. That had been the moment when, after crossing the Talpa Mountains alone, he prepared himself to enter the enemy stronghold of Castell Rhyngill, armed with nothing more than a set of false papers, a declaration of intent, his quick mind and the ability to lie through his back teeth. His stomach had churned as he had walked, outwardly confident, up to the huge castle guard and declared that he wished to see the King. Yes, now. It's very important and no you may not enquire as to the nature of my business. No, I'm not a salesman, I am the Lord Snydewinder and that is enough for you to know. Jump to it, man. Show me to His Majesty. Yes. Right now!

From then on, he had almost convinced himself that he was the Lord Snydewinder and not the ex-Chief of Cranachan Internal Affairs. As far as the world was concerned Fisk was dead, long live Snydewinder. In the next few years, power had corrupted him, absolutely, and after a series of devious and expert power-base building manoeuvres, too complicated for the young King Klayth to grasp, Snydewinder had eased himself into a position where he controlled all aspects of life in the castle. Anybody showing the slightest suspicion was 'disappeared' and everyone else was dismissed. He was in charge. Not Klayth, he thought, not that puppet King that learnt everything he knows from me, who I guided, who I manipulated along with everything else in this rotten little tinpot kingdom. His thoughts carefully censored the less than savoury dismissal from Cranachan and the scene as King Grimzyn and the committee had illustrated, in no uncertain terms, the fate that would befall him if his plan didn't come to fruition, or if he even so much as thought about setting foot in Cranachan again.

But it had worked, it was a success. The more he thought about it the more confused he became. It didn't make sense to him. He'd done his job, kept his side of the bargain. Cranachan got its tithes from Rhyngill, and he'd prevented this place being invaded, and all for what? What thanks did he get? After thirteen long years of slaving over a hot throne they send giant, door-smashing knights here to scare me, he thought. Well it won't work. They won't get away with it. Oh no. I'll show them! They won't succeed . . .

Under his breath, the Lord Snydewinder grumbled and moaned and complained as he clutched his knees tightly and rocked back and forth on his chair.

'Listen!' said Hogshead urgently. His voice rang hollowly in the long, gloomy corridor.

'What?' asked Courgette.

'There's someone coming.'

'At last,' sighed Firkin grumpily. 'We've been walking down this corridor for ages!'

'It's not been that far,' said Hogshead, defending Courgette.

In the distance, the regular thump of footsteps grew louder.

'Maybe we can ask this someone for directions,' Firkin said sarcastically, looking pointedly at Courgette. His comment hit home.

'Look! It's not my fault if I've never been here before!' shouted Courgette, stamping her foot. 'It's a big castle.'

'So you *are* lost again?' continued Firkin. The pressure was beginning to show. He was tense. Courgette looked away.

The pounding footsteps grew even louder. Firkin scowled.

'Now, now, please! This is no way for you to behave!' Merlot stood between the two teenagers and rustled melodically. 'No way at all, what?'

Arbutus nodded his definite agreement.

Firkin turned and looked up at the brightly robed Wizard. 'And what would you suggest?' His temper was beginning to fray visibly around the edges.

'We should be working together,' shouted Hogshead.

'By George, he's got it, eh, Arbutus?' declared the Wizard. The owl nodded sagely.

187

'But who, or what, owns the feet that are makin' all o' tha' noise?' asked the Pieman, bringing the conversation back into the realms of the present – and all too real – reality.

The footsteps echoed, regularly, down the corridor. The small group looked towards where they expected the sound to be coming from. The Pieman screwed up his eyes, Merlot squinted into the gloom, Firkin and Hogshead looked confused and Arbutus slowly opened one eye, peered down the corridor for a few seconds, then closed it again and waited.

'I can't see anything,' said Courgette.

'I'm not sure I want to,' whispered Hogshead.

'But it's not that dark in here,' added Courgette. Then, 'I'm scared.'

'What I want to know,' said Firkin quietly, 'is why this person is running . . .'

'Mmmm,' answers Hogshead helpfully.

'. . . and whether we should be looking for somewhere to hide,' finished Firkin.

Merlot stared hard at him, silently.

'I mean . . . er . . . what if they're coming to arrest us . . . What if they know we're here . . . ?'

The steps echoed around them. They stared down the empty corridor. The pounding grew louder. Echoing off the rocky walls. It almost sounded as if it was echoing *through* the walls. They should have been able to see someone now. Someone very big, by the sound of the footsteps. They grew louder. They grew closer. And closer . . .

'Is this Castle haunted?' shouted Hogshead above the pounding din.

'I'm scared,' squeaked Courgette.

. . . And closer. The thing should have been upon them by now.

'I can't see anything,' added Hogshead.

They tried to focus on the sound source. It still grew closer. Closer. Too close. It was on top of them. As one, the group looked up and followed the pounding of the invisible feet as they clattered across the ceiling and began to fade away.

Dimly, from the corridor directly above, a ghostly yell filtered down through the stones. 'It's alreet, luv. I'm comin'!'

188

The two guards ran down another of the thousands of empty castle corridors. Burnurd was excited. An invasion meant something to do. He was also annoyed with himself. He'd taken a direct order from Snydewinder. He knew that, in the normal scheme of things, he had to. Snydewinder was the Lord Chancellor after all. But Burnurd was annoyed at himself because he'd taken a direct order from Snydewinder without creating much of a fuss or even really trying to annoy him. The only part about taking an order from Snydewinder that Burnurd enjoyed was the few moments of fury that could be released from the horrid little man when, having given his order, Burnurd was almost in charge of the proceedings as he 'hummed' and 'hahhed' and watched him go redder and redder. Burnurd had the art of timing his agreement to carry out the order to perfection, causing the maximum annoyance to Snydewinder with the smallest degree of personal risk. It was the nearest thing to a perk that Burnurd had. He mourned once again the lost opportunity for Snydewinder-baiting.

The only reason he had passed up his perk, this time, was the unsettling expression on the Lord Chancellor's face. In all the years that he'd been here Burnurd had never seen fear on Snydewinder's face. Not real fear. Not bulging eye and quivering wreck-type real fear. Not like just now.

The prospect of meeting someone or something that could instil such abject fear and panic in Snydewinder filled Burnurd with intense excitement. He wanted to shake them, or it, by the hand and buy them, or it, a pint.

The two guards turned a corner and stared at the junction of corridors ahead.

'Which way?'

'Er . . . right,' replied Burnurd decisively.

The guards turned and ran off, looking ahead for signs of the intruders. Clues like chalked arrows, or fragments of clothing snagged on a sharp bit of stone, or even a long piece of string for them to follow on the way out would have been really nice. There weren't any, of course. That would be too easy.

'How many d'you reckon there'll be?' asked Burnurd, his deep voice booming in the echoey corridor.

'. . .' came the reply.

'How many d'you . . .' asked Burnurd over his shoulder. Abruptly he stopped in his tracks and looked around. Maffew had disappeared. Burnurd stood alone in the corridor and scratched his head. Where had he gone? He looked ahead. Nothing. There had been no junctions since the last one, so . . .

He looked back the way he'd come and there, on the far side of the junction, was the distant figure of Maffew, shrugging his shoulders and waving sheepishly.

'No sense of direction!' muttered Burnurd. 'Next time I'll just say "Follow me"!'

There is a place in every castle where the architect stamps his mark of individuality. Some add dead ends to corridors for no apparent reason, some make one doorway, in a series of ten or twelve, three inches smaller than it should be, and add witty signs saying 'Duck or Grouse Ha Ha!'; others choose rows of obscenely gesturing gargoyles high on overhanging parapets; and others still, play visual jokes by adding wings to the flying buttresses.

None, however, could be counted on to stamp their mark so stunningly as Emsee Yescher, the inventor of the vertical take-off buttress, the self-refilling waterfall and the Möbius escalator. He was, without doubt, the undisputed Master of 'Artytechture', as it came to be known. Even as a child it was noticed that Emsee had unparalleled genius in 3-D cognitive reasoning and hyper-spatial interpolatory rearrangement. One summer's day, out on a picnic with his parents, he was playing with his building blocks. His parents went over to investigate when they heard him giggling quietly to himself, and couldn't believe their eyes when they found that the reason their picnic had not been plagued with ants was that hundreds of them were doggedly climbing a four-sided spiral staircase, with one level, that led nowhere. Years later, Emsee Yescher had been given free reign in Castell Rhyngill's design and construction, and had produced the most masterful example of an artytechtural conundrum ever to be conceived and successfully built.

'Vertigo Alley', as it had been nicknamed by the constructors, was situated in approximately the centre of the Castle and was the main nexus of all the corridors. If you stood at the bottom and looked up, corridors appeared from all directions and angles. Some were connected by short sets of stairs, others by Möbius escalators, others still by longer sets of stairs at ninety degrees to the short ones. Some corridors just ended in a vertical drop. It was a masterpiece in 3-D hyper-spatial geometrics. Some philosopher mathematicians even held that it went beyond mere 3-D, and allowed access to other more mysterious dimensions. simply by standing at the 'top' of the 'highest' staircase, they said, closing your eyes and relaxing backwards into free air, one could fall paradimensionally and transcend all the laws of conventional geometrics to find oneself in a world where who knew how many dimensions were at play. Strangely enough, nobody had ever plucked up the courage to find out for sure.

Sadly, the design and construction of 'Vertigo Alley' took its toll on Emsee Yescher and tipped him into a 'downward' spiral of madness. Eventually, after years of being found at the bottoms of staircases in a state of utter confusion, he was put into a home for manic architects and spent the rest of his days quietly attempting to tessellate reptiles with frogs.

Meanwhile, the small band of intruders walked into the huge open space and stopped. Suddenly, they felt very small. Almost as one, they looked up at the web of interconnected stairs and passages and wriggly escalators. Firkin's mouth fell open in awe. Hogshead felt very dizzy. The Pieman fell over.

'I'm . . . I'm . . . sorry, Courgette,' whispered Firkin as he realised the size of the castle. 'It's huge!'

'Told you,' she whispered.

'I bet you haven't got a clue where we go now.'

'No.'

'Merlot, how many fingers have you got?' asked Firkin.

'Not enough, what?' the Wizard replied as the Pieman struggled to his feet.

'That corridor looks nice,' said Hogshead and pointed to one with more torches than the rest.

'But it's up all those stairs,' whined the Pieman.

'Yeah. The King wouldn't live on the ground floor, would he?' explained Hogshead.

The Pieman shrugged his shoulders and they all moved off.

'If we're going up there,' said Merlot, 'keep your eyes on the stairs in front of you. There's Magick at work here.'

Firkin led the way and began to climb the narrow flight of stone stairs.

In a few moments, they reached a small landing and then headed off at a tangent to their initial direction. They climbed on. The stairs began to get steeper.

Firkin looked 'up' and suddenly felt the step beneath him heave as if he was riding a camel in an earthquake. He grasped the hand rail and felt horribly dizzy, and not a little sick. He knew he was looking up because gravity told him this, but all his other senses screamed that he was looking down. A very long way down. He shook his head and looked sideways into the void. A bad move. His head reeled and his stomach churned as he stared into a chasm that seemed to fall down and up at the same time. He stopped climbing and gripped the wall tightly, hugging the solid stone and placing his cheek against it for reassurance. His pulse raced as he suffered from an immense art attack. The wall moved, he was sure it moved. Or was it him swaying? Up and down became vicious rumours that he had once heard about, long ago. He began to spin. Toppling round and round in a spiral dive, down into the sky, or was it up towards the ground? A hand reached out and grabbed his shoulder . . .

'Are you alright?' asked Hogshead.

'D . . . d . . . don't look down . . . or up?' answered the pale, quivering Firkin.

'Why not?'

'D . . . d . . . don't! Don't. It's horrible!'

Firkin clutched the wall as if he firmly believed that if he let go he would fall up or down or somewhere into a whirling void, never to escape. Dante's *Inferno* was alive and well and standing three feet behind him.

'Come on, get out of the way!' said Hogshead. 'You're in the way! Move, will you?'

'Which way?'

192

'Up.'

'Which way?'

Hogshead pushed Firkin gently up the stairs, guiding every footstep and talking him through, until gradually they reached the next landing. It was slow progress. Firkin fell on to the ground and kissed it as if it was a long-lost friend that had been abroad for a holiday, liked it there and settled down to stay, only coming back reluctantly because the money had run out. He lay down, whispering pathetically, his eyes firmly shut, and felt gravity's reassuring pull. In one direction. He called this 'down'.

Over the next few minutes, the rest of the group assembled with the Pieman bringing up the rear, puffing like a steam engine.

Merlot stared at Firkin and said, reproachfully, 'You'll never learn, will you?'

Ahead of them the corridor stretched away and curved out of sight, and to the right another smaller corridor led away. Firkin shrugged and crawled pathetically into the corridor. He sat with his back against the wall. The cold stone made him feel secure, and he gradually calmed himself down. His senses beegan to recover and soon he became aware of a conversation.

Courgette's voice floated wispily into his mind. 'What are you eating?'

He heard Hogshead reply, 'Biffcit.'

Confused, Firkin opened his eyes and saw Hogshead chewing a large golden-brown oat cake.

'Where did you get that from?' asked Courgette.

'Er . . . I . . . er, found it!' he lied and swallowed hard.

'Where?'

'It was lying around and . . . er . . .'

'My Dad will go mad if he finds out.'

'Well, there were too many for six of you.'

'Oh! That's stealing.'

'No, it's tax!' answered Hogshead defiantly. 'Its about time we got something back, isn't it, Firkin?'

Hogshead smiled and handed him a biscuit. Firkin took a bite.

'Oh, my pies not good enough now?' asked the Pieman, teasingly, from the back.

'I just felt like a . . .'

'Shh!' Firkin signalled with a finger on his lips.

'What?' whispered Hogshead.

'I can hear voices.'

Deep slow mumblings were coming from round a corner in the corridor. Firkin crept forward and peered round. In a moment he came back.

'Two Black Guards,' he said with a slight quiver in his voice.

'What do we do now?' asked Hogshead, fear rearing its head again.

'Leave this to me.' said Merlot firmly, 'I'm trained in such matters.' With that he strode forward melodically, the bells on his shoes tinkling gently. Firkin, Hogshead and the Pieman stared open-mouthed as the Wizard turned the corner.

'Ooh, isn't he brave?' whispered Courgette, awestruck.

As he disappeared from view, they listened carefully, awaiting the sounds of thaumaturgical destruction as Merlot let off thunderbolts of energy at the enemy. However, instead, around the corner floated the warm and soothing voice of the Wizard as he quietly asked, 'Good day, gentlemen. I wonder if you could tell us where the King is, what?'

Burnurd and Maffew turned, looked at each other in disbelief, nodded in silent agreement, then ran forward in hot pursuit of the fleeing Wizard as he turned the corner, cloak-tails flailing and Arbutus flapping alongside him.

'That way,' shouted Merlot to Firkin and pointed down the little corridor off to his right. In a moment they were up and running, hell for leather, away from the two huge guards as they appeared round the corner.

'They went down there,' said Merlot, helpfully pointing down the smaller passage. The guards nodded their thanks and flashed past without slowing down.

The racket from six pairs of running feet and yells of "Ere, I want a word wiv you' or 'Come back' and, quite frequently, 'Help!' faded into mere echoes in a surprisingly short time.

'OK, Arbutus,' said Merlot leaning nonchalantly against the wall and listening to the rapidly receding sounds. 'That's taken care of them. Now for some real work.' He rubbed his hands together enthusiastically.

'Aye, aye, Captain,' squawked Arbutus foolishly.

'Now would you like to go and talk to some pigeons . . . ?'

King Klayth was back in his favourite place again. The library. Doing the thing he liked doing most. Reading.

But something wasn't right with him. A large book was open in front of him on the massive table and he was looking intently at the pages, but his mind was definitely not on the story. He was leaning over the open book with his head in his hands, his elbows propped either side. He scratched his head, stared at the ceiling and absently drummed his finger on the table top. He sighed heavily. His mind drifted way off the story, out of the library and into the tithebarns. He still couldn't quite believe the size of those things and he *really* couldn't understand why they were empty. He stood up and began to wander aimlessly around the rest of the library. Vacantly he drifted through the rows of musty books, stacked high on dusty shelves, with only tiny letters to give any indication of what they held. Dazedly he wandered on, occasionally picking a book out at random, then tutting and returning it to the shelf. Finally, he arrived at a section where he had only been once or twice before. This part of the library was called 'Records'. Huge black leather-bound ledgers stood in rows, like blackened teeth. He looked along the aged spines at their names. Things like "Accounts receivable", "Livestock OG 993 to 1014" and "Employees".

He reached out, pulled "Accounts receivable" off the shelf and stared glumly at the page at which it fell open. Columns of tiny handwritten figures filled the page and were totalled up at the bottom right-hand corner. Some he recognised as dates, and after a little while he figured out that 'b.f.' probably meant 'brought forth', but the rest of it may as well have been written in hieroglyphics. Grumbling sulkily, he closed it and replaced it on the shelf. He then pulled down "Employees", in a moment of idle curiosity. The heavy ledger fell open at a page in OG 1025. Klayth stared at it for a moment and tried to divine what it was. Again there were columns of figures, but this time they were words, not numbers, and all were written in the same small neat writing as in "Accounts receivable". There were names and addresses, a list of

195

job titles, a column of figures for wages, a column for a start date and one for a finish date and a wide column called "Reason for Leaving". He was curious about this book so he took it to the nearest reading-table and sat down.

As he looked at the huge tome he felt that he was looking into another world. Lists of names and addresses that he had never heard of before lay in neat little lines, on page after page. He looked at the third column and read words he had never seen: ostler, farrier, smith's assistant, cobbler, armourer, knave – the list went on and on: maid, seamstress, courtier. His head swam with new words. Pages of names of jobs. He turned the page and almost gasped in surprise. Gone were the neat letters. In their place lurked a script so untidy and scrawling that it spilled over the dividing lines, dug into the surface of the page, had almost complete disrespect for the subtle nuances of style and grace, and looked disturbingly familiar. It looked like the type of mess that a spider would make had it been submerged completely in a pot of ink, hurled on to the virginal page, and then thrashed about in a wild frenzied attempt at removing the ink from itself.

And there at the top of the page, the first entry in the new hand: 'B. Scrivener, Pott Street, Rhyngill, Scribe, OG 1012 to 1025, Dismissed.'

Suddenly a thought hammered into him; he stopped reading and looked up. All those words were jobs. All those names were people. All those people worked here. He looked down the column 'Reasons for leaving' and apart from the odd 'died' or 'deported' they all had the same reason. Dismissed. And they all happened in the latter half of OG 1025. Questions fluttered around his mind like moths to a summer candle.

Where were they now?

Who had dismissed them?

Why was the writing horribly familiar?

Why did he feel that something was very definitely not right about all this?

What was the word for an uneasy feeling brought about by certain fragments of information, events and gut feelings (see Hunches) all appearing to point to one conclusion or identity. Begin with 'S.' Nine letters. Middle letter 'i'?

If he had a dictionary to hand he could have looked it up.

Suspension. No, too long.

Subterfuge. Good word, but wrong.

Centrifuge. No, it begins with S.

Sausage. Don't be silly!

S . . . i . . . That doesn't help.

Sus . . . i . . . Got it!

Suspicion.

He stood up and, unsure why at the moment, ran off towards the tithebarns just as, at the far end of the library, a tall figure entered and begin to look for something that he felt sure he remembered finding in there in a few minutes time.

The sound of a couple of wing beats and the scrape of talons on a stone window-ledge heralded Arbutus' arrival at the top of the tallest tower. He hopped forward, looked around, then flew up and perched on a dusty wooden shelf.

The wreckage of the large oak door still lay where it had fallen and only a few footprints disturbed the thick layer of wood chips and dust.

Thirty odd pairs of eyes stared out of cages in dull avian curiosity.

Arbutus settled his wings behind his back, flexed his legs at the knees and uttered a series of cons and dull trills; the pigeon equivalent of "Ello, 'ello, 'ello. What's been goin' on 'ere, then?'

'AAAAAAAAAaaaaaah!' yelled Hogshead as he fled past, arms flailing, down the dimly lit corridor. Hard on his heels were Courgette and the Pieman, who would have been yelling something similar if they had the breath. Firkin brought up the rear and tried to think of something other than the two huge Black Guards behind him and what they would do if they caught them. He failed. But not for long.

A junction approached. In a millisecond a decision was made. They cannoned round the corner to the right.

'AAAAAAAAAAAH!' repeated Hogshead but without the doppler effect.

He stopped suddenly and looked down. Vertigo Alley stretched vertically away in a stomach-churning vista between his toes. He stepped back from the edge just in time to grab Courgette and swing her round to a safe halt and save himself from a viciously nauseating bout of intense vertigo. He gestured furiously to the other two as they sprinted toward the sheer drop. The Pieman had his eyes tightly closed in fear and ran in a curiously loping way so that he could hold his tray and yet not lose any pies. Firkin suddenly realised that ahead of him, just beyond where Hogshead stood, in fact, was another entrance to Vertigo Alley. At almost the same time he also realised that the Pieman showed no signs of slowing down. Suddenly, Firkin accelerated, leapt desperately and brought down the Pieman in an expert rugby tackle. The two landed heavily and slid along the floor, face down, locked together. Firkin felt as if he had accelerated as the force of the Pieman's inertia tugged at him. He held grimly onto his ankles and gritted his teeth. He knew that a few short feet ahead of them lay a lot of long feet between here and the ground below. In a flash he recalled the stomach-wrenching experience he'd had on the way up here. At least it would be shorter on the way down.

'Oh! Friction don't forsake me!' prayed Firkin in a moment of desperation.

A greasy trail spread out behind them from the Pieman's apron, lubricating their progress. They weren't going to stop. Firkin dug his toes in. It hurt like hell. Gradually, and far too slowly for everyone concerned, they began to slow. Firkin looked up. The opening was approaching. The drop was too close. Firkin felt as if his toes were about to explode. The edge moved inexorably nearer. He was going to fail. It was too close. Hogshead reached out and grabbed the strap of the Pieman's tray. He tugged with all his might trying desperately to stop them. With the slowness of an insurance company paying a claim, they slithered to a sticky halt with the Pieman's shoulders pointing out into mid air and Firkin jammed underneath his feet. He stared into the chasm below and watched in horror as a pie rolled past him and tumbled slowly away. It took a very long time to stop falling, and left a thin greasy patch hundreds of feet below. Both of them shook terribly. From that moment, the Pieman vowed only ever to use low-fat pastry. A decision based entirely on the desire to maintain a long and healthy life.

Firkin lay on the ground panting and wished he could disappear. He knew that any moment now, not far behind them . . .

'Hah! Got you!' boomed Burnurd. 'Nobody move. There is no escape!'

'That was fun. Can we do it again?' enthused Maffew.

'No. We've got to get Snydewinder.'

'Oh! That's not fair!' whined Maffew. 'I like runnin' and shoutin' and . . .'

'Orders is orders! Go on.'

The huge guard moved away slowly, mumbling.

'Wh . . . wh . . . what are you going to do with us?' panted Hogshead,

'Me? Oh, nuffin',' answered Burnurd. 'Snydewinder'll do all that other stuff.'

'What other stuff?' asked the Pieman, then regretted it.

'Torture an' intergot . . . interry . . . inter . . . questionin', an' some other stuff.'

Courgette burst into tears.

Maffew appeared at the corridor junction and grinned sheepishly.

'Oops! Wrong way,' he muttered, and disappeared after receiving a swift kick from Burnurd.

Not for the first time since he had left Middin, Firkin wished fervently that he had had the good sense to have ignored all those worthy feelings of heroism and righteous indignation and done what any sensible person would have done: stayed in bed, thrown the covers over his head and hoped it would all go away.

An uneasy silence fell over the group, broken only by Courgette's pitiful sobs and Hogshead making noises which he hoped were comforting.

Burnurd stood motionless at the end of the tiny corridor. The Pieman looked out into Vertigo Alley and briefly considered if he would have been better off had Firkin not prevented him from forming a flat greasy patch hundreds of feet below. He decided not. He also briefly considered leaping up in an act of unparalleled bravery, attacking and overpowering the guard, and leading everyone to safety. But, as he was still having difficulty catching his breath after all this running about, he decided against that too.

199

He settled down and chose option three. If it's inevitable, relax and enjoy it!

A few minutes later Firkin looked up. The massive bulk of Maffew returned and stood expectantly next to his colleague.

'Move, you idiots. Let me through!' shouted Snydewinder attempting to force his way between the guards. He pushed, pulled and hit out at their backs. Burnurd stepped sideways and Snydewinder lurched between them, fighting for balance. He shot the guards a withering look over his shoulder, straightened his leather armour and stared at the captives.

'Ok, the game is up! Throw down your weapons!'

Silence.

'All of you.'

Silence.

'Now! On the floor. Over there!' he yelled and pointed behind him.

The four captives stared at him.

'Come on. What are you waiting for? Do as I say!' he shrieked. His face grew redder.

'B . . .' ventured Hogshead.

'Your weapons. Now!'

'Erm, what if we . . .'

'No excuses. No bargains. No deals!'

'. . . didn't have any weapons,' finished Firkin.

'Lies! Invaders always have weapons . . . unless,' Snydewinder tapped his chin as he thought, 'unless . . . you're spies. Yes. That's it. Spies! Guards arrest them!' He turned to Burnurd and Maffew and ushered them forward.

There was no escape. They were well and truly cornered.

As the guards finally moved in, hope moved out.

Ch'tin stared about him in disbelief. And hunger. The largest, most appetising leather-bound book, that he had ever seen in the whole of his three-quarter-inch existence, was lying next to him. And it was open. The aroma of well-matured lignin wafted across the table. His digestive juices were working overtime. His stomach rumbled a tiny wormy rumble. It was hard being surrounded by more food than he could ever imagine. He squirmed surreptitiously forward.

A tall figure stared hard through the gloom of the library as he pored over the book. He issued only the occasional sound. A thoughtful 'Hmmm' or a more inspired 'Aha' as his fingers found an interesting entry.

Arbutus stood on a shelf and watched the old wizard chewing his beard thoughtfully, as he preened his flight feathers. The trip to the dusty pigeon-loft had left him feeling distinctly grimy.

'How much longer are you going to be?' asked the owl, around a particularly filthy primary, with a hint of irritation.

'Eh? What?' Merlot had heard something being said but was so engrossed he'd missed what it was.

'How long?'

'As long as it takes!' snapped Merlot. 'You should learn to appreciate books, you know. This is good,' he added in a lighter tone, looking up at Arbutus for the first time. Ch'tin agreed as he chewed at the corner of the book. It was very good.

'Glad to hear it,' muttered the owl, folding his wings pettishly.

Merlot reached under his hat, threw the owl a mouse, and carried on reading. 'Stop that!' he shouted as he spotted Ch'tin. 'Don't destroy the evidence.' He pulled the book away, threw the worm a scrap of parchment and continued reading.

This leather-bound book fascinated him. It was a record of all the people that had been employed at the castle over the years, what they did and, most importantly, why they left. It was the same volume that Klayth had already looked at. Now he was finding the same things. The story was all there for all to see. It was deviously hidden and perfectly executed. Almost. Merlot couldn't believe the arrogance of the man. He'd even initialled all the evil deeds.

Snydewinder, over the last thirteen years, had authorised over two hundred dismissals of castle employees, enabling himself to be promoted to the positions of Chief Strategy Advisor, Chief Accountant, Bookkeeper General, Tax Advisor, Lord Chancellor, Teacher, etc., to name but a few.

In short, he'd successfully managed to manipulate and remove the castle employees so that he could now advise the King to do exactly as he wanted. And there was no one to disagree. Merlot still needed more answers. He had two major questions.

Where did Snydewinder come from? And why had he manoeuvred himself into such a position of authority?

He knew where he would find the answers. Arbutus would probably have the confirmation, after his visit to the pigeons. Ch'tin watched ravenously as Merlot replaced the book on the shelf.

'Please! Food I am needing,' he whimpered.

Merlot chose a harmless love-story from off a nearby shelf, picked up Ch'tin, shoved them both in his pocket and headed off for the tithebarns saying, 'Food, enjoy and inwardly digest, my little green friend! *Bon appetit*, what!'

Arbutus flapped gently on to the Wizard's melodic shoulder.

'Now tell me,' said Merlot, 'what did your avian cousins have to say . . . and don't say "coo"!'

Snydewinder babbled animatedly as his imagination ran away with itself, fuelled on the high-octane prospect of inflicting pain on the four captives trudging miserably before him. They had walked down corridors, climbed down stairs, and fallen down to the ground as they stumbled in the poor light offered by the guards' torches. Always down, down, down. They were now far below ground level. 'Get a move on!' Snydewinder yelled. 'I've got tons of preparation to do before dawn! There's knives to sharpen, irons to heat, gallows to get . . .'

'Shut up! Shut up!' shouted Hogshead defiantly. 'There's no need for this.' He put his arm around Courgette's shoulder.

'Aw! Isn't that sweet?' mocked Snydewinder. '*Stop it*! I want *none* of that sort of thing whilst you're my prisoners!' The change in his character was frightening as he taunted them from behind the massive bulk of Maffew.

Courgette was close to tears.

'Don't you think 'incarnate' is a good word!' mused Snydewinder out loud as they neared the dungeons, 'or "imprison" or "inflict", you know – like pain!' He shrieked wildly in the gloomy flickering light.

Firkin ground his teeth together and clenched his fists.

'Personally,' continued the Lord Chancellor, 'I've always liked the sound of the word . . . "*hang*"! Hah! It always sounds so . . . Final. Don't you think?'

It was too much for Courgette. She wept openly as they trudged solemnly on.

Snydewinder rubbed his hands together. The leather creaked evilly. 'I see I'm going to really have some fun with you four. You will learn the lesson: never to mess with me or the King of Rhyngill. Even if it kills you. It probably will!' Snydewinder howled with laughter. The cruel shrill wail of a cowardly sadist who loved his job.

Firkin risked a look round. Something that Snydewinder had just let slip began to make him think. He counted. Four!

Suddenly, he realised that since they had been captured he had only thought of himself. Me, save Me!

Where were Merlot and Arbutus? He hadn't noticed they'd gone. He felt sickeningly ashamed. They could be lost or hurt or dea . . .

'Here we are,' shrieked Snydewinder as they rounded a sharp corner in the dim passageway. 'Home, at last!' He ran past into the little – used dungeon and opened the doors to the cells, in preparation for their occupants. Small groups of black, shiny, scuttling things fled from view. They had sense. Snydewinder laughed cruelly.

'Come, come. Your rooms await.' In the dark, his eye shone with madness, like mercury on a midnight oil slick.

In the cells, the smell of dampness was overpowering. The walls oozed carpets of mould that glistened green and orange in the torch light. Juvenile stalactites formed shining nodules on the bare stone ceiling and, in the drier corners, countless unseen spiders lurked. There was a constant background noise of echoing drips.

Snydewinder's gloved hand pushed a horrified Firkin into the first cell and slammed the door behind him. He pushed the creaking bolt home. Rust made its movement difficult.

'There is no escape,' he reminded Hogshead as he was pushed into the next cell. The guards pushed the last two cell doors shut; their hinges creaked and squealed in corroded protest.

'Come on. Hurry up. We have a trial and a gallows to prepare.

A verdict of guilty awaits. Time and trials wait for no man!' He ran
out of the dungeon laughing horribly.

The two guards followed, carrying their torches, leaving the
prisoners in the dark to the sound of dripping, scuttling and
Courgette sobbing.

In the Conference Room of Castell Rhyngill, a small handbell
rang. Its sound echoed clangorously as it collided with stone walls,
bounced off pillars and ricocheted off the panels of weapons that
lined the walls. It was trying to escape.

A few moments later, Rhyngill's black-leather-clad ruler
entered the Conference Room.

'Sire, I crave audience!'

'It had better be worth it!' shouted the King, waving a large
ceremonial beheading sword in the traditional manner.*

'Oh, it is, it is, excellent, excellent . . .' babbled the Lord
Chancellor excitedly under his breath. He breathed heavily as if
he had been running hard. He had.

'Well, are you going to tell me? Or do I have to guess!'

'Your Highness. I come post-haste from the dungeons.'

'What were you doing down there?'

'Spies!' The Lord Chancellor revelled in the word.

'Spies?' Klayth put down the sword. It sounded as though,
unfortunately, it was going to be worth it.

'I have captured four spies,' cried Snydewinder excitedly. He
was so pleased that he was forgetting his 'Sires' and 'High-
nesses'. 'I found them on a routine patrol. They were plotting evil
crimes. I apprehended them!' No mention, credit or even vague
hint was made of the essential part that Burnurd and Maffew had
played.

---

* A tradition begun by King Stigg, the first and, so far, cruellest King in
Rhyngill's history, after the then Lord Chancellor had thought it worth raising
him from his bedchambers for an audience on a matter of pressing importance.

Unfortunately for the Lord Chancellor, the King had not seen the matter as
quite so important, when weighed against the pleasures of bed, a bottle of
whisky and his favourite and extremely lusty concubine. The four-foot
ceremonial beheading sword hanging on the wall was swiftly pressed into action,
and the Lord Chancellor was duly dismissed. Permanently.

'Who are they? What do they want? Why are they here?'

Confusion and fear rang in Klayth's voice. He didn't like it. Spies and suspicion. It just wasn't right.

'Three unknowns and one insider, the cook's girl,' answered the Lord Chancellor, stiffly trying to control his inner madness.

Klayth was shocked with the answer.

'Their mission – unknown,' continued Snydewinder, almost in control of his wild mixture of anger, fear and desire for retribution, 'their target – unknown! They are in the cells awaiting trial!'

'When?' asked Klayth, afraid of the answer.

Snydewinder took a dramatic breath. 'Dawn.' His voice was eerily flat. Almost calm. Inside he boiled.

Klayth collapsed in his throne.

'It is my firm belief,' said Snydewinder, holding his voice steady, 'that these are dangerous spies. I am counting on you tomorrow, Sire, to pass full sentence.' A wild twitch flashed across his face, betraying the pressure within. He had to leave, he could feel his grip slipping.

'I have a lot to prepare for the torture . . . er . . . trial tomorrow, Sire. I beg leave to sharpen up my knives, er, knowledge of legal procedures!' He rubbed his gauntlets feverishly. The manic glint in his ferret's eye began to shine. The eye of a terrifying storm to come.

He turned and tore out of the Conference Room as if driven by some wild demon. Klayth stared at the space where he'd been.

'Dawn. No, not a dawn trial!'

His head fell into his hands.

'I can't do it!'

Hundreds of feet below the King, Firkin shivered uncomfortably on the slatted wooden bench in the dripping, stinking cell. He listened to Hogshead as he continued to offer words of comfort to Courgette. He was doing a brilliant job. She now only sniffled and sobbed in short, isolated bursts.

Firkin felt empty and could offer no words of comfort. No words of solace.

The whole situation was his fault, and he knew it. Words of comfort from him would only add insult to an already critical injury and would, more than likely, be slammed back in his face. He would be open to the high-tempered backlash of the combined anger, fear and frustration of them all, including himself. He hated himself. He had failed. He squeezed his eyes shut and tried to hold back the emotions inside.

There was another, and more tangible, reason he could offer no comfort. He was fighting back a lump in his throat bigger than he had ever imagined possible. He felt as if something was trying to get out, something alive. It was hard to breathe. He dared not open his mouth. If he did it would be to cry out and scream with pain and fear, not to offer consoling words in the dripping darkness of their desperate cells.

He clenched his teeth. He pulled tighter and strengthened the grip on his knees; any more pressure and they would explode, showering him with hot synovial fluid. Desperately, he tried not to think of tomorrow. He failed.

How ironic and fitting it should end at dawn. The start and the end. The full circle. He thought of his sister, the last time he had seen her smiling and laughing, the hopes he had then, the stupid pathetic juvenile dreams. It all seemed so far away, so long ago, like experiences from another age, another world. Gradually, as tiredness added its weight to the already overwhelming burden on his emotional shoulders, increasing his vulnerability, heightening his already mountainous susceptibility, slowly he succumbed to the war of attrition and lost the battle with his emotions.

Gently, down his grubby cheek, a warm salty tear of despair sparkled on its way to freedom and leapt into the grimy green puddle below.

Unsurprisingly, in the dead of night, the castle was quiet. It had been quiet for the last thirteen years but tonight it was very quiet. It was as if the castle was holding its breath, waiting for dawn. Everyone was asleep, more from sheer emotional exhaustion than anything else. Hogshead tossed and turned fitfully on the wooden bench in the cell. Courgette tried to bury her head in her hands. No one snored. It is difficult to snore when only hours remain before a fixed appointment with almost certain death.

Only one room rang with the sound of industry. A dark room,

deep in the bowels of the castle, far, far below ground level. Four large torches produced huge flames and turned the stone walls crimson, giving the air a thick smoky taste. In this room, a thin black-clad figure put the final touches to his own private version of hell and tested out the final rack. Sleep was one of the last things on Snydewinder's mind, his body coursed with adrenalin, his mind ran with plans and lists of things done and still to do. He'd been up all night and had stripped and regreased the other four racks so they now ran with an exquisite smoothness. He had also sharpened all the spikes in the iron maiden, polished the thumbscrews, cleaned the manacles and built up the fires so that the pokers now glowed in deadly scarlet readiness.

He finished with the rack and pushed it back, its wooden feet squeaking on the bare stone floor, so that all five stood in a neat row. When it comes to torture, thought Snydewinder, neatness and attention to detail are essential. He ran wildly to the far end of the torture chamber and picked up several small cases and five gleaming scalpels that shone with icy sharpness. He shook the cages and watched the scorpions flick their tails aggressively. He arranged the cages on a table, talking to himself all the time, and placed the scalpels next to them. Next he wheeled out a tray of polished steel dental equipment. Pliers, clamps, drills, he ticked them off mentally, laughing quietly and maniacally all the time and never staying still, even for one second. At any given instant some part of the his body was twitching, or tapping, or fiddling. This was not under his conscious control; it was his body's way of using up the massive amounts of pent-up nervous energy that were surging through it. If he sat still at all he would, more than likely, explode. He stood over by the heavy, dark, oak door and looked around the room, surveying his work, ensuring that the first impression was just right. He moved one of the torches slightly in its holder, so that the dental equipment would flash with attention-grabbing sharpness as the prisoners were brought in and strapped to the racks. Details, he thought, essential details! He rubbed his hands together and licked his lips.

'Ready!' he said and smiled humourlessly. The wild glint showed strongly in his eye, feeding on the anticipation. 'Time for business!'

He clapped his gauntleted hands together, flew out of the torture chamber and up several corridors to the Guard Room, where he poked his head inside, barked several orders at the bewildered guards and whirlwinded on.

A few moments later, and only panting slightly, he entered the King's Public Chambers.

The King sat waiting. He had been there for hours. His face was pale and drawn with worry. He hadn't slept last night; his thoughts kept reminding him of the real significance of a dawn trial. He shivered as he thought of what the next short hour would bring.

A dawn trial was the only trial where a sentence of death could be passed. The main reason being that a sentence of death is the only sentence allowed to be passed at a dawn trial. This became law in the reign of King Stigg the Unmerciful, who always passed death sentences at dawn trials, even for the most trivial offences. When asked why, he had replied, 'Mornings. I hate mornings. I always feel like death first thing in the morning.'

It was now King Klayth's duty to continue that policy.

The strained voice of Snydewinder rattled into his consciousness and shattered his reverie.

'Sire, your Imperial Presence is requested to oversee the trial and pass sentence upon the prisoners captured yesterday.' Snydewinder blurted.

'Nonsense. I haven't had my breakfast yet!'

'Erm. Your Majesty, there will be no breakfast this morning.'

'Explain!'

'The cook's daughter was caught yesterday with the aforementioned spies and so last night, at my request, the cook Val Jambon was arrested, and will appear today as an accomplice. He will receive as fair a trial as the others.' A twitch of wildness flashed across Snydewinder's face.

'This is ridiculous. Are you trying to destroy the workings of this castle? Isn't a death sentence for being found in the castle just a little excessive? How can you justify this?' He would dearly have loved to yell this at the top of his voice. Suspicion, doubt and a large dose of fear of passing judgement piled up to make him want to say these things. But he held his temper and said none of them. Yet.

Instead he said, 'Very well. Let's get this over with.'

King Klayth swallowed hard and, with the dull woolly feeling of someone who hasn't had a wink of sleep all night, walked down to the torture chamber. Snydewinder followed close on his heels, rubbing his gauntlets together noisily, grumbling under his beath and almost skipping all the way.

Firkin's arms were already aching. He was lying on the rack, his hands and feet shackled to the rotating drums above his head and below his feet. The slack had been taken in. The other four were in a line stretching away on his left. At the far end Courgette was crying as she explained it all to her father. He lay there and listened with a mixture of pity, confusion and sadness. Anger wasn't far behind.

In the flickering torchlight Burnurd and Maffew stood guard. They waited for the King and the Lord Chancellor. Maffew looked at the table of dental equipment before him and fidgeted uncomfortably. He liked being a castle guard. He was proud to be able to look after the protection and well-being of the King and the uniform was nice. But when it came to inflicting pain on people, well, it just wasn't on . . .

Suddenly the huge oak door to the torture chamber was flung open and Snydewinder burst in. He wore his black leather armour and huge gauntlets with metal-capped knuckles, freshly polished. His steel-toecapped boots chinked as he stomped about on the cold stone floor. He glared wildly at the prisoners with his one good eye.

'All rise! Ha ha ha! If you can! His Royal Highness King Klayth of Rhyngill.' He bowed an overlong bow and ushered the King towards the throne prepared for him, facing the row of five racks.

The King wore full judicial body armour, consisting of a long black leather cape, lined and edged with moleskin; black thigh-length studded boots, each with its own perfectly balanced throwing-knife within easy reach; a standard black leather body-armour and, instead of a crown, he wore a long wig that fell down in tight rolls just beyond his shoulders, made entirely of white leather. He walked slowly in past the prisoners and remained looking straight ahead. His eyes were red, the result of his restless night.

Firkin strained to see him. His adversary. The purpose of his journey. The reason for all of his, and his sister's, and Hogshead's and everybody's misery. He couldn't believe his eyes. The clothing looked right. The setting looked right but . . . he couldn't be that young!

The five prisoners glared at the King as he sat in his black robes and creaked uncomfortably. He was unable to bring himself to look to his right where Courgette and the Cook were lying. He took a small hammer out of his pocket and raised it reluctantly. He glimpsed the equipment arranged on several tables around the room and felt sick. Snydewinder glared at him.

'We are all gathered. Let the . . . the trial begin,' said the King quietly.

He hit the arm of his throne with the hammer and hated himself. He had no choice.

Snydewinder took what would have been the spotlight and paced up and down in front of the five racks. His gauntlets gripped his chest as he strutted about.

'I take it we all know why we are here?' shouted the Lord Chancellor and listened as his harsh voice echoed away to cold silence. No one answered.

'We are here for a trial! The trial of you five loathsome creatures. You stand, oh sorry, lie before us, charged with being Cranachanian spies. Now, think carefully before you answer this. How do you plead, you snivelling creeps?'

'Not guilty!' they cried together.

'So. You want it the hard way! Well I intend to prove otherwise. You all, of course, know the penalty for . . . spying?' They did. He'd told them enough times during the night as he'd stood outside their cell doors whispering hoarsely to them. They nodded and shuddered. Tears rolled down Courgette's cheeks.

Snydewinder moved up close to her ear and whispered, 'The gallows are ready!'

Everyone heard him. Courgette screamed. Snydewinder cackled and rubbed his gauntlets together, making the leather squeak noisily.

'Yesterday afternoon, you four were caught inside the castle without permission. *Why*?'

210

'We were . . .' began Firkin.

'Spying!' shouted Snydewinder, 'Guilty. Ha, ha, ha.'

The King shifted uncomfortably in his throne.

'No,' yelled Firkin as Snydewinder tightened the rack one notch. 'We're not sp – spies! We're not interested in your secrets.'

'So you know about our secrets!' yelled Snydewinder joyously. 'You are spies! Only spies know about our secrets.'

The Lord Chancellor turned away from the racks to reveal the design on the back of his judicial cloak. Painted in red, on his leather cloak, was a woman wearing a thin dress and wearing a crown. In her outstretched arms she held a sword vertically and in her left hand, dangling down, a small noose. A dawn trial was a very fair trial. You could choose how to die. –

'We're not spies. We are devoted servants to His Majesty the King and we wanted to see how he lived,' shouted Firkin.

'How touching,' scorned Snydewinder. 'Well now that you're here, you can have a full, hands-on demonstration of the judicial system!' He leapt quickly to the rack and swung on the handle, tightening it another notch. Firkin's body made a sickening cracking noise. Maffew cringed and bit his lip.

'But . . . why did you not crave an audience, a guided tour?' asked Klayth, hating every minute of this.

Firkin thought quickly 'We were being shown around . . .'

'By your accomplice,' cut in Snydewinder quickly. 'Her!' He pointed dramatically at Courgette.

'No!' shouted Hogshead. 'Leave her alone!'

'I've never seen them before,' she sobbed. 'It was their owl. He was lovely.'

'*Owl*? There is no owl,' Snydewinder shouted.

'. . . dear Arbutus . . . He was Merlot's . . . and . . .'

'Owl? Merlot? Ramblings,' yelled Snydewinder. 'The ramblings of a mad woman! We cannot trust a word she says.'

'Leave her alone,' shouted Hogshead in impotent fury.

'I wanted you to see him,' whispered Courgette to her father. 'He was lovely. I'm sorry . . .' She broke down again and sobbed quietly.

Despite himself Snydewinder was beginning to almost believe

her. He could never handle sobbing women. Doubt began to creep in. If she is innocent then why are these three here? He had to get rid of them. They were after him. Those three. They had to be. Maybe the King, his King, had worked his insult out. Maybe he had choked on it. Maybe they were here to get him. For choking King Grimzyn. His face grew red with rage. He turned to Klayth, his lip quivering with nerves.

'Sire, I have seen no owl. It is a ploy to divert the cause of these proceedings. These people are undoubtedly Cranachanian spies.'

Courgette wailed in fear. Klayth had had enough. 'I have seen no evidence!' he shouted, staring fixedly at the overanimated Lord Chancellor.

'They are dangerous! Kill them! Exterminate them!' Snydewinder flung wild accusations about and tightened Firkin's rack another notch. Firkin screamed.

'Where is the evidence?' demanded the King.

'There, in front of you. Physical evidence. They were found in the castle. They are spies! They'll tell me. Don't worry. They'll tell the truth!' He fingered a sharp scalpel blade and made it squeal as he scrapped it across his leather finger.

'You caught these "spies" as you call them, yourself?'

'Yes, yes, oh yes! Red-handed.' he babbled, grinning a hollow death's-head grin.

Burnurd scratched his head and looked at Maffew.

'Where?' snapped the King, rapidly losing what little trust he may have had in the Lord Chancellor.

'Top corridor, near Vertigo Alley.' He stared at Hogshead, and waved the scalpel threateningly across his face.

'And what do you think they were doing up there, when you caught them?'

'Spying!' he yelled. 'They are spies!'

'Sire . . . ?' said Burnurd quietly.

'There is nothing up there worth looking at.'

'Who knows why they were up there. They were, and they shouldn't have been. But for my watchfulness, and quick arrest, we could be invaded now. Or under siege!'

Klayth's mind flashed out to the tithebarns.

'Sire . . . we arrested 'em. Maffew'n'me.'

212

'Ha, well yes. Of course I wouldn't risk my personal health on a matter of security,' answered Snydewinder grinning slimily. 'Who knows what dangers there would be. Cranachanian spies always have weapons. The guards can take care of that. It's their job. And a fine job they do too.' He fidgeted uncomfortably, his fingers working constantly.

'Did you find any?' asked Klayth suspiciously. An uneasy feeling started to grow within him.

'Any what, Sire?' Snydewinder's face flashed a momentary panic.

'Weapons.'

'Er, well, not as such. No.'

'Well, they're not spies then.'

'Not spies! Ridiculous!' The Lord Chancellor's teeth ground together audibly.

'Sire, we're not spies,' shouted Hogshead desperately, panic fringing the edges of his words. 'Release the others and I'll tell the truth!'

The others looked at him.

The King shifted uncomfortably on his throne, unsure where the truth lay. Burnurd and Maffew looked expectantly at him.

Snydewinder boiled with range. 'Lies!' he cried, 'They're spies, they're bound to deny it. It's basic training. Kill them. Exterminate them now before it's too late!'

Another fragment of unease added itself to Klayth's gut-feeling.

'The truth!' shouted Hogshead above the shrieking Lord Chancellor. 'We came about the tithes!'

The King instantly thought again of the twelve enormous tithebarns. The twelve empty tithebarns. He sat up. Why were they empty? Could Snydewinder be right after all? Could these be spies come to steal all the tithes?

Snydewinder's whirling mind had it. He knew why they were there. Now he'd get rid of them. And clear himself.

'Your taxes are too high!' shouted Firkin.

'So you came to steal it all back!' accused Snydewinder.

'What?' Firkin had to think hard. He couldn't tell the whole truth. 'How could we? There'd be too much.'

'Wagons,' shouted Snydewinder. 'Load up the wagons and take it all back!' Got them, he thought.

Pieces of a strange jigsaw began to coalesce inside Klayth's mind. It was murky but something was definitely not right here. The image of a carrot in a muddy wagon-track crossed his mind.

'We have no wagons. We have no food,' cried Firkin. 'This is all lies!' His voice strained in desperation.

Courgette was confused. 'But I've seen wagons,' she said quietly through a blur of streaming eyes.

'What did you say?' said Klayth, shocked.

Her father urged her on. 'I've seen wagons,' she repeated, sniffing.

Several pieces of information spun in Klayth's head. It was as if he was watching a one-armed bandit spinning fruit at him. But instead of fruit other, more real, objects spun before his eyes. Empty tithebarns slowed and locked on the far left. The other drums still spun.

'Nonsense!' shrieked Snydewinder. 'Ramblings.' This was going wrong. Horribly wrong.

'Carry on,' urged the King.

Firkin and Hogshead were bewildered. They knew nothing of this.

'Two men come in a big wagon. They come every few weeks. They came yesterday morning,' said Courgette quietly, between sniffs.

Wagon tracks in mud locked next to the tithebarns. The fruit machine spun on. Klayth remembered the hastily arranged hunting hack yesterday morning. Hadn't that been arranged by the Lord Chancellor? Another drum slowed and locked in.

Snydewinder began to look very worried. He hopped from foot to foot. He rubbed his hands together feverishly. He was losing control.

No one else could have arranged the hack. No one works in the stables. The column of job titles in the book in the library locked in on the fruit machine.

Courgette continued, 'They load up their wagons and ride away.'

'We only have one wagon in the whole of Middin,' squealed Hogshead, close to panic. 'We walked here, I'll show you my blisters if you like!'

King Klayth ignored him, his attention fixed on Courgette's sobbing tale.

'. . . Two great big men drive it. I hate them. They're not nice. They have big sticks and they beat the horses and shout at them in funny accents. And, and that's not nice.'

'Nonsense!' exploded Snydewinder. 'They love their horses. All Cranachanians do! And there's nothing funny about the Cranachan accent! It's so refreshing to hear it again, once in a while. It's a nice accent . . . oh!'

All eyes were fixed on the Lord Chancellor. He suddenly looked very much like a small boy with his hand in a biscuit jar. The floodlights of truth had been turned on and were blazing down in kilowatt floods of righteousness.

'What did you say?' shouted the King, standing up. 'You know these thieves? You know who has been emptying my tithebarns for years, starving my Kingdom? Ruining everyone's lives?' Each question caused the Lord Chancellor to twitch and writhe as if he had been stabbed with a long sharp stick. His eye rolled, like a goldfish in a storm. The cracks were beginning to show.

'Why?' Klayth stepped off the throne and moved towards Snydewinder. 'Why do you find Cranachan so refreshing? Does it remind you of somewhere perhaps? Somewhere over the mountain?' He pointed in the general direction of the Talpa Mountains.

Snydewinder's lip twitched as he thought furiously. Serious structural repair and underpinning were required if a major disaster was to be avoided.

'Well?' shouted Klayth.

'Lies. All of it. I deny it all . . .'

Snydewinder trembled as if he was fighting an overwound spring deep within him. It was a fight he was rapidly losing. The mental equivalent of complete landslip, caused by erosion of the underpinning substrata, was happening inside his head. The remains of the courage commanding his feet to stand firm left him. His body was saturated and dripping with adrenalin. Suddenly, there was nothing left for him to do. Panic reached out and held open the door. He ran. His steel-toecapped boots clanked as he fled towards it, occasional sparks leapt from them as he struck the cold stone floor. Arms flailing wildly over his head, he screamed a succession of choice Cranachanian oaths. In a moment he was through the door, slamming it shut with the whirlwind force of a madman. And all that remained was the sound of running feet and a wild high-pitched shriek of laughter, echoing with harsh madness.

As the yells faded and just before Burnurd and Maffew realised that it might be a good idea to try and stop Snydewinder, the oak door was flung open, there was a small explosion and a cloud of blue smoke floated in. 'Stop this travesty of a trial. Now!' cried the tall figure as he stood in the doorway, rustling melodically. An owl was perched on his shoulder.

'Arbutus!' shouted Courgette.

'Merlot!' shouted Firkin, with a huge sigh of relief.

'Owl? Merlot?' said the King. 'So it's true!'

Arbutus flew over to Courgette and perched on the rack next to her shoulder. She grinned for the first time in what seemed like forever. 'These people are innocent!' cried Merlot.

'These people are innocent!' cried Klayth at the same time. 'Release them, now.'

Burnurd and Maffew turned, and with a huge sense of job satisfaction, began to release the ex-prisoners.

'Snydewinder!' shouted Firkin, desperately, one hand free. 'He's getting away. Catch him! Stop him!'

'Yeah, stop him. It's all his fault!' agreed Hogshead.

Merlot stood motionless. His eyes fogged over and he appeared to stare into the distance. His brow furrowed in concentration.

Burnurd smiled foolishly as he untied Courgette. 'I'm sorry,' he whispered. 'I had to do it! I . . . orders.'

She looked up at him, still with tears in her eyes and smiled, 'I know,' she said simply.

Merlot rustled gently, in E major, as he opened his eyes and grinned at Firkin. 'It's alright,' he said. 'He'll turn up. Trust me!'

Courgette threw her arms round her father and buried her face in his stomach, sobbing with relief. Val Jambon patted her head and made gentle comforting noises.

Firkin stood up and looked at Merlot. He reached out and hugged him.

216

'Oh, Merlot, when I realised you weren't with us I thought you were de . . .'

'Oh, no. Not me! Calm down, it's alright now, what? Ooh, fuss, fuss, fuss.' He straightened up his cloak and looked faintly embarrassed.

A few minutes later they were all free and sat on the floor next to Merlot and the King. The stress of the last few days showed on Firkin and Hogshead's faces. They nursed their wrists and ankles and almost exploded with questions.

'Who is Snydewinder?' asked the King, bursting to know if his suspicions were correct.

'Quite simply, in a nutshell, as concise as possible, without any preamble . . .'

'Whooo?' said Arbutus.

Merlot glared at the owl, '. . . the most loathsome of creatures, what? He is a spy. A special agent sent here from Cranachan.'

Firkin and Hogshead looked confused. Klayth nodded.

'Thirteen years ago,' continued Merlot, 'you were at war with Cranachan over the lemming crop. And, as history will tell you with stunning clarity, you lost. In two and a half minutes, I believe. In the normal course of events, they would have invaded *en masse*, taken over your Kingdom and amused themselves with a bunch of rapes and pillages. But they'd got what they wanted – the lemmings – so they were happy. Cranachans are inherently lazy and their Kingdom is almost overcrowded, which means that any farms they have are small and remarkably inefficient, what? The extra burden of feeding the prisoners of Rhyngill was too much. They didn't need your Kingdom. Just your farms. They knew that your Father had left you on the throne, a young and vulnerable King, so an agent was sent to facilitate the removal of the food sent to the tithebarns. Of course, once the castle was almost empty, it was easy. For the last thirteen years all the food taken as tithes has been shipped out over the mountains and nobody, except you, young Klayth, suspected a thing.'

But what about the Black Guard?' asked Firkin, looking curiously at Burnurd and Maffew.

'Disbanded thirteen years ago. Now a rumour kept up by gossip and Snydewinder.'

Klayth sat with his head in his hands. 'I feel so awful. So stupid. I've been used and tricked and . . .'

'We all have,' said Hogshead.

'But what are we going to do?' asked Firkin desperately.

'Don't you worry,' said Merlot confidently. 'We've got a plan, haven't we, Arbutus?'

The owl, perched on Courgette's shoulder, nodded smugly.

He ran blindly, his breath echoing down cold corridors as he panted with exertion and blind panic. His world had started to unravel, like a cashmere jumper caught in the arms of some arcane farm machinery. But faster. Thirteen years of safely manoeuvring, controlling, and manipulating the occupants of Castell Rhyngill were suddenly over. It was as if the small poodle that you have nurtured over years turns round snarling, fangs dripping with saliva, and sets about systematically ruining everything you own, including your ankles. He couldn't believe what had happened. He'd been discovered and now panic, like a wildly intransigent squatter, had moved in. His steel-toecapped boots clattered along the dark corridors as he fled from the torture chamber. His mind raced, filled with questions. What to do? Where to go? How to get there? What the . . . oomph!

He stopped suddenly after rounding a sharp corner. He was face to chest with a wall of highly decorated solid metal. He didn't remember that being down here. It looked down at him through two piercing blue eyes. To Snydewinder's unbelieving surprise it held a very large, and very sharp looking, two-handed sword. Its edge shone in the dim corridor. Snydewinder thought quickly about his next action. Plans came and went in very quick succession. He chose one of the many available to him and immediately pressed it into action. He took a deep breath, and screamed. Panic had settled in, it had just opened a beer and was getting itself comfortable to enjoy reading a good book. Snydewinder tried to run but the knight had him in a vice-like grip, his huge metallic hands clamped about the ex-Lord Chancellor's shoulders like galvanised clams on a deep-sea diver's boot.

''Ello.' said Prince Chandon. 'Where the bloody 'ell are y' 'idin' all yer maidens?'

'D . . . d . . . d . . . d . . .' was the best reply he got.
'What y' tryin' for t' say? Dorn't knor . . . ?'
'. . . d . . . d . . . d . . . d . . .'
'Dorn't 'ave none . . . ?'
'. . . d . . . d . . . d . . . d . . . dd . . . du . . .'
'Give us a clue. I'm 'opeless at morse code!'
'. . . d . . . d . . . d . . . dd . . . ddun . . . dun.'
'Oh, I norr. Dunjunns in't it?'
Snydewinder, completely lost, nodded pathetically.
'Alreet. Tek me t'dunjunns then!'
Percy turned the gibbering Snydewinder round and frog-
marched him back along the corridors to the dungeon and the
torture chamber.

As King Klayth listened to Firkin telling of the misery and
starvation throughout the ruined kingdom of Rhyngill, his face
dropped and he sank lower in his chair.

'I had no idea about all this,' said the King, quietly shaking his
head. 'I've grown up through it all. I thought it was normal. The
way things were meant to be.'

'It's not your fault,' said Firkin.

'I need to put it right,' said Klayth, not listening. 'But I don't
know how!' he said as he pulled the judicial headwear off and
threw it onto the floor. 'I don't know how.'

'You're the King. You can do anything!' squeaked Courgette.

He stopped and looked up. Courgette's words floated in his mind.
'You're the King. You can do anything!' He said them over and over
to himself. 'You're the King.' He mouthed them, tasted them. 'You
can do anything! You can do anything!' For the first time he realised
that he was the King. The one in charge. *Le Grand Fromage*! The
full weight of rulership had settled on his shoulders. He could make
the decisions. Not Snydewinder. The future of the kingdom was in
his hands. Not Snydewinder's. A cloud of doubt was suddenly lifted
from his heart. He knew that he could order people about, if he
wanted to. He knew that he could give people back the food they
grew. He knew he had the power to make Rhyngill great again. He
knew he could do it. He was the King. He could do anything!

But . . .

How?

Suddenly, his thoughts were shattered as the door was hurled wide open and Snydewinder was flung through it.

Anger, betrayal, hatred, retribution and a few other less savoury emotions welled up inside Klayth and fought for supremacy.

'Get him!' he exploded, pointing to the pathetic creature on the floor crawling away as fast as possible.

Burnurd and Maffew needed no second bidding. They had waited years for the chance to get back at Snydewinder.

The two huge guards moved fast, faster than even they thought possible, gathering momentum as they ran towards the whimpering man. They hurled themselves upwards in a terrifying, slow motion, rugby tackle, hovering like two humpback whales in an Alaskan sound, until gravity pulled and they landed, with devastating accuracy, in a bone-crunching heap . . .

As the dust settled, people risked timid glances from between fingers and behind chairs. They saw Burnurd and Maffew sitting side by side on the floor, smiling broadly. One foot and a skinny arm poked out from underneath the combined might of the castle guard. They twitched occasionally.

Maffew bounced once or twice for effect.

'Er, 'scuse me, yer majesty, I realise this may not be t'right time to ask but 'ave you got any maidens y'want savin', damsels in distress an' th'like?' asked Percy shyly from the doorway.

Klayth looked at the huge knight, then across at the satisfied grins on Burnurd and Maffew's faces. His shoulders twitched. A grin began to grow. Relief flooded the young King's body, as for the first time in years he could see a way forward. He could see a purpose in his life. He opened his mouth and laughed. The others watched in baffled silence. The King laughed again, his eyes closed, he held his stomach.

A smile stole surreptitiously across Merlot's face. Firkin smirked. Hogshead spluttered. And very soon the torture chamber echoed to the sound of laughter.

The combined relief of all, but one, of the occupants of Snydewinder's private hell, attacked the tension of the last few hours, pulled it off the walls, ripped it into tiny little pieces and merrily jumped up and down on the bits.

220

*

A few days later, on the other side of the Talpa Mountains, inside the Great Hall of King Grimzyn's Imperial Palace Fortress in Cranachan, the trade discussions were drawing to a close.

The delegates from Rhyngill sat facing their opposite numbers across the highly polished wooden table. Men in long black coats applied themselves diligently and efficiently to the business of supplying the delegation with coffee and biscuits. As soon as they had finished, they vanished quickly and quietly through the small door at the far end of the hall.

'Before we outline our final proposal,' said His Royal Highness, King Klayth of Rhyngill, 'my Commercial Advisor will briefly review the points we have already discussed at length, to reacquaint us with the facts.'

A portly figure stood, bowed his head slightly to both kings, and started talking.

'Over th'last ten years, Rhyngill's suffered from a significan' decrease in its farm produce output, 's I'm sure y' are aware.'

He carefully avoided any hint of an accusation of Cranachan's recent activity. Both parties knew that the others knew. And both parties knew that the others knew who was ultimately to blame.

'This 'as been mainly due t'the lack o' financial investment in farm machinery'n'seed stock, 's well as decreasin' efficiency o' th' labour force owin' t' increasin' age an' decreasin' 'ealth.'

The Pieman paused to gaze significantly at the eight crystal chandeliers hanging above the mahogany table, lighting the sumptuous tapestries in the great hall, and took another bite of the ginger biscuit that had come with the coffee.

'Given a significan' monetary injection,' he continued, 'f'r use in a carefully organised farm improvemen' scheme, coupled with a stengthenin' o' th' labour force by th' injection o' approxima'ely three thousand 'ealthy men, Rhyngill's farm produce output'll rise significan'ly in a very shor' period o' time allowin' a simple mutually-useful market tradin' system t' be set up between our two countries.'

King Grimzyn frowned and looked toward Gudgeon, the Scribe of Trade and Industry, as he furiously scribbled on a piece of parchment.

221

'Well?' whispered King Grimzyn.

Gudgeon shrugged his shoulders and stared at his piece of parchment again. Frundle fidgeted with his fingers. There was an air of mistrust emanating from the Cranachan side of the table.

'Well,' begin the Pieman, 'what d'y'think o' fit?'

Klayth watched as Frundle leant over and whispered to Gudgeon, who then, after a few moments, nodded, scribbled on the parchment, nodded again, leant over and began whispering to King Grimzyn, gesturing animatedly. A carpet of cautious silence covered the room, broken only by the constant crunching of the Pieman as he ploughed his way through the plate of ginger biscuits.

'C'mon,' he urged, 'we ain't got all day.'

King Grimzyn held up his hand and continued listening to Gudgeon's whispered advice, nodding once or twice and occasionally whispering a question. Gudgeon nodded, King Grimzyn nodded, something seemed to have been settled.

The Cranachanian Scribe of Trade and Industry looked across at his Rhyngillan counterpart, cleared his throat and began: 'Are you suggesting that, if we give you some money and return your men to you, you will grow lots of things and sell them back to us?'

'Yeah,' replied the Pieman, 'That's wha' I said.'

'Oh good.'

'Well, what d'y'think?'

'It is a splendid idea,' answered Gudgeon. 'On behalf of Cranachan, I accept.'

'Here, here!' cheered King Grimzyn. Secretly he breathed a sigh of relief. Thirteen years of housing three thousand soldiers as prisoners of war had become very expensive indeed.

'Having agreed to that in principle I think we can leave our Commercial Advisors to thrash out the final details, eh, young Klayth? Fancy a nice game of croquet?'

'I'd love to!'

The two Kings stood and strolled through the open doors and out into the warm midday sun.

High on one of the toes of the foothills of the Talpa Mountains, a thin, bony figure with a black leather eyepatch struggled with a heavy pickaxe. He sweated, cursed and swore profusely. In that order. Gone were the trappings of his office, no more did he wear black leather armour, no more gauntlets, no more shouting and ordering people about, no more glory!

A small hollow in the rocky ground indicated all the progress he had made that day. He looked up toward the mountains, at the work ahead of him and spat derisively into the red soil.

The two Castle Guards sat on a huge rock finishing off their supper of a freshly cooked turkey, watching their prisoner with amusement.

Snydewinder, the ex-Lord Chancellor etc. of Rhyngill, made up the smallest chain gang in the Kingdom's history and at that rate it would take him a very long time indeed to upgrade all the Trans-Talpino Trading Routes from Rhyngill to Cranachan.

Burnurd pointed down the hill and across the valley to Castell Rhyngill. The sun picked out the tall towers, sparkled on the circular, lily-filled moat and glowed red behind the curtain wall. It could have been out of a fairy story.

'Ooh, isn't that pretty?' said Burnurd.

'Yeah,' agreed Maffew, holding a turkey leg. 'It's . . .'

They looked at each other and grinned.

'. . . Boooootifull!' they chorused.

'Dawn, you've got someone to see you,' said her mother in complete shock. She stood in the doorway to Dawn's room and gestured feebly to the visitor. He walked in, his heavy riding-boots clumping on the bare floorboards.

Dawn struggled and sat up. The worst of her illness was over; the package that Firkin and Hogshead had stolen had worked wonders, but she was still weak.

The rider walked forward, smiled and said, 'Special delivery.'

He placed a large box on the floor next to Dawn and then handed her an envelope. It had a seal of red wax and a blue ribbon on the back. She looked up at her parents, who shrugged, then urged her to open it. She felt excited.

After a few moments of struggling, the seal was broken and Dawn removed a piece of parchment from the envelope. It looked very nice. There was a gold edging, a fancy border and two types of writing, although one of them was a little scruffy. In big letters, nicely written, was a message that Dawn shakily read aloud, with her finger under every word.

'In honour of the ree . . . sent new all . . . eye . . . i . . . ance with the king . . . dom of Cranachan, you are all in . . . vit . . . ed to a celly . . . cel . . . cellybrashun at Castell Rhyngill. Ruzzvupp.'

Shurl squealed with excitement and then stopped.

'I haven't got a thing to wear,' she said. Then, 'Why us?'

'It's Firkin, mum. He's done it. And everyone's invited.' Dawn looked up at the rider and asked, 'What's ruzzvupp?'

'It means you've got to answer.'

'Yes, yes. I want to go. I want to see Firkin.'

'I take it then that you will attend,' said the rider.

'No, we're going!' decided Dawn. 'What's that?' she said pointing at the box, her excitement rising.

'A little something, with the best wishes of your host,' replied the rider.

'Ooh, Firkin!' she squeaked.

The box was placed on the bed and she struggled with the string to open it. Quite soon several pieces of frayed and terribly knotty string hung around the sides of the box. She looked at the lid. Slowly she lifted it and looked underneath. She took a quick breath. 'Is it?' she asked the rider.

He shrugged.

Dawn opened the lid a little further and caught a waft of something inside. 'I think it is?' Her eyes were wide with wonderful excitement. Her finger snaked over the edge of the box and into the dark inside. It withdrew with a cargo of frothy white stuff on the end. She put her finger in her mouth.

'It is! Lemming Mousse! Firkin's sent some Lemming Mousse!' Dawn's face was a picture of joy.

'I feel I must clarify a point here,' said the rider, 'The gift comes from your host. King Klayth. He sends is apologies and looks forward to making amends.'

Shurl quietly fainted, whispering, 'The Kinnnn . . .' Wyllf caught her.

'I shall go about my business and issue this decree on to your

224

Post.' The rider turned and left, stepping carefully over Shurl and Wylff. Dawn took another fingerful of mousse and smiled.

She looked at the invitation and noticed the other writing again. She read it carefully to herself.

'Mission a disaster. Long live the King! See you soon. Party to get ready. Love Firkin. P.S. Look in the envelope.'

She reached across the tipped up the envelope. Two slightly battered, but still pretty, snowdrops fell out onto her bed.

She grinned and dipped, once again, into the bowl of mousse.

On one of the lower foothills of the Talpa Mountains, a small group of people stood in an uncomfortably awkward silence. Nobody was quite sure what to say. Nobody was quite sure what to do. Firkin knew that very soon the three companions who had helped them through the most trying time of his, and Hogshead's, life were going to leave. Forever. Firkin had never, in his short life, come upon this experience before. He'd said goodbye to people but every time he knew that he would see them again, maybe in six months, maybe a year, maybe longer; but sometime, he knew, they would come walking through the door, or round the corner, or over the hill. They would be back.

This time it was different.

Far below the little group, crowds flooded from all directions towards the castle. They had responded quickly to the invitations and were streaming from all directions, in all sorts of carts, on horseback, on foot; anything that moved and could carry people, they were in it. Some carts were festooned with ribbons, covered with gardens of flowers and acres of brightly coloured parchment. All the people seemed to be wearing their brightest and loudest clothes. From up on the foothills it was a magnificent sight. It should have stirred a slight flicker of happiness in even the hardest of cynically pessimistic hearts. The fact that it was all because of them should have made Firkin and Hogshead's chests swell with unashamed pride and their hearts soar with unfettered joy. In normal circumstances it would, but now, here on this bare foothilll, cooled by a gentle early-evening wind and watched over by a solitary singing skylark, all thoughts of happiness seemed a distant rumour.

'But why?' protested Firkin again with a throat that felt strangely difficult to talk through.

'Stay here forever they can not,' explained Ch'tin. 'Stories of incompleteness too many will there be!'

'But they're our friends now,' protested Hogshead. Firkin sniffed.

'Yes, know that I do.'

The huge knight shuffled uncomfortably. 'I 'ate sayin' 'bye,' he said, in a subdued voice. For a fleeting moment, a sparkle in the corner of his eye glinted brighter than his armour.

'Yes. Let's jus' go,' agreed the Pieman, surprisingly quietly. He fidgeted with the straps on his tray.

Merlot stared at Firkin. The early evening sun glinted magnificently off his stars, moons and sigils and even, somehow, made his long off-white beard shine. His cloak rustled melodically in E major. He looked every inch the Wizard. Arbutus opened his eyes and joined Merlot's stare. Firkin swallowed hard, blinked and then sniffed.

'Still don't believe in magic, what?' whispered the Wizard smiling wonderfully, a glint of light shining in his eye.

Firkin looked sheepishly at his feet and forced a grin. He quickly wiped his eyes with the back of his hands, and hoped that nobody saw him.

Three decibels below the threshold of human hearing a sound began. It was unannounced, it was unbidden and, for all there, it was highly unwelcome. The brandy-glass cicadas were back. Hot on their tails were the tiny silver fragments, accompanied by the choir of mosquitoes, and the irritating itchy feeling. Suddenly they were everywhere. A silver swirling cloud of spinning argent fragments. Nobody had seen them arrive, they just seemed to explode into being from nowhere, one minute there were none, then . . .

All around the three men they flew. They flashed and sparkled and glinted in the dusky light and magic. As the four youths watched, a glow began to centre, to coalesce, to concentrate itself on each of the three bodies at a point just below their hearts. It was as if millions of silver bees were swarming from a hive in the hollow centre of the figures' chests. The swarm grew gradually, spreading in all directions. The children stared open-mouthed at

226

the men. It enveloped them further, as if a light-speed spider spinning tinsel was hell bent on cocooning them. The children stared open-mouthed through the men. Faintly, indistinctly at first, the hill behind began to show. Then the silver swarm had enveloped them completely, turning them translucent until slowly, almost painfully, they just stopped being there anymore. The exact moment they passed over the space–tome continuum was unknown, like the exact moment the sun finally dips over the far horizon, but Firkin and his friends realised that they were staring out across the hill, through where the wizard, the knight and the pieman had been, past where they had stood. All that remained was a slight smell of ozone, a gentle tingling in their ears and a glowing afterimage burned into their retinas.

And a huge sense of overwhelming emptiness.

Their friends had gone.

Hogshead sniffed. Firkin wiped away a tear. Courgette made a small whimpering sound.

'I wish they could have stayed,' whispered Firkin.

'Oh, Arbutus,' sighed Courgette, millimetres away from tears.

'I'll miss his pies,' sniffed Hogshead, attempting to lighten the mood with a feeble attempt at irony. But, like a tarpaulin on a winter's day, the mood stayed the way it was, dark and heavy. Klayth said nothing, he just tried to look regal.

How long they stood there they couldn't tell, but each of them remained just long enough to begin to try to accept that the figures had, in fact, gone. In one of those moments that happen all too rarely, the foursome turned and moved, each in their own thoughts, in their own world, but somehow all together. They walked, in silence, away towards the castle.

'Oi! You lot! For me wait, will you?'

Dreamily, almost reluctantly, Hogshead looked back to see Ch'tin wriggling towards them as fast as he could squirm. Hogshead reached out, picked the tiny worm up and carefully held him gently in his hand.

'Oh, Arbutus,' sighed Courgette, and sniffed as she tried to ignore the fact that he wasn't there anymore.

The now sadly depleted group marched disconsolately on toward the castle.

'Oh, Arbutus!' squeaked Courgette, in a very different tone of voice. 'Look, look, look!' It was a tone of voice that was completely out of place in the present company. She leapt up and down in sheer joy. The others stared at her.

'Look everyone!' She pulled a large brown flight-feather out of her pocket and waved it joyously. 'Ooh, it's so pretty!'

The others said nothing, they just stared in sheer disbelief.

Hogshead let out a startled cry as, out of the thin mountain-air, a hot steaming pie appeared in his hand and Firkin jumped when a small furry peach appeared and floated gently before him. The three of them grinned wildly with surprise and sheer joy. Courgette waved and swished her flight feather.

Klayth looked rejected. The others suddenly stopped. They felt embarrassed. Hogshead tried to hide his pie. Klayth, their new companion and friend, had nothing. Ch'tin looked shyly down at where his feet should have been. Nobody knew what to do. What to say. They all felt for Klayth.

For a brief moment a bearded face appeared where Merlot had been.

'. . . and you, young man, have not been left out,' it said, looking hard at Klayth. 'What have you got, eh?'

The young King looked in his hands: nothing. He fumbled in his pockets: nothing. He looked up at the translucent face of the Wizard and shrugged his shoulders.

'Where haven't you looked?'

Klayth stared stupidly at a nearby rock and made to look under it.

'Don't be silly,' said Merlot's floating face. 'Try again.'

'I don't know,' said Klayth, completely baffled.

'Honesty,' said the Wizard, 'That's good in a King, what?'

The face of Merlot floated down the hill toward the tiny group, like a sentient balloon, and hung in the air close to Klayth.

'Look around you,' he said conspiratorially, 'go on, have a look and tell me what you see?'

The young King squinted his eyes and looked into the far distance. He saw Castle Rhyngill, but he had that before. He saw the people, that was good but he felt somehow that wasn't really what Merlot meant. Firkin smiled quietly to himself, then

228

nudged Hogshead and Courgette and made a gesture with his hand. The others grinned.

'What? said Klayth as he saw them grinning at him. 'What, is it behind?'

He turned quickly to face the opposite way.

'Yes!' cried the others to the back of his head.

The face of Merlot grinned.

'I can't see it!' moaned Klayth.

'Them,' said Merlot simply, 'can't see them.'

With his feet still facing the wrong way, Klayth turned and grinned sheepishly at his three new friends.

His three friends. He liked the sound of that.

'You have all the friends you've ever wanted,' said Merlot, his voice fading like the colour from a dying rose.

Klayth's eyes filled with tears as he suddenly realised how true it was. His heart felt huge. He wanted to shout and yell and jump up and down. He knew then it was going to be good to be King.

Silently, the face vanished.

He ran across and hugged Courgette.

Ch'tin beamed. Hogshead reached down and put him gently in his pocket.

'C'mon. We've got a party to go to,' said Firkin, looking down the hill on to a vision of hope.

People were still arriving from all corners, like ants to a banquet, to herald a new age. Klayth felt incredibly proud. Firkin thought eagerly of seeing Dawn again.

They all started off down the hill towards a celebration in the fairy-tale backlit castle, their hearts soaring with joy. It seemed like their feet hardly touched the ground, as if they walked through clouds of swirling dry ice. They didn't say a word, although that would soon change, they just revelled in their feelings. Feeling complete again. Simply feeling wonderful.

Courgette and Hogshead brought up the rear, walking slowly and smiling at each other.

She held her feather and thought fond thoughts of Arbutus.

He held her hand and thought very fond thoughts of her.

THE FROGS OF WAR

Andrew Harman

Never mind anti-anti-anti missiles or thermonuclear chilled eels, the Ultimate Weapons are Rana Militaria: The Frogs of War. Have your head off as soon as look at you, they would. Hidden in the forgotten village of Losa Llamas, they are discovered by the slimy Snydewinder, ex-Lord Chancellor of Rhyngill and a thoroughly bad lot. And after a temporary halt, his world domination plans are back on track.

Little do Firkin and his friends know that, when they attempt to help King Klayth out of a hole, they will fall headfirst into a whirl of time travel, Thaumaturgical Physicists and extremely unpleasant amphibians!

THE TOME TUNNEL

Andrew Harman

Kings have been known to get a bit shirty. Beheading
jugglers for spilling gravy on the royal sleeve, murdering
firstborn sons throughout the kingdom and so forth.
Standard operational procedure. But Firkin's friend,
young King Klayth? Surely not. Things Cannot Be
What They Seem.

Returning from their previous adventure, Firkin, Hogshead
and Dawn find themselves dumped unceremoniously in the
smoking wreckage of a village. Their village. Now they have
to unpick the twisted stitches of Time which they caused in
the first place. Unless they act quickly, the entire fabric of
the Space-Tome Continuum could be at risk. Oh yes, they
also have to find their friend Courgette. And their only tools
are magic, blind stupidity and a sword called Exbenedict!

Orbit titles available by post:

☐	The Frogs of War	Andrew Harman	£5.99
☐	The Tome Tunnel	Andrew Harman	£5.99
☐	101 Damnations	Andrew Harman	£5.99
☐	Fahrenheit 666	Andrew Harman	£4.99
☐	The Scrying Game	Andrew Harman	£5.99
☐	The Deity Dozen	Andrew Harman	£4.99
☐	A Midsummer Night's Gene	Andrew Harman	£4.99
☐	It Came From On High	Andrew Harman	£5.99

The prices shown above are correct at time of going to press, however the publishers, reserve the right to increase prices on covers from those previously advertised, without further notice.

ORBIT

ORBIT BOOKS
Cash Sales Department, P.O. Box 11, Falmouth, Cornwall, TR10 9EN
Tel: +44(0) 1326 372400. Fax +44 (0) 1326 374888
Email: books@barni.avel.co.uk

POST and PACKAGING:
Payments can be made as follows: cheque, postal order (payable to Orbit Books) or by credit cards. Do not send cash or currency.

U.K. Orders under £10	£1.50
U.K. Orders over £10	FREE OF CHARGE
E.E.C. & Overseas	25% of order value

Name (Block Letters) _____

Address _____

_____

Post/zip code: _____

☐ Please keep me in touch with future Orbit publications

☐ I enclose my remittance £ _____

☐ I wish to pay by Visa/Access/Mastercard/Eurocard

☐☐☐☐☐☐☐☐☐☐☐☐☐☐☐☐☐☐   Card Expiry Date

_____